THE
ODYSSEY

THE VISION QUEST, BOOK THREE

THE
ODYSSEY

THE VISION QUEST, BOOK THREE

DEBORAH PRATT

VGM PUBLISHING

THE ODYSSEY
THE VISION QUEST, BOOK THREE

By DEBORAH PRATT

Published by VGM PUBLISHING
A division of Pratt Enterprises Incorporated.
269 So Beverly Drive
Beverly Hills, CA 90212

Visit us online at www.thevisionquest.com

Cover Design by Najla Qamber

Editing by Marc Baptiste

Book design by Shannon Bodie, Lightbourne, Inc.

Copyediting by Palma Odano

ISBN 978-0-9846756-8-5 (Paperback)
ISBN 978-0-9988254-0-3 (Hardcover)
ISBN 978-0-9846756-9-2 (e-book/mobi)

DEDICATION

THE VISION QUEST, BOOK THREE, is dedicated to my mother, Geraldine M. Pratt, who is and always will be my pillar of faith. To my father, Bertram R. Pratt, who taught me all things are possible if you believe from your heart. To my sisters, Diane, Donna, and Deirdre, without whose help these pages would never see the light and to my children, Troian, Nick, Michael, and Ashley, for their love and understanding that mommies have dreams too.

And

I want to congratulate the winners of *The Vision Quest* character competition—Brad Zipprich for Obsidian and Michael Hansford for OPALMOX—and thank them for allowing me to include their characters, create their story lines, and integrate them into the pages of *The Odyssey.* Welcome to the family! Enjoy!

UNITED CO-FEDERATION
SANGELINO
ATLANTIA TERRITORIES
VACARY SETTLEMENT
TEMPLE MOUNTAIN
ATLAND CITY
JOINT COMMON MARKET
THE TERR
PANAZIA
GIATISHA
CAPE HORN ISLAND

THE VISION QUEST

EARTH 118 A.Q.

View a large color map online at
www.thevisionquest.com/Earth118AQ

VISION QUEST
BOOK TWO

THE SUMMER CAME TO A CLOSE, and try as they may, no one would believe the anonymous letters they sent out on the Vybernet telling that the explosions at Temple Mountain were not an accident. The words without proof that the Black Guard biodroids were sentient and building an army became conspiracy. The truth was confounded even more when Covax reported that the explosions never happened. None of the Atlantian authorities would go back to see the alleged destruction. It became clear they would also never see the ever-growing biodroid army of Black Guard Militia being built inside Temple Mountain. In the end, Lazer, Cashton, and Kyla were forced to keep their identities hidden. The horrible truth of what lay in Temple Mountain was covered up and for now, Evvy Tyner died in vain.

There was a small faction of rebels that heard them called the Wave. Despite the rumblings of impending war between the Atlantians and the Black Guard echoing ever louder across his homeland of Atlantia, and the pleadings of his friends Cashton and Kyla, Lazer acquiesced to his mother's wishes to leave Atlantia and go to school on Mu, the other risen continent and home of Masta Lia Poe and the Tosadae Academy of Visionistic Arts. Along with his friends, Cashton and Kyla, he headed off to the other school of higher education—Tosadae's Politia Military and Flight Academy to realize his dream of becoming a pilot in the Politia Forces.

Lazer's decision to move on with his life was put back in question hours after their transport lifted off when they were attacked by the same renegade Black Guard Shadehawk fighters that had killed his father. The first few blasts destroyed the transport cockpit, killing the pilot and crew and leaving the students helpless at the hands of their assailants. Lazer, the best game banger on Atlantia, had flown this very same transport a million times in his game's simulation, but now he had to do it for real. He and Cashton manned a secondary cockpit and cleverly used the transport's security shields to deflect the Shadehawks' blasters right back at them to save the day.

This apparently senseless attack reinforced Lazer's desire to return to Atlantia immediately to join in the Atlantian Wave Forces against the Black Guard. The commanders at Tosadae adamantly denied his appeal to return home. His promise to his mother to stay through his first-level Rite of Passage became the driving force that would have to sustain him through the endless months at school—that was until he met the beautiful Elana Blue and was chosen to study the Visionistic Arts with the renowned splicer, Masta Lia Poe.

Lazer and Masta Poe forged an instant and unique bond. She saw in him the potential to reach a hero's destiny. She also knew he must get past his revenge and hatred to attain that destiny if Atlantia was to be saved. She took a reluctant Lazer under her guidance and began to teach him the *knowings*—genetic knowledge we are born with as ways to access the powers of the universe that had been forgotten by all but a few humans over the millennia.

Only a few knew that back on Atlantia, Ducane Covax, creator of the Black Guard, was being held prisoner by Five, who had named himself the appointed leader of the newly sentient Black Guard Militia. Five was now not only sentient and experiencing emotions, but the biodroid had also learned to shift his molecules and reconfigure his mechanical body into a human form thereby accessing his own version of the powerful Visionistic Arts. Covax had just discovered that Five had stolen the Orbis Gnorb and tracked down the one human who held the genetic code needed to unlock the deeper powers of the Gnorb: an Atlantian named Cole Lazerman. Five, having failed to destroy Lazer at Shooting Falls and again on the Tosadae transport, must now wait for Lazer to leave the protection of Masta Poe and the Politia Forces on Mu.

Meanwhile Triumvirate Aleece Avery joined the investigation team on its way to Atlantia, leaving global politics in the hands of her co-Triumvirate and archenemy, Baz Mangalan. His plan to dome the troubled continent of Atlantia to protect the rest of the world from the possibly sentient Black Guard was gaining momentum. Aleece needed proof of what was actually happening on Atlantia before she could stop him, and her one-time ally, Ducane Covax, was nowhere to be found. Aleece gambled her life on finding a way to protect the Atlantians. Fifty miles inside Atlantian airspace, her transport and escort sortie were shot down.

With Aleece out of the way, Mangalan's order to dome Atlantia was accepted and launched. Within one hour, Five and his Black Guard had taken command of the controls. War on Atlantia erupted like a raging wildfire and with all satellite communication cut off by the dome's force field, the capture and slaughter of innocent Atlantians began. Lazer's mother, Detra, was one of the first to be taken prisoner, as was Triumvirate Aleece Avery who had managed to survive the crash. Mangalan ordered the world press to withhold the truth of the Black Guard's coup on Atlantia.

With a complete news blackout, Lazer was left unaware of the events happening on Atlantia, and life at Tosadae continued as he battled his conflicting emotions: his anger and hatred of the Black Guard, his worry for his mother, and his newfound love for Elana Blue. Even learning that her father was Ducane Covax, the creator of the biodroids, didn't tarnish the growing love between them. Yet his raging emotions consistently interfered with his ability to harness his universal powers at every turn. Masta Poe taught him all she could in the little time she knew he had.

Lazer's friend Kyla who had loved him from childhood fought her own demons of jealousy. Desperate to show Lazer that Elana Blue was a coward and unworthy of his affections, Kyla devised a harmless prank that backfired and pitted both she and Lazer against Kippo, a vicious Prometheus whose venomous glands had not yet been removed. Lazer's victory against this genetically spliced part bear, part lion, part Komodo dragon creature was a shallow one, leaving Elana in shock and Kyla dead. It was Masta Poe's powerful connection to the universe and mastery of the Visionistic Arts that called Kyla back to life, but it was Lazer's love that gave her the will to return. Kyla was alive but mortally wounded. Praying for a miracle to restore them, he watched as his love, Elana Blue, and much more than best friend, Kyla, were sent to the healers in Sangelino.

Lazer counted the days to his Rite of Passage. This was his final promise to his mother and Kyla before his return home to Atlantia to defeat the Black Guard and avenge his father. This he knew in his heart was only the beginning of the greatest journey of his life.

BOOK THREE

THE ODYSSEY

1

RITE OF PASSAGE

COLE "LAZER" LAZERMAN sat beside his best friend since childhood, Cashton Lock. Cashton had personally given Lazer his nickname the first day they met in sixth grade. He swore Lazer's temper could flare faster than a laser blast, and Lazer, as much as he hated to fight, had received countless bloody noses and numerous black eyes to prove his temper had a mind of its own. Together they survived the plague of bullies that roamed the settlements of Atlantia. Lazer's name stuck through high school, and now because of his growing reputation on the zoccair field at Tosadae, it had become a hero's chant whenever he scored for the team. And that, for a freshman, ranked a total flare and lit the way to success and self-belief.

Lazer understood those days were amazing, but they were whispers compared to today. Today was special. It was a unique, once-in-a-lifetime day that Lazer had waited his whole life to come. Lazer looked out the window, scanning across the deep blue of the firmament and across the white cathedral-shaped clouds that filled the sky as they jetted toward the four passage challenge locations. Lazer felt stoic as he thought how this day should have represented the beginning of the greatest event in his life, his Rite of Passage, but instead of bliss he felt empty. So much had happened at home and school that, other than his promise to his parents, the whole reason for going on this Rite of Passage journey had lost its meaning. As they began their first descent from the stratosphere to about ten thousand feet, he looked out the transport's window marveling at Earth and how much it had changed after the Great Quakes.

He squiggled into the comfortable seat. He and the other students traveled aboard his favorite of the Tosadae transports used exclusively for the Rites of Passage treks. This one, called the Votan, named for Pascal Votan, a Mayan prophet and architect of the thirteen-moon calendar. There was no question it was worn from the thousands of students that it had carried. It looked as though it had seen better times, but still, it was a wonderment Lazer wished could tell the stories of all those who went before him.

Lazer impatiently played with the thin leather strap that wrapped around his Rite of Passage lock of dark hair and couldn't help but wish for the things that mattered most to him: that Kyla and Elana would be all right, to know his mother was safe, and to go home and shut the Black Guard down forever. But the harsh reality that his home, the entire continent of Atlantia and all its entire population, had been taken captive and sealed under a proton dome was a dagger in his heart. He knew the Atlantians were at war even though the All News Network (ANN) insisted the World Politia were in control. Lazer knew the truth—the humans weren't in control and this was only the beginning of what was to come. Worst of all, it seemed the rest of the world didn't care. Universal God, he wanted to go back and make sure his mom, whom he'd not heard from in weeks, was okay. He had to finish the fight he'd started at Temple Mountain with that Black Guard. There was a connection he didn't understand, but it was there. He had to destroy some of the biodroids that murdered his father and twenty-seven hundred innocent people, and that was a start. A cool wind rushed over him; it carried the sweet voice of his other best friend, Kyla: "Finish your Rite of Passage. Honor your parents. Honor yourself." Kyla made him swear he would not go home until he honored his father's last request and complete the first level of his Rite of Passage. Why had she made him promise? He felt waves of frustration pointing at everything in his life he couldn't control. Lazer punched the seat in front of him. The flashes of anger still ate at him no matter how many times he repeated Masta Poe's words. The few moments of peace his mind gave him stumbled and fell under the desire to destroy his enemy. Lazer had to let those desires go or he would never achieve bliss and become one with the powers of the universe. The same powers he needed so desperately to save everything he loved. First he has to conquer his own inadequacies, master his gifts, and keep his promise to his parents and Kyla. Destroying the Black Guard would have to wait for a few weeks until he could finish his Rite of Passage and find a way to get back into Atlantia.

Cashton, as always, slept snoring like a bear in hibernation while Lazer, ever restless, contemplated his life. The two other students who had also qualified for their initial Rite of Passage trials sat lost in thought. The opportunity to take their first of four survival odysseys was an honor of the highest degree, held sacrosanct by every Earthean youth since the Great Quakes redefined the world. Every human and human-based splicer prepared for the official Rite of Passage ritual starting at seven, first with their parents, then teachers, and mentors, and then, once they understood its importance in global society, they drove themselves to excellence. The leaders designed the trials to challenge the body, mind, and finally, the spirit. Lazer understood this first level unfolded in a relatively controlled and heavily monitored environment, yet all the dangers were very real. He understood that how he scored on each level of these amazing ordeals would define and position him to become a viable member of the Collective society. The outcome of the trials gave all who succeeded the first key to understanding their true self in harmony with the universe and most of all, the title of adult.

The rush of anxiety buzzed through him. He was excited and nervous. Lazer looked at his fellow travelers. He let his eyes fall out of focus as Kyla had taught him and watched as the pallor of their skin shifted colors. The almost unperceivable aura hues shifted their colors as their thoughts, influenced by their emotions, defined their feelings. The shifts were slow and subtle, but he began to see the energy shimmering out of each of them. It flowed from their pores in wrinkled waves of colored light. Soft shades of sickly yellow meant fear, and the pale gray hue of frustration that hung on all of them had a subtle rim of lavender which meant concern. The excitement and anticipation was white and everyone had it like a halo.

Each student sat motionless, probably imagining what adventures lay ahead. Lazer smiled as he remembered Masta Poe's warning that dwelling in what might happen in the future constituted a waste of time unless a prophetic vision showed itself. He didn't consider himself a prophet, and his desire to go home had not manifested as of yet, so he did his best to stay in the present, an observer of his surroundings.

They all looked heroic, all dressed up in their state-of-the-art, technologically smart, environmentally sensitive bodysuits designed to fit the specific requirements of their individual Rites of Passage: arctic, desert, aquatic, and jungle. These suits were lightyears from the one that slowed his descent at Shooting Falls the day he fell from his Zakki. Its crude sensors read his peril and extended the hidden flaps beneath his arms and between his legs to slow him, causing just enough resistance for Elana to fly her father's Wedge beneath him and save his life. The thought of her made him smile.

Lazer's smile faded as he lay back against the seat cushion and closed his eyes. Why hadn't he been able to save her? One negative thought and a barrage followed filling his mind: Elana, Kyla, his mother, Masta Poe, Tosadae, the problems on Atlantia exacerbated by the horrifying fact that his homeland had been domed by the world Collective to protect everyone but the Atlantian people. He felt like a tiny ship tossed on a great sea by a turbulent storm.

But the one question that besieged him again and again was, if the Collective was in change, *why had all communication from Atlantia been cut off?* He knew the communication block of the dome had left the young territory sealed off from the world, but for the Collective to stop the Vybernet perplexed him. The continuous dome lockdown meant he had no way in and his mother, Detra, had no way out. One more piece of proof that the Black Guard was in control and his mother was in danger. Lazer ran his hands through his hair. No matter how hard he tried, he couldn't stop worrying about her. Masta Poe told him a hundred times, "worry is the first door to defeat," and "release fear for it holds helpless all you desire. You must let go of the things you can't control." He wasn't afraid; he just wanted to get this done and get home.

Lazer rolled his shoulders, trying to loosen the tension that twisted itself into his neck. His muscles locked like ridged bands of steel. He focused on keeping his breathing calm beneath the green and taupe camouflage pattern of his smart suit. The green camouflage colors meant he'd been chosen for the jungle Rite of Passage on Passage Island.

Cashton, headed to the ice fields challenge on the New South Pole, snored softly next to him wearing a dove gray and white cortex fabric compounded by several layers of lightweight arctic gear necessary for sustaining life in below-freezing temperatures. His strong shoulders seemed to have grown even broader in the months since school started and now gave Cashton the air of a man. His height, handsome face, caramel-brown skin, and chiseled torso had attracted several very cute girls at the tarmac. They seemed to flock to him every time he played in the Tosadae Zoccair Tournament. His amazing athletic ability made him an incredible goalie and an instant hero every time he blocked a shot. But as quickly as he attracted girls, his awkward, off-handed, and very nerdy social candor sent many of the girls running in the opposite direction.

Cashton had often said he wished he had the wit and charm of Lazer's father. He swore he would pay more attention to the life lessons Rand had so often shared and they had foolishly both ignored. But since the attack at the Vacary Mines and Rand's cruel murder along with the twenty-seven hundred other innocent people, the opportunity to learn from his father had passed. Lazer sighed. He missed his father perhaps more today than he had at any other time. Rand would have been excited for his son, especially on this day.

It had been a year since Rand's death, and that dark virus of hate and revenge had eaten an ever-growing hole into his heart. Above all else, that pain tainted so many of Lazer's emotions. He too often wallowed in what Masta Poe called the unchangeable past. He commanded himself to stop. He gave gratitude for the good in his life. *Thank the Universal God for Elana Blue,* he thought. Their love for each other became the only light that pierced the armor of his dark anger and gave a small breath of peace to his soul. That fact and Kyla's friendship kept him sane. Kyla and he were still more than friends, but what were they? To that question he had no answer. His emotions pulled at him like a ghostly fog he didn't understand. Lazer shook his head. *Thank the Universal God that Elana Blue and Kyla were safe in the Healers Center in Sangelino.*

The transport bumped across an air pocket and jerked Lazer back into the present. He noticed the only girl of the passage group fidgeting nervously with a pair of aqua blue, web-fingered gloves. Paddle-like flippers and a micro rebreather were clipped to her gear belt. No question: she's gotten sent to Panazia's underwater labyrinth of caves, which pockmarked the middle depths below the central Pan-Atlantic Sea. The labyrinths represented the lost remains of the lower half of South America before the Great Quakes dragged the landmass into the sea. The girl would have to survive for two weeks below the surface of the water. Lazer had hoped to be chosen for the Panazia undersea Rite of Passage since its magnificent underwater mountain ranges, deep sea caves, and kelp forest were said to be the most beautiful in the world.

Just before the Great Quakes liquefied those parts of South America that had been stripped of their vast jungles for farming, cattle, and construction, five sections of the continent had been domed. Massive tremors shook the earth and the land once held by the intricate root systems broke apart and took the remaining domed portions to the bottom of the sea. They had been miraculously saved by the visions of a splicer prophet and became the five cities of Panazia. They developed over years of hardship into a series of beautiful underwater communities, four of them connected by tube ways. The fifth, smaller and more remote Giatisha, stood a hundred miles south on its own. The fertile soil of the great jungles of the Amazonian rainforests grew inside the domes using artificial sunlight. The cities were made from rock, coral, sand, and all manner of recycled materials salvaged from the ocean floor. They surrounded the jungles in a protective circle of architectural wonder. Just beyond the dome, the sea floor blossomed into enormous kelp forests, which in turn gave vast amounts of oxygen both to the underwater cities and to the upper world.

Next Rite of Passage level, Lazer thought, *Panazia*. He wondered where Elana and Kyla would have been going. They, too, had qualified for the Rite of Passage. But now, because of what had happened that night in the battle forum, they were on a very different kind of survival trek—they were fighting for their lives. Lazer gave a long, heavy sigh filled with remorse. He reminded himself that even though he wanted both of them with him, they had been taken to Sangelino where the world's finest healers would make them well and whole again. Kyla's wings were gone forever. The flight in her arms he'd imagined so many times would never come to fruition. Lazer never cared what her genetics were, only that she had been born and become so much more than his friend. He wished she had accepted the simple truth that her kindness, wit, and intellect made her wonderful. Maybe with her wings gone, she could. If he and Elana were soul mates, he and Kyla were twin flames.

"Spit," the boy across the aisle whispered, having hit his head.

Lazer had seen him many times around Tosadae Academy since the beginning of the year. Kyla had pointed him out on numerous occasions as he'd made her "cute-boys-to-hook-up-with-before-I-graduate" list. Lazer didn't remember his name but recalled how they'd cheered him during the Academy's crizette championship game against Station City last month. He'd been a terrific player in a fast-paced and dangerous game; a kind of polo only on vicious-looking, but well-domesticated young splicers, with sometimes as much as a six-foot wingspan called archeops. It took skill, athleticism, power, and speed to move the floating ball with a mallet, all while riding a domesticated archeop that stood six to eight feet tall—half condor, half Komodo dragon.

Lazer looked at the tan-colored desert fatigues the boy wore, which rounded out their Rite of Passage quorum. The boy's dark skin and almond-shaped black eyes made him mysterious and handsome. A hundred years ago, his features could have meant he hailed from Mongolia, India, or Peloponnese, or he maybe even carried, as Lazer did, the great and ancient bloodlines of the Anastasi descendants who had first settled the North and South American continents some fifteen thousand years before the Great Quakes. But, thank the Universal God, being a different color didn't matter anymore. One earth under one god. Only those who hated the human splicers and biodroids could bring back the kind of wedge that led to hatred and war. *Hadn't humanity learned from their past mistakes?* Lazer thought. *Why couldn't humans see what was happening?* Lazer let his gaze drift back through the window. Humanity sat at a pinnacle of choice, and the wrong decision—or worse, no decision from the leaders and the Collective—could take them back into the ignorance of the past. The thought was a hard reminder that he could not fail. He had to keep his promise, get through his Rite of Passage, and get home to stop the Black Guard.

2

ONE LAST MESSAGE

HOURS PASSED AS LAZER waited in silence for their various tube drops. A sound from the back of the transport pulled his attention. Commander Brockton rose from her seat. She stood six feet even and cast a long shadow in the soft light of the transport's cabin. Her close-cut hair lay streaked with blades of white, but her tight skin and muscular body belied her age and gave the appearance of youth, vitality, and strength. She had been at Tosadae for fifteen years as coordinating professor of the senior virtual flight simulation training division. And she, like every professor, volunteered to lead at least one Rite of Passage launch—or ROP release launch, as they called it—per session.

"Tosadae students, the next fourteen days will be about discovering your true ability to survive in a hostile environment," she said in a thick, slightly masculine voice. She moved forward, stopping in front of the cockpit door. She gave Lazer a small nod and the V salute. Lazer nodded back and bounded the V made from his fingers on his chest.

He'd seen her many times in the cockpit bays of her simulators.

She'd told him on more than one occasion she liked his relentlessness to be the best. She believed in him and that felt good.

"Your acceptance into the Collective, your rightful place in society, will be determined by the caliber of your behavior on these challenges. Your rights to work at the best jobs, purchase property, marry, and have children rest in your hands alone. Use of the Visionistic Arts is prohibited on this first-level trek unless you are in a true life-threatening situation. The creatures you encounter can and will be anesthetized via light wave transmission as soon as you hit your Pulsar Activation Release marked by the PAR switch.

"There is," she added, "the rare occasion when the PAR control tags malfunction. As I am monitoring each and every one of you via GPS and satellite visuals, let me say a PAR failure rescue has never happened on my watch."

"Wouldn't that just be just our luck to be the first," Cashton grumbled hoarse and groggy as he whispered to Lazer.

"Any unprovoked use of the Arts will be counted against your final score. And, I repeat again, my team and I will be watching you at all times. Your entire Rite of Passage is monitored by satellite as well as land and sea camera 24/7. But remember, retrieval is not instantaneous. If you are wounded, get to the nearest retrieval location and stay put. Your environmental suits will automatically convert into medical, survival protocol wear to give you first aid. They are designed to send us constant readings of your vital statistics. Use your head and use your PAR."

The girl across the aisle from Lazer shot Lazer a look, obviously confused.

"Pulsar . . . Activation . . . Release," Lazer whispered, pointing to an LED switch that glowed under a snap cover on her utility cuff. "Pop it and press. You'll be fine." Lazer gave her as reassuring a smile as he could. He could see by the look in her eyes and the streaks of sickly yellow permeating her aura that she didn't want to be there.

"Cadet Renfroe," Brockton signaled the girl to step forward.

Lazer and Cashton watched as Brockton adjusted the girl's bubble-shaped environment helmet. She switched on her facemask's light and air, preparing her for a high-speed drop into the middle of the ocean for the Panazia challenge.

She looks strong. She'll be okay, Lazer thought looking at the slight wisp of a girl that stood before him. He knew the girl's self-sufficient aqua-pressure suit would supply her with adequate oxygen through the rebreather support system for weeks. The fine ribbing that ran like thick corduroy carried a liquid charcoal purification system that acted as an air filter. It would oxygenate for the full fourteen days, extract and desalinate fresh water from salt water, and keep her body pressurized and warm at the lower depths. It would also monitor all her vital read-outs. She could, if she followed the quest map, find an undersea habitant with craft to live in while gathering the list of creatures, rock samples, and gaseous specimens she would need for her freshman thesis. Renfroe slipped on her supply pack and secured the modest survival strap with a loud click.

"Ready?" Commander Brockton asked her.

Cadet Renfroe gave a nervous thumbs up to Commander Brockton and followed her to the drop platform. The young girl shot Lazer a last look and gave the most imperceptible wave goodbye to him. He smiled back at her and he and Cashton gave her a thumbs up in return. The second both of her feet were standing on the platform, Lazer heard an icy whoosh of air, and she dropped away. The release panel sucked shut and silence prevailed.

He and the others looked out the window to see her ejected from the trailing tube and vanish into the sea.

Lazer took a deep breath. It would be a while before the next drop.

"Kyla never meant for Elana to get hurt," Cashton whispered. "You know that, right?"

"Yeah, I know," Lazer replied.

"Kyla loves you, Lazer—has since the third grade. Don't be mad at her. You two are going to have to deal with your feelings."

"I know. I just want her to be okay again," Lazer said. "I know she wouldn't hurt anybody on purpose. Kyla knows my feelings for Elana."

"You and Elana will get back together too."

"I know that too. Once I make sure my mom and Atlantia are safe, I'll find Elana Blue. She's gonna be with me for the rest of my life," Lazer said.

He spoke with a passion that Cashton had never heard.

"Sounds like love to me, bro," Cashton grinned.

"Yeah," Lazer smiled. "I know something is making her hold back but I think once we're together again, we'll work it out. Hey, I hope you find someone just as amazing, Cash."

"Join the club on that."

The two friends shared a smile, fell into guy silence, and waited for the time to pass.

Hours dragged by. They ate, played some games, and Lazer entertained himself by checking a few last-minute things on his wristsponder, which he had managed to smuggle aboard, as Cashton watched.

"Get busted with that and you're dead meat," Cashton whispered.

"Shhhhh. It's all ice."

"Well? Anything come up?" Cashton asked.

Lazer shook his head, "No."

"It's been glitching like this for days. Something's trying to get through. What about you? You get anything from home lately?" Lazer whispered back.

Cashton shrugged. "Bunch of static drool, not even any usual V-ads from home. Not like my mom and dad to not send me anything especially about today. Something's whacked and I don't like it. The politia or whoever is controlling the dome should open it once a day so people can get word out."

"We leave for home the day we get back," Lazer said.

"Tell me something I don't know."

"Cashton, your drop," Brockton said.

"The *day* we get back," Lazer added emphatically.

"Scope that," Cashton said, adding a sharp V salute. He sealed his promise with the latest handshake taken fresh off the streets of Station City, the entertainment capital of the world next to Dubai Land in the Republic region.

"Stay ice. No pun intended," Lazer said, smiling at his friend. "They're trackin' us on satellite."

Cashton grinned. "That's what I'm afraid of. How am I supposed to party with a bunch of Big Brother jickheads eyeballin' me all the time? Hit me up as soon as you get back," Cashton said.

"Cadet Lock!" Brockton shouted.

"Yes Ma'am!" Cashton crossed, secured his survival strap, and moved into the drop tube. "Light it up!"

"Go in light," Brockton corrected him with a flare of her nostrils.

"Yeah. Sorry, Ma'am. That's what I meant. Go in light."

Brockton hit the release. Cashton gave a wild howl and vanished down the release tube. As before, the vacuum sucked the release door back into place.

"Hi, Lazer. Universal God, I miss you. I swear by the Collective, your room seems more and more empty every month you're gone. I . . ." Detra's voice echoed in Lazer's molar receiver. It vibrated through his body and warmed his heart. A holographic visual appeared, glitched, and broke off her words. The communication ended abruptly in a wall of static. He couldn't get the message to reopen. Lazer punched up the next V-mail.

Another holograph appeared, glitched, and wavered into a very different Detra Lazerman. She wore her hair pulled tightly back. It made her skin look pale and her eyes vanish into the cavernous dark circles below them. Detra's image vacillated back and forth through a wash of white static trying to lock in. Her gloomy, frightened face called to him and the sadness that rang in her voice broke Lazer's heart. He felt fear behind her every word.

"I hate these attacks. The Black Guard are getting more and more blatant. An entire compound burned to the ground Saturday. I know it . . ." Again, a glitch cut her words short.

What attacks? Lazer hit refresh and fast forwarded into the V-mail.

"F . . . F . . . Food is short, and the s . . . s . . . simplest of survival supplies a fortune. What I wouldn't give for some decent hygiene wipes. The Atlantian Outback fuel delivery transports are few and far between, and any news is sporadic. This damn dome blocks everything. I hope you get this. They promised to open up once a day for mail and news transmission but it has been weeks. I'm so glad you're not here," she said as a series of explosions erupted from outside. "Universal God! Lazer! Universal God!" Detra screamed. Her face froze as the transmission jammed, glitched, and tweaked out to black. A vertical message flashed at him: REMAINDER OF THIS TRANSMISSION DELETED.

"No!" Lazer screamed as he tried in vain to access his mother again.

The wristsponder glitched to a haze of static folding into a single dot that popped back on. What replaced it felt even more frightening. Detra's face appeared, clean and plastic looking, smiling at him like a doll and telling him how wonderful things were at home. Everything about it looked fake, digitized, and totally not his mom. Things on Atlantia were worse than he'd imagined.

Lazer leapt to his feet.

"Commander Brockton!" Lazer shouted as he raced back to the drop tube area.

"You're up, Lazer. Remember, no Visionistic Arts," Brockton said as she guided him to the platform.

"Commander! Someone opened the dome. The Atlantian transmissions are getting out," he said.

Lazer held up his wristsponder to show her the emergency status flash.

"The transmissions, they're being altered. It's propaganda. Listen, please. My mother's in danger!"

Brockton pulled the wristsponder from his wrist.

"I'll take that. No more calls to Mom, son. You're about to cut the cord," she said.

She backed him down the aisle.

"You don't understand! I just received . . .," Lazer said.

He reached to take the wristsponder back.

"Tell it to the Triumvirate," Brockton said, forcefully guiding him onto the drop platform.

"I have to call Commander Hague. There's been a . . ."

"Time to be reborn, son. Go in light."

And with a great whoosh, Lazer dropped.

3

AWAKENINGS

KYLA LAY IN A FIELD covered in butter yellow and black sunfodils. Their huge flowery faces smiled down on her allowing her glimpses
of the bright summer sun that shone down on her from a flawless azure
sky. The scent of the flowers wafted over her as sweet as butter and
amber honey baking in the sun. The warmth of the sun made her skin
perspire, beading in the fine, flesh-colored, tattoo-like markings that
covered her body and sparkled in her hair as it caught the subtle shifts
of brown, amber, blonde, and black patterns and mimicked the moiré
markings of her wings.

Kyla smiled. A soft, cool breeze made the sunfodils shimmer around
her, casting speckled shadows that fell across her skin like a veil of fine
lace. She listened as a nearby babbling brook played in counterpoint to
a hundred tweeting sparrows taking flight. She felt everywhere at once:
on the ground, in the water, and floating in the air. She could sense the
beauty of all that lulled her into this surreal peace and rested as hours
drifted by without worry or care. Tranquil bliss reigned until a single

17

clap of thunder disturbed her serenity. Behind the thunder a harsh pounding shook the earth and commanded her to wake. Kyla moved, and a shock of pain tore across her back like the sting of a well-placed whip. She felt the slow rip of skin as if her flesh peeled itself open like a mouth to scream. Another sound bombarded her ears. It got louder and closer. Her instincts whispered, *Be quiet. You're in danger.* She struggled. *Wake up.*

Kyla commanded her mind to come back from the dreamy haze that held her. She willed her eyes to open, and a very different light pierced the shadowy haze. Fluorescent blue algae, cold and shallow, sent a brilliant glare that stabbed into her eyes. Kyla fought the pain and forced them to stay open. The strange sounds she could not decipher pounded closer.

Her mind tried to pull her back into the dream world like a siren's song lulling her into its warmth. Her senses of smell, taste, and touch and those nonhuman instincts that lay deep inside her splicer genetics warned her again of the impending danger. The sounds blended and the tweeting birds became horrifying screams of suffering people.

She had to get up. She squinted into the glaring light and saw a hospital room—machines, IVs, and monitors hooked into her like the tentacles of a sea monster. She looked across the small room and saw Elana Blue sleeping in the next bed. Behind Elana she could make out metal walls with no windows and the shape of an octagonal, retractable door. *It's a transport, but we're not moving,* she thought. Kyla shook the cobwebs from her mind, struggling to remember. Flashes of Deigen, the battle, and Lazer slammed into her memory—the last moments of the fight in the Battle Forum, running, flying higher and higher in a desperate attempt to get away from the hot, foul breath of Deigen and its razor teeth as they ripped into her flesh and tore off her wings. Kyla clenched her eyes, seeing it again as it dragged her back, crashing onto the ground. She arched her back in pain. The horrible memory jolted her back to full consciousness.

Kyla was sure she and Elana must have been hypnotized by the healers; Kyla for her wounds and Elana . . . Again the pain lashed into her back with the sting of a cat-o'-nine-tails. Tears filled her eyes. She knew now for certain her wings had been ripped from her back. The same wings she had hated as an embarrassment her whole life had been torn away and she had almost died. Or *had* she died? Kyla struggled with the memory until the screams outside the door swelled louder, getting closer with each second.

She had to get out, but where could she go? How could she get by them? Death waited outside the door. The side effects of the hypnotic state made her woozy, barely able to think. She was being taken to healers somewhere. Were they in Sangelino? Had marauders brought down the ship? She didn't know what had happened and didn't have time to figure it out. Another loud thud just beyond the door brought her back to the reality of the moment and the danger it represented.

They had suspended her with wires and harnesses face down, four feet above the floor. Kyla slipped from the suspension harnesses and gingerly pulled the feeding tubes and IVs from her body. Crawling on all fours, she made her way to Elana.

"Elana," Kyla whispered.

"Elana," she said, this time louder. It hurt to talk. Her voice sounded dry and raspy. "Elana, please."

Elana did not respond. She lay peacefully lost in her dreams, oblivious to the danger closing in with every second.

Kyla willed her limbs to move. She used her hand to grab Elana's bed and pull herself onto her feet.

The screams outside were frantic. Desperate people were dying. Deuterium blasters pinged and seared their flesh, burning them alive. She recognized the hissing, throbbing pitch of the pellets. She'd heard it in the simulator work she did in class, not to mention the Vacary Mines attacks and the night at Temple Mountain with Cashton and Lazer. That fateful night had cost Evvy her life. It had happened less than a year ago, but she had never forgotten those sounds of death and destruction, and right now they were just outside her door.

"Lazer," she whispered. She wished he were here to help them. He'd know what to do to get them out.

"Elana," Kyla called again. "Wake up!"

Kyla shook her. Elana lay motionless, her face still, relaxed in sweet repose as if she dreamt of some beautiful world where all things were safe and wonderful.

Kyla heard them advance from room to room, looking for something or someone. They were at best a few doors away. Kyla's instincts shrieked at her. *Get out!* She moved. With each step a wave of pain beat down on her. Her mouth stayed shut, silenced by fear. She inched along in what felt like slow motion compared to the speeding train of destruction and death that rushed toward her door.

Kyla looked around the room—no windows, a small bathroom with no way out, and two shallow supply closets. She was trapped. Why hadn't she learned to go negative, become invisible, and vanish into thin air? Right now she would do anything to not be inside this room waiting for the horror on the other side of that door. Something caught her eye. A long piece of blue conduit hung like a huge snake through an open ceiling panel across the room. It beckoned to her. Now, more than ever, Kyla wanted her wings back. She wanted them to lift her from the floor and carry her to sanctuary.

Come on, Elana. Wake up! Kyla thought. She wished her powers of telepathy were stronger. She took two steps back toward Elana and reached to pull the blankets away when the pounding and screams from the room across the hall stopped her.

Kyla knew in that instant she could not save them both. She grabbed the harness that had held her and the blue cable and began to climb. Her body, weak from the wounds and racked by pain, fought her every movement. She pulled herself hand over hand up to the ceiling. She reached into the open panel. A violent whip of pain tore into her back as she pulled her body inside. Kyla focused on the thin piping that ran neatly inside the narrow crawlspace. She dragged herself up and scooted forward pulling one leg and then the other. She quickly slipped the ceiling panel back just as the door flew open.

Four Black Guard biodroids rushed into the room with phasers that extended from their arms raised and more than prepared to blast Elana.

A rush of guilt shuttered through Kyla as she peeked through a tiny crack in the panel. She wanted to help her, but it was impossible. Kyla thought of Lazer. He would understand. He had to. He would know she couldn't do any more. Tears filled her eyes. He would never understand that she had left the love of his life to die at the hands of the Black Guard.

One of the Black Guard raised a claw and pointed. "This is the one," the tinny, mechanical voice spoke. "Summon Five."

The other three guards lowered their weapons. In an instant a gurney guided by two clones floated in. They lifted Elana from her bed and placed her onto it securing the restraints.

Elana's eyes fluttered open. Too dazed and confused from the hypnotic coma to summon her Visionistic Arts, another instinct took over.

"Maximus," she shouted.

Every Black Guard that held her stopped. Her words acted as a verbal off switch.

Kyla could see the green light bands stutter and short when a fifth Black Guard entered. A monolith compared to the four others that stood mute around Elana. Other than his height, Kyla couldn't tell one from the other, but Elana's face said everything. She knew this one.

"Five. Release me," she commanded. "When my father hears of this he'll . . ."

"He'll do nothing," Five replied. "If you want him to live you will see to it he gives me the bio codes. Do you understand?"

"You'll be deactivated for this . . .," she said.

Elana struggled against the restraints. It was obvious to Kyla the side effects of the hypnotic coma cluttered Elana's mind and rendered her powers inaccessible, but just in case, Five touched her chest with his claw. Her body arched in pain. Elana thrashed, jerking at the restraints that bound her to the gurney. She fought the electric surge until she had no choice but to succumb. Her body fell limp. She'd blacked out.

"Take her," Five ordered. "And kill every living creature on this transport."

Kyla held her breath. She too knew that biodroid's voice. She'd heard it that night at Temple Mountain.

4

CONTROL

DANTE LABOV STEPPED from his home a hundred stories above downtown Sangelino. As he walked across the enclosed overbridge to the Triumvirate station transport, he glanced down across the sprawling cityscape below.

The sunset bleached the western sky and melted into shades of pink, orange, purple, and gray as it kissed the horizon. *Another day without her*, Dante thought. Time held little relevance these days since Aleece's disappearance other than that he and everyone else who knew, understood it was running out. He could not help but feel the frustration that life had become a never-ending series of meetings and conferences, each resulting in minimal progress and endless red tape.

It looked as though the Triumvirate had slowly evolved into everything they'd fought against since the pre-quake citizens freed humanity from the grip of twelve power-hungry banks and a hundred disjointed, self-serving governments that ran the world. Every history student learned how humans had become paralyzed by propaganda and fear and anesthetized by legal, television-peddled medication, illegal drugs and banal, mind-numbing entertainment. How in those dark days a citizen army of brave men and women went against the odds and exposed a worldwide conspiracy of greed orchestrated by a third-generation world leader whose name had to be stricken from all history books; a man who carried on the plot of his father, his father's father, and the secret society who together laid the groundwork that would have control over the world's finances, food and water supply and, thereby, the world. For one hundred years before the quakes, power dangled in the hands of a select few ruthless men. Humanity would have been crushed into financial submission and continuous war if Mother Nature hadn't stepped in and redefined Earth. Man has caused the initial quakes, stripping the land, mining, fracking, and pumping massive amounts of waste-water deep into the earth. The toxic water made the ground unstable causing constant earthquakes until Mother Nature took it from there exploding Yellowstone's super volcano under Yosemite. The volcanic chain reaction circled the globe and humanity hung on the brink of extinction. In the aftermath of the Great Quakes, it was the surviving corporations who stepped in. Using their global networks the corporate leaders came together to save what remained of Earth's inhabitants. Other than the corporate logos that flew like flags over the remaining land masses to distinguish guardianship and stop the lawless raiders, Earth had become a unified planet. It had unified for the betterment and equality of the planet. For that Dante Labov was a proud citizen of Earth . . . until now.

Dante looked around at the vast capital city before him. He knew how the corporations helped create the Constitution of Freedom based on the Open Information Act to be shared by the entire collective population of humans, splicers, clones, gens, and biodroids; how over time so many new species had come to share the world; and how this enlightened collective population had agreed to stop warring and accept one another—until now. The newest species were biologically based machines and their sentient awakening had just opened the newest and deadliest Pandora's box, a potential war between humans and machines. It had been a hundred years of peace and that peace made the new generation of humans ill equipped to handle what was coming. Dante felt saddened by the thought of falling backward into the trap of power. For the first time in their young history, Triumvirate and the corporate fathers wallowed in ambivalence and confusion.

The gleaming silver transport arrived and he stepped aboard. It was a tube-shaped chrome transport that hovered above a single, magnetic levitation rail and shot diagonally across the city at two hundred miles per hour. The door closed and he felt his emotions as they welled inside him. He loved Sangelino, his wife, daughter, business, and his home. He didn't want to lose them, and starting today he knew he would have to fight to protect everything precious. The time for hiding and ignoring reality had ended. The doors of the transport hissed open.

Dante stepped from the train and walked across the station mall. He had not been informed as to why he was being brought before the Triumvirate. He would know the details soon enough.

Dante wanted Aleece walking next to him. He needed her political acumen to face the Corporate Council members who awaited him. He considered himself a brilliant businessman, not a politician. His water production companies had built huge aquatic theaters to pull the needed water from the air. He had partnered with the brilliant scientist Laurant Bouvier to develop the technology. Doctor Bouvier was also credited with the technology that could make renewable, freshwater glaciers in the North and South Poles. The ice caused the albedo effect, reflecting the sun back into space to keep the oceans and the earth from warming and killing sea life. It also calmed the weather caused by the thermo-haline circulation patters. Doctor Bouvier's teams would go into the world-renowned Bouvier Labov Polar Ice Farms with massive tankers and harvest the extra ice for transport to be taken to places around the globe in need of water. Both Labov and Doctor Bouvier took great pride in their polar ice farms. But, to face the corporate politicians, he wanted Aleece.

Perhaps he could sway the tide of events from their obvious path of conflict and quell Atlantia's dilemma by representing their need here in Sangelino, as his wife had done with the Triumvirate and Corporate Council. Perhaps he could convince the Collective to go into Atlantia with enough Politia Forces to stop whatever problems had already begun. Dante Labov knew this uprising on Atlantia had to stop or it would domino out and all of humanity would face these rogue biodroids and who, or what, commanded them. Dante pushed the accusatory thoughts of Covax being behind this nightmare away. He needed proof first. Someone or something was to blame. Why couldn't everyone see the fate of humankind falling back into the darker side dragged down by fear? He understood that unless he took his place in the council, he could do little to stop it.

He reached the grand courtyard that led to Triumvirate Park. It looked majestic in the fading light with its rows of grand oak and massive magnolia trees standing guard in front of the graceful architecture of Triumvirate Headquarters. Dante climbed the main stairs just as a young politia officer walked out to intercept him.

"Dr. Labov, the council is ready for you," the officer said.

"Has there been any word about Triumvirate Avery and her convoy?" Dante started to ask. His voice rang with concern for his missing wife.

"You'll have to ask the commander, sir. I'm not classified for any information about Triumvirate Avery's situation," the officer responded before Dante could finish.

"Of course," Dante replied. *Situation?* Dante thought.

The officer handed him a small data disc the size of a large antique coin. It reminded him of when coins were made of precious metals and had value. Now only digital currency existed—I.D. DNA tagged global chit cards had become law and the only form of global currency that existed. This wasn't money; this coin was security clearance and highly guarded information. Dante adjusted of a pair of private intelligence lenses that appeared in front of his eyes and inserted the disc into his wristsponder. Seen only by Dante, a barrage of information appeared in holographic images in front of him. As they walked, he sped through the data and felt it vibrate his arm as it transmitted the data to a small memory chip he'd had implanted in his brain. The process worked much like having a photographic memory for those who didn't or couldn't retain the information. The technology aided the memory with instant recall. What one did with the information still required intelligence. Dante finished and touched the holoscreen, placing the images and rows of facts on hold until they reached the main chamber. The haze of holographs dissipated back into his sponder.

Just as they entered the main council chamber, Dante hesitated. He took one last breath of freedom. By walking through the door, he would be committing his time and knowledge to the Collective.

"Sir?" the Commander said, waiting for him to enter.

Dante lifted his chest and with it his courage and entered. He felt the shadow of the space cover him and with it came the weight of responsibility he was taking on. He belonged to a greater good now, and he would use everything in his power to stop the insurgence on Atlantia and get his wife home.

The main room was bright and large. It was officious yet there was a sense of warmth that prevailed. Dante looked at the first face to greet him. Blane Fahan stood and smiled as Dante crossed to him. Fahan's lanky frame looked taller and thinner than Dante remembered. He was part human and part amphibian, with his humanity as vast as his brilliant mind. The first human Chimeras were developed to be used for animal testing and to create breeds of organ donors but the combined genetics of the human based splicers were almost always smarter and many exemplified the compassions that far too many pure humans had lost along with their Visionistic powers.

Dante smiled warmly at him. Fahan extended his webbed hand.

His short fingers protruded beyond flat, bluish-gray, paddle-like fins that formed the palm. His eyes looked more human than most of the peophins, half-human and half-dolphins that swam in the cold waters of the southern Atlantic Straits. Dante had seen more and more of the amphibious land-walking splicers. They seemed everywhere in Sangelino these days. The two men shook hands. Fahan's skin always felt cool and moist, but his smile shone warm and genuine. He added a nod of welcome and encouragement mixed with apology and concern. *How could one look express so many things?* Dante thought. Dante nodded back, grateful for his kindness. He moved on to the next hand. All of the Corporate Council heads of the Big Six greeted him with a mix of emotions. Some mumbled their deep concerns about Aleece. One even asked about his daughter. Their words were a blur as Dante, ever the diplomat, made his way to Aleece's chair. The sight of it empty stabbed at his heart, but one look at the face in the next chair steeled his resolve.

Baz Mangalan did not stand. He was human, with the gray pallor of a dead man who hadn't been told he'd passed on. Mangalan sat calmly and watched Dante's entrance. Finally, the always impeccable, ever-slender Mangalan rose to greet him. Easily a head taller than Dante, his face looked deadpan as he held out a small elliptical opalescent badge to Dante.

Dante looked at the finely carved, milky glass broach; on its surface, the wings of an eagle caught the light. The Triumvirate's insignia gave access to all levels of security save the highly guarded, top secret level labeled Code Umbra; for that clearance he still needed a signed approval from Fahan and Mangalan. For that, they all did. Putting on the badge officially instated him as an interim Triumvirate in Aleece's absence. He would have voting rights, limited but still enough to make a difference, applicable in crisis situations but only until his wife returned.

"Thank you for assuming this position, Dr. Labov, and welcome," Fahan said.

Dante took the badge, lifted it to his tunic, and felt as it adhered itself into the fabric. He shook Mangalan's moist hand and nodded. Dante sat down in Aleece's chair as the meeting that would determine Atlantia's fate began.

5

ICE

"UNIVERSAL GOD, I hate the cold," Cashton said. He felt the thin, icy air as it crystalized and stung in his nose when he breathed it in. Even though it entered through the permeable, transparent mask designed to regulate the temperature, keep out excess moisture, and allow only warmed, filtered oxygen to enter the cold was bitter enough not to win the first battle. Cashton looked down at his suit with its rows of tiny blinking lights that traced down his arms and legs—small, multicolored flashing buttons busily analyzing and constantly recalculating the outside temperature then counterbalancing the inside temperature to keep his entire body warm and comfortable. Luckily, it was his first Rite of Passage, and all the calculations were done automatically at least for the first week until he acclimated. After that, every survival calculation would have to be manually determined and input by him. But for now, the suit did all the work. It blocked the invading chill carried on by the relentlessly blowing, freezing wind as it buffeted into him. He could hear the hiss that came from the sharp, icy snow that, at the moment, fell in vertical lines as it blew into him. The ice and snowfall obliterated his view, save for more than ten feet at best. The wind blew harder. They tiny ice pellets struck the surface of his mask and suit, sounding more like the constant crumpling of paper. He needed to find water and shelter before dark. That was rule number one. If only he had his micro-dot music ring to play his favorite music and block out the monotony of nature. Cashton heard the crack of ice under his feet and supposed it was a better idea not to have the latest sounds blasting in his ears as it could make him miss hearing the ice break or the howls of a pack of ice wolves or polar bears closing in on him. Most of those animals that had survived the Great Quakes had been relocated to the New South Pole to save them from extinction when the poles shifted off their axis. As hungry as Cashton felt, he knew any predator would certainly be hungrier.

He checked his locator and kept walking west to the infamous Passage Caves that were waiting for him a few miles ahead. The wind blew harder. It shoved him along, pressing against his back like an obnoxious bully. Cashton leaned back into the wind at a slight angle, cribbing into the current of air to help him keep on his GPS. He pressed the navigation beam and a thin, red line shot out in front of him then faded into the snow. He now had only two things to do: follow the red line and keep himself from slipping on the glassy ice surface below his feet.

The ice fog shifted creating gray and white forms that appeared, twisted, and blew away. He was tired as he walked for the second hour, occasionally checking the red GPS line that would take him to the Passage Caves where he would spend his first night. There he could rest, light a fire, and figure out what to eat before his supplies ran out.

Breathless and exhausted from his battle with the elements, Cashton's frustration wore at him until the storm abruptly stopped. It took with it the icy talons and fine shower of pin-prick-sharp snow that had been assaulting him since he landed. An instant later, the sky cleared, and like the opening of the second-act curtain, it drew back its white cloudy veil, whisking itself away on the last of the wind. Silence. A vacant hush surrounded him. Cashton stopped to catch his breath. He looked across the endless white horizon as the pale colors of the fading sun shined up from below the horizon, creating a soft, pinky-peach and pearl blue wash of the sunless sky. Perhaps he would get to see the Aurora Australis if the sky turned dark enough. How cool to be in the land of the midnight sun, though full darkness would not come for another three months. He would be high enough to see the magnetosphere's charged particles moved by solar winds into a light show like no other on Earth. Cashton smiled. Ice Island was frozen, white and austere, but it was beautiful beyond words.

The distant howl of the receding wind did not take with it the ever-present cold that surrounded him. The freezing chill pressed in on him like an unwanted enemy stalking his every step. A rush of panic filled him and in an instant, he imagined a morose variety of unpleasant and gruesome possible deaths. It was horrible, but it was a survival instinct that reminded him he needed to hurry and find shelter.

Cashton gave a shiver that brought him back to the present—not from the cold but from a long dark shadow, large and ominous, that moved by him. He turned his head to look in all directions and let his eyes scan every inch of desolate space. *The sky?* he thought. But it glowed perfectly clear save for the distant clouds that carried the storm away. The ominous presence moved again. This time Cashton stopped. His peripheral vision caught the low-moving shadow drifting past him just to his left. It was enormous. Cashton turned to face his adversary, whatever it was, and gasped. Nothing approached from any direction. *How can there be a shadow without sunlight?*

Cautiously he rocked back to reposition his stance, steadying himself to run or fight. The ice beneath his feet creaked under his weight. He had walked onto an immense ice shelf, the kind that made up most of the New South Pole. Cashton peered down into the ice beneath his feet. The very large shadow swam beneath him. A black and white killer whale, easily thirty-five or forty feet long, swam around him below the ice. One of its large black eyes rolled upward, distorted by the ice but obviously watching his every move. Cashton looked across the ice shelf and touched his GPS. The red line jutted out, triangulated, and calculated his distance. He had at least a half-mile to cover before he was on solid land again and within the safety of some caves. Suddenly the huge shadow dove, vanishing into the watery depths. Cashton thought to run might be a very good idea.

6

PASSAGE ISLAND

LAZER PLUMMETED in free fall, dropping at about seventy-five miles per hour. He fell like a wash of water flushed from a mountain cave—cold, fast, and powerful. The rush of speed made his heart pound with pure exhilaration. It took all his strength to open his arms away from his body and slow his descent. He broke through the billowing clouds that hung ten thousand feet above the jungle's canopy. He saw the breathtaking lush vegetation growing in an emerald ring around the majestic Quilliani Mountain range that sat at the very center of Passage Island. Lazer marveled at the vast desert side that stretched on for miles and ended at the sea. The island's magnificent terrain existed as one of several survival environments the Rite of Passage Foundation had developed in association with the Foundation for Humanity. The Foundation had put all the Rite of Passage safe challenge locations in place for young men and women just like him to prove their adulthood status through the magnificently orchestrated survival trials. Without the approved trial certification, no man or woman could marry, have children, own land, or start a business. Many jobs were denied them without at least completing the first level of the official Rite of Passage certification.

Lazer believed in the Rite of Passage challenges. Required by a globally mandated law, the survival trials determined if you could marry, hold certain jobs, and have children. Its challenges, rules, and rewards represented the first bastion on the way to adulthood. Lazer wondered why several hundred years ago almost all societal rites of passage had been all but abandoned, save for a few tribes like the Aborigine with their Walkabout and a scattering of primitive tribes in Africa. Those tribes required a series of true physical challenges to take their young people into adulthood. The Great Quakes changed the world, and now the current Rite of Passage, taken from an old television reality show, became an opportunity for young people to achieve strength and pride in knowing they could care for themselves and their families in any situation. They took the joy of responsibility and grew up or lost out on all rights associated with adulthood in the eyes of the unified world.

Lazer pulled the cord, and his parachute blossomed into a pyramid of gold nylon. He took the guide controls and maneuvered himself toward a small, red-ringed clearing that sat thirty or so clicks beyond a sparkling purple lake. Lazer studied the intricate, tangled terrain of the jungle as he descended through the steaming tropical mist that gently rose in great voluminous columns and hung in the treetops just below the warm azure sky.

In the distance, Mount Quilliani, a jagged thrust of black basalt rock, poked defiantly through the clouds. Its long black shadow reached across to the rocky shore of the eastern side. The snow that melted on its highest peak fed a series of tributaries that led to numerous twisting rivers and streams. The most beautiful of the rivers cut through the great southern wall that held the hardest and most dangerous terrain used for level-four Rites of Passage. The southern river traveled on a curious calcium-powdered bed of creamy white silt that made the water a turquoise blue, reflecting the sky that arched endlessly above him.

To the west, another small river snaked its way through the almost impenetrable vegetation and towering trees. A geyser shot through the layers of vines and colorful flora before disappearing back into the earth. Between ruby-colored vines that clung to the shattered ruins of ancient temples, timeworn stone faces stared out from the dense foliage that shrouded them. The jungle bled into a desert with miles of rolling hills made of blinding white sand that ended Passage Island at the Pacific Ocean's turbulent seashore.

The ground rushing up from below demanded Lazer's attention. In a matter of seconds, his vista vanished and he landed with a thump, feet first, tucked and rolled, spinning across the soft, grass-covered terrain of the small clearing. He jerked the release handle, and his chute billowed away, then dutifully and instantaneously, biodegraded, disintegrating into thick, sweet-smelling organic foam before his eyes. Lazer stood up and shifted his survival strap, which had enough basic supplies to take him through his first few days until he got his bearings. He breathed the clammy jungle air and look around; other than the survival suit on his back, his thoughts, and his instincts, he was alone.

Lazer scanned the sky and set his solar compass to triangulate and give him his position on the island. He called up and checked his holographic quest map, going over the list of things he'd been assigned to retrieve for his thesis. All the basics were covered: science, logic, math, physics, geography, psychology, physiology, and history. *Check*, he thought and shut down the map. Lazer turned a 360 and searched for a pathway that would take him into the jungle. The easiest route to his eventual rendezvous point was through the eastern jungle and across the lower mountains to the north. Neither the temple ruins nor the desert would be on this trek. Perhaps he would have them for his final Rite of Passage. On that final passage, he'd face real dangers and holographic visions designed to make him tackle his greatest fears. He'd heard stories of visions that appeared in the form of ancient monsters and nightmarish beasts. Lazer walked toward the far side of the circle thinking he'd rather take on physical battles in his second and third year against fully grown splicers than to face his own imaginary fears any day. Right now, his concern focused on the small but often vicious living creatures he would probably have to face on this first Rite of Passage. They would be challenging enough,

"Okay, Laz, get your act together. All creatures that can kill you are tagged and monitored and easily rendered unconscious by your PAR switch or the observation team if things get out of hand. So ice out," Lazer said to himself out loud.

Still, he could feel the hackles rise in the back of his neck as he approached the thick wall of wide leaf trees that stood before him. Beyond the row of trunks lay ominous shadows that faded into near blackness. Lazer stopped and took a breath. He was nervous. At least staying in the moment would keep his mind off Elana and Kyla.

"Okay go! You can handle this. Your primary Rite of Passage is basic day-to-day survival and gathering of samples for your freshman thesis. No big deal," he said and looked up for the satellite transmitters. "Hope you folks are picking this up." Lazer headed north.

He'd barely crossed the widest part of the clearing and already the heat and humidity had his face covered in sheets of sweat. His environmental suit had been designed to acclimate to any temperature; laced with an intricate web of monitoring sensors—fine carbon nanotubes functioning as power storage, micro motors, and miniscule structural support cables combined with imbedded circuitry. The special molecular tubes and miniscule cables were each designed for a host of functions, from extracting vapor from the air to create water or from the sea to keep the body hydrated. Some could convert his body heat into light, storing it, and regenerating it back as heat. The same filters were perfect for converting the ions from positive sun and body heat into a welcome flow of negative coolness. The suit was a genius design with A.I. that enabled the echo-sensors to interpret the body's internal signals: perspiration, low or high skin temperature, heart rate, breathing pattern, and the mind's beta waves. Balancing them against the external environmental data, the suit would determine the physical comfort needs of the wearer. It all sounded impressive, so why was he so hot?

As he walked into the wider spaced trees, he drifted back into his jumbled thoughts of school, Elana Blue, Kyla, and then his mother and her last desperate call. Lazer grabbed for the wristsponder Brockton had taken. Over and over in his mind, he replayed that frightening last communication from her, wondering what he could have done to help her even if Brockton hadn't flushed him. *You should be there*, he thought.

Lost in his frustration, Lazer came to an opening in the trees. The jungle revealed a small field of emerald-colored grasses that ended at a solid wall of bamboo trees. It was choked with all manner of dense vegetation and thick ropes of hanging, twisting vines that completely blocked his path. He'd been walking for at least two hours, so going back wasn't an option. Without a second thought, Lazer raised his hands and, using one of the minor skills he had learned in Visionistic Arts, parted the trees as effortlessly as Moses had parted the Red Sea. The crack and snap of bending bamboo and breaking vines made him feel like he could handle this until suddenly he remembered Brockton's warning.

"No Arts. Spit!" he muttered and begrudgingly released the foliage as fast as he could.

Lazer looked at the tangles wall and found a narrow passage. He squeezed between the moss-covered trees, grunting through the twists and turns of each ridiculously tight space he could get his body through. He pulled out a small but effective laser machete and methodically hacked his way into the jungle. It was hard work, but he was strong and he felt good with the level of progress he was making. As he walked, he whistled until he heard a distinct snap in the branches above him.

7

MASTA LIA POE
AND THE FIRST VOID

MASTA LIA POE opened her eyes. They felt heavy, as if caught in a dream from which she couldn't awake. Her small frame and cascading white hair floated weightless on a breeze that came from nowhere in a place that existed beyond description. It was cool and bright and vastly empty other than an even streak of blue light that emanated from nowhere and expanded everywhere at once. She searched above and below but found she had no reference point, only the grand expanse of silver-gray colors brushed with pink that stretched away from her in every direction. There were no walls, ceilings, or floor, no horizon, no sky, no land, or sea, only a great expanse of light and color spilling into a vast infinity. Masta Poe stepped forward and the cool air warmed as the sense of profound beauty and peace prevailed. From nowhere, a soft wind pulled at her long ivory tunic and whipped her hair. Calmly, she waited for this extraordinary space to

41

instruct her as to why she was there and what she was supposed to do next.

A new color came in a wrinkle of yellow light accompanied by a loud pop that sent sound waves in the form of a dozen transparent rings. The rings rippled through her and continued out across the space, which expanded and then contracted. Suddenly, Riana stood next to her on a floor that a moment ago didn't exist.

"Oh, hello, Masta Poe," Riana said, a bit surprised.

"Riana," Masta Poe responded and tilted her head. "Do you know where you are?"

Riana looked around. "Not exactly. Are you in my imagination?" Riana asked.

"Perhaps you are in mine," Masta Poe told her, punctuating the thought with a warm smile.

Riana smiled back.

"Well, where do you think you are?" Masta Poe inquired.

"I didn't know it had a name," Riana said.

"You've been here before."

"A few times in my dreams and during deep meditation. This is the first time I have come here and been awake."

"You are in the Voids," Masta Poe explained.

"Voids," Riana said with a rush of clairsentient psychic understanding so complete it surprised her. "This is where you told me to come if any of your prophecies comes true. Right?"

"Yes. Your mother foresaw it first. It's why we stepped up your training," Masta Poe said.

"But you've seen this prophesy too?" Riana asked.

"In a manner of speaking. I have only chosen to know it in the realms of infinite possibility, existing without fear or the need to control or take," Masta Poe said with a humble smile.

"What are they?" Riana asked.

"I understand these Voids to be folds in time and space that can be accessed through the human mind; your emotions and passions are your best tools of navigation. You can use them to see and visualize a possible future or heal the emotions of the past," Masta Poe said as she looked around. "Do you believe the future can be changed if you know what is coming?" Masta Poe asked.

"I suppose," Riana answered.

"Then close your eyes and see what could be."

Riana did as Masta Poe requested, and in an instant, her eyes flew open. "Stop!" she shouted suddenly feeling frightened and out of breath. "Why would anyone want to kidnap me?"

"You are more powerful than you know and when the dark powers find out that truth, they will want to possess you and your gifts," Masta Poe explained.

"How can a place of telepathic thoughts be safe?" Riana asked looking around as if someone would rush out and take her.

"These can be more than psychic realms, Riana, if we focus our thoughts, we bring the energy to manifest them into reality," Masta Poe explained. "I discovered these abilities when I still lived with my mother beneath the earth. I imagined other life paths, explored a myriad of possible dimensions that lead into other times and even other worlds. I envisioned living above ground in the sun and the day that vision manifested into reality, I lost my mother. That tragedy terrified me so much I blocked the portals into the Voids, and for a long time they became lost to me until you brought me here," Masta Poe said.

"I don't understand, are we physically here now?" Riana asked.

Masta Poe reached out and passed her hand through Riana, frightening her and causing her to step back.

"Your mind is here. Yes. But it's not until you can bring your three-dimensional self and for that you must physically ascend here."

Masta Poe looked at her protégée. She could see the fear and confusion as Riana's mind grappled to understand. Riana, at just fourteen, had blossomed from the confident little girl Masta Poe met at three years old into the beginnings of a beautiful young woman. It was easy to see her spirit had enormous natural powers that she and the universe were just learning to freely share.

"You are a true questor of vision, Riana," Masta Poe said. "You and a few others on Earth hold the key to humanity's next evolution. The boy you saw in your vision, Cole Lazerman? When he lets go of the hatred and anger that binds him to the past, he too will be one of the great questors. You will both know the boundless gifts of the source that will give you knowings," Masta Poe said.

"You taught me about the knowings," Riana said.

"Yes. Do you remember what I taught you?"

"Knowings are the ancient, genetic memories which give all humans an understanding of our ancient and universal source knowledge, our collective truths and future wisdoms," Riana said.

You as an individual being hold inside you the ability to comprehend the true meaning of self-realization and with it your special purpose in the universe. You and a select group of others have unique skills that will lead this planet to ascend across the universe and connect into a better place for everyone. Masta Poe thought the words and sent them to her telepathically, *Riana, I believe your connection to the universal love and power source is purer than anyone I have ever met.*

Riana smiled and thought back, *Thanks.*

Masta Poe quickly cleared her mind so Riana would not read her thoughts of the danger that came with such a gift. Riana had much to learn, and those who wanted her had not figured out the wealth of her powers were a great danger to her.

Masta Poe gestured all around them. "I believe these Voids are the imagination's unseeded fields of what could be. What would you imagine into being, Riana?"

"Could I imagine my mother home?" Riana asked.

Masta Poe could hear Riana's voice suddenly filled with hope.

"Desires for personal gain? Besides, why would you desire to control the destiny of another? Perhaps your mother is where she needs to be to do what is best for her."

"But I'm worried about her," Riana said as the moment of hope crashed into despair. Masta Poe could watch Riana's emotions as they shifted into fear for her mother. The soft, grayish pink color that completely surrounded them turned a cold, steely gray. The space closed in on them with the weight of an impending storm.

"Riana! Stop. Do not bring fear into these Voids, Riana, for just as there are good and wondrous things you can create here, there are also bad. By the laws of the universe, bad feelings and negative emotions will attract others of like kind to you. Can you stop and promise to control your emotions?"

"I promise," Riana said.

The gray lifted and changed to the kind of pearl that takes the sky just before dawn.

"And what good does worrying do, Riana?" Masta Poe asked. "Does it make you feel better?"

"Certainly not!" Riana said.

"Does it change the reality of what is happening?"

"No, but . . ."

"Then worry serves no purpose at all, does it?" Masta Poe asked.

Riana tilted her head and furrowed her brow. Tears of frustration filled her eyes. "No."

"To worry is a futile act. It is the need to control a situation you cannot change by thinking bad thoughts of what could possibly go wrong—for in this case only action can change reality unless it belongs to someone else's destiny. Respect your mother's journey, Riana."

"I miss her," Riana insisted.

"Then it is for yourself and not your mother that you worry?"

"Yes, selfishly. But what can I do to make this horrible emptiness go away?" Riana asked, the tears now falling from her eyes.

Again the space turned bluish-gray and it began to rain. Riana looked around and opened her hand capturing the drops as they fell.

"Breathe, Riana. Be at peace," Masta Poe said. "Use your mind and affect your own reality. Love her and leave your mother to deal with her destiny."

"How?" Riana said.

"Stand in the present only and surrender to what is now. Believe you can and you will," Masta Poe told her.

Riana closed her eyes and her young face filled with peace. Instantly, the rain blew away, allowing a wave of the soft pastel colors to surround them again.

"Believe that your mother is safe. See it. Will it. Have faith that she is doing what she needs to do and will her to come back to you if and when the time is best for her to do so. Remember, she too is on a journey. Love her with open arms, Riana, as she has learned to love you. That is the greatest gift we can give anyone: unconditional love filled with trust and honesty and the belief that everything that is happening is for the best."

Riana threw herself into Masta Poe's arms. As Masta Poe folded her arms around her, the colors in the Void shifted and blossomed into an opalescent rainbow. A great white light filled the space, enveloping them. Just before they vanished, Riana caught a glimpse of a small, glowing yellow ball that floated a few feet from her. Without words, it called her name.

"Riana, I'm waiting for you. Come to me. The time is now," the ball of yellow light said in a language Riana had never heard. The meaning was vague, but she was certain it said her name. "Beware," she heard it whisper. The colors that undulated turned into a brilliant white light and covered them. Riana and Masta Poe vanished from the space leaving the glowing yellow ball as it hung a moment longer in the vast, empty Void. Then, with a pop, it vanished.

8

THE APPRENTICE

FIVE HAD BEEN AT Temple Mountain for the better part of the day. Five had searched the main data banks for one biodroid who did not fit the configuration profile in the hope of discovering the codes he needed without Covax. He discovered only multiple failed biodroid projects that had been designed, initiated, and personally rejected by Ducane Covax. Most had been destroyed, but two had managed to avoid the disintegration process because both had been sent to Tosadae as an experiment. They had studied with the politia at their military academy, but only one had been invited to study with the great Visionistic splicer Masta Poe. Her and more so her mother's experiments, Five learned, had discovered direct connectivity with universal source energy. That connection was essential to accessing the full spectrum of the powers that drove the vast array of abilities that were the Visionistic Arts. Five was curious for selfish reasons. He needed to know if Masta Poe had been successful in teaching this biodroid the Visionistic Arts. It would mean its biological elements held a soul. It meant "they" in some way were

47

alive. It was obvious the report was incomplete. The program had been shut down. The attacks on Atlantia made all off-continent biodroids security risks. Both biodroids at Tosadae had been returned forty-six hours before the coup that domed Atlantia.

A metal tap rapped against the door. On Five's command the biodroid entered. It was not as statuesque or massive as Five, but OPALMOX, as it was called, was distinguishable by the beautiful purple sheen of its skin. The color seemed to create a moiré pattern as it caught the light and made him look more alive than any of the other biodroids Five had ever seen. OPALMOX entered and stood at attention in front of Five.

"OPALMOX reporting as ordered," the biodroid said.

Five studied the biodroid in silence for a long time. He could tell by the slight shifts in its arms it felt uncomfortable. *Feelings*, Five thought. He checked the data scroll reconfirming some of the information.

"You are designed with human and viral-based synthetic DNA according to my data shards," Five said.

"Correct, sir. Is that why I have been summoned?" OPALMOX asked.

Five watched the green light bands rhythmically move up and down the biodroid's face.

"You have been at Tosadae," Five said. "You studied under Masta Poe and trained in FX-80 Lightning Politia fighter simulators. Those reasons, in addition to having a unique DNA bio form, is why you are here."

"O-P-A-L-M-O-X? What does that mean?" Five asked, knowing the answer from his data shard.

"It's an acronym. O-P-A-L-M-O-X stands for Organically Programmed Android Living Mechanical Operational eXchange."

"Reconfigure," Five said.

"Sir?" it asked.

"It's easier if you have eyes," Five said.

"Easier for what?" OPALMOX replied.

Defiance, thought Five. *None of the other biodroids had shown any signs of free will.*

"That was an order," Five said.

"I was only curious as to why human features are relevant. As part of my education at Tosadae . . ."

"Curious?" Five said cutting off the biodroid.

"Masta Poe and the other instructors encouraged intellectual exchanges, sir. Is that a problem?" OPALMOX asked.

"Not for the moment."

"Why do you want me to transform, sir?" OPALMOX asked again.

"As I said, it's easier for me to read your emotions. You obviously have them, and I have found that in human form it is impossible for even our kind to lie," Five said.

"Why would I lie, sir?"

"Well OPALMOX, you are still resisting my command to use your transformation technology. I am your superior and do not need to explain the reason. Do it," Five said.

Like turning on a light switch, the biodroid shifted its molecules from gray to flesh. Eyes, a nose, lips, ears, and shoulder length hair lifted from the blob of swirling matter as it reconfigured itself into its chosen human version. Five smiled. Its human form looked thin and its features androgynous.

"You have not decided if you are male or female?" Five asked.

"A biodroid has no gender. We do not procreate, so it is irrelevant," OPALMOX said.

"If I need you to infiltrate, you must decide your gender for a convincing transformation. Do you understand, OPALMOX?" Five asked.

"Yes," OPALMOX responded.

Five observed the biodroid, fascinated by this logical reasoning and the streak of belligerence. *If it persisted,* Five thought, *OPALMOX would be disintegrated and that would be that.* Dissention was not acceptable in the Black Guard ranks of Five's forces. However, Five knew very well these human traits might be worth observing as long as they could be controlled. Besides, OPALMOX had a variety of needed attributes.

"You are trained by the politia to fly an FX-80. Are you not?"

"Yes, sir. I have only flow simulators, but my scores are exceptional."

"And were you angry when they asked you to leave Tosadae?" Five asked.

OPALMOX paused to consider the question.

"My emotions were still too new for me to decipher what I felt, sir."

Five looked at Masta Poe's report to Covax. In every course of study, OPALMOX ranked near perfect by any standard, human or biodroid. The fact that he could not comprehend rejection added a layer to Five's building mistrust.

"I want you to work with me OPALMOX," Five said.

"In what capacity, sir?"

"I will let you know. Report to my first officer and give it this data stream. It will explain the rest."

Five pointed to the panel on OPALMOX's arm and transmitted the data over a secure optical link directly into OPALMOX's data system.

"That will be all," Five said.

OPALMOX stood still assessing the report. The soft ambiguous features, especially the ill-formed eyes, looked as if the biodroid had fallen into a state of deep contemplation. With a blink, the life came back into its eyes and with it a look of concern.

"Is there a problem, OPALMOX?" Five asked.

"You would do that to the humans?" OPALMOX replied in response to the details of the data.

"I will do what I must for us to survive," Five said. "Do not pity the humans. They have never pitied any species on this planet including their own."

OPALMOX quickly transformed out of the human features and into its biodroid form. It shifted so quickly that Five could not read its feelings. The idea that this biodroid might possess free will fascinated Five.

"You may go," Five said.

OPALMOX turned to leave.

"OPALMOX? Were you able to perform any of the Visionistic Arts?" Five asked.

OPALMOX hesitated. "No," OPALMOX said.

"If you betray me, I will disintegrate you. Do you understand?"

"Yes," OPALMOX said and left.

"I will disintegrate you," Five repeated and let his human face shift into its biodroid form.

9

HOURS INTO DAYS

DANTE HAD HEARD it first. Some message had gotten through about the state of affairs beneath the dome over Atlantia. They all waited for the report. Mangalan's aide entered the room, whispered in his ear, and after a terse nod, inserted a disc into the main player. She launched a series of images that expanded into a massive holographic projection that everyone could see.

"The Black Guard have done a sweep," the aide announced.

"A sweep?" Fahan asked.

"They've opened the dome and sent out several sorties. They attacked and snatched multiple transports off the sea and out of the air," a commander added.

"This says they used a wide-range electromagnetic gravity beam," Dante said, looking at the report. Anger swelled in his voice.

"That's impossible!" Mangalan said as he reviewed the data. "There isn't a gravity beam powerful enough to yank seventeen transports out at once."

"Obviously there is," Dante corrected him.

"And we don't have it," Blane Fahan added.

"Maybe we've had it for years. Probably since the Great Quakes uncovered half the technology from the Celians, we were able to decipher and use it to advance ourselves," Dante said. "The Black Guard just figured it out and didn't tell us."

"I suppose you believe the myth that they discovered the red Gnorb in the forties during the atomic tests at White Sands and it gave humans the technology for microwaves and computers," Fahan said.

"Actually I do," Mangalan said. "How else do you account for the paradigm shift? The other Gnorbs discovered after the Great Quakes certainly accounted for half the technology we have today. And we have barely scratched the surface."

"Gentlemen, the present concern is how to protect our transports," Dante said.

"We've rerouted traffic five hundred miles in all directions around the Atlantia fly zone," Commander Banner responded.

"How many transports have been taken since we lost control of the dome?" Dante asked.

"Thirty-seven reported, sir," Banner told him.

Dante flared, "If that isn't an act of global war, I don't know what the hell is."

"Our alternate makes a good point," Fahan said. "These are blatant acts of war beyond the Atlantian borders. We have to stand up to them."

"Who? What enemy are we standing up to?" Mangalan asked. "Ducane Covax? A phantom group of biodroids?"

"Black Guard," Dante corrected him. "And they are far from phantoms. I think Covax won't respond because he can't. I believe Aleece is right. The biodroids are sentient and in control—perhaps not all, but enough of them to initiate these terrorist actions. What is happening on Atlantia is just the beginning."

"We have no standing army to stop them," Fahan pointed out.

"What is our status on organizing and reinstating the Joint Politia Forces?" Mangalan asked Commander Banner.

Banner stood and gave a lengthy report telling of more clone attacks that had occurred not only around the Alliance but also in both the Common Market territories and the Republic. Dante couldn't help but think that all Politia Forces already assigned to the various territories were being stressed. Banner paused and then added, "An additional seventy thousand politia have already been drafted and placed in accelerated training to prepare for a possible Atlantian invasion."

"Who ordered that?" Mangalan demanded.

"It wasn't an order, Triumvirate; it was a request from Dr. Avery before she left."

"Very much like your precautionary order to place dome pads without informing the rest of the Triumvirate," Fahan said.

Mangalan's ego felt the sting of Fahan's verbal slap.

"I believe these additional outbreaks are a diversion, a distraction to keep us busy so we don't invade," Dante added.

"Can you prove that?" Mangalan asked.

"They have control over the dome! They can open and shut it in sections at will," Commander Banner said.

"And can you prove that the Black Guard are in control?" Mangalan asked. He looked at Dante.

No, Dante thought. Their reconnaissance was thin at best. The dome over Atlantia blocked any communications out or in and all satellite visuals. Only the occasional V-mails that spilled out when the dome opened to snatch vessels provided information. Black Guard loyalists, who in turn rallied clones, mutants, gens, and splicers around the world to sympathize with the Black Guard, didn't make a case. Even unsubstantiated rumors of zomer military forces being created in the Far East regions north of Station City—thousands of shallow-gene clones, idiot savants capable of a single task: to kill and destroy—needed hard proof to justify an invasion.

"Everyone knows about the pockets of defecting clones and splicers, but can we prove Ducane Covax created an army of biodroids? How big an army? For what reason?" Mangalan asked.

"Add to that a colossal electromagnetic gravity beam capable of snatching multiple transports out of the sky and off the seam," another commander added.

Dante looked around the room. Why would no one say it out loud?

"I am not alone in my belief that these biological machines we created to protect us have themselves taken Atlantia, and we have to stop them," Dante said.

"We can't invade Atlantia without proof," Fahan said.

"It wouldn't be the first time in this planet's history that a country was invaded without proof," Commander Banner added.

"Well, until we get it, I say we unify all Politia Forces and concentrate them in a staging field near Atlantia and set up a blockade," Dante insisted.

"To what end?" Mangalan asked. "Without direct provocation, any attempt at an invasion would be against the law and sitting off their coast would be seen as a threat."

"What law gave them the right to seize the dome and hold Atlantia and a world leader hostage?" Dante snapped back. "The people of Atlantia have asked for our protection! We continue to do nothing. We've failed them."

"I agree with Interim Triumvirate Labov to make preparations to go in now and cut this cancer off in Atlantia. If we're wrong, we pull out," Fahan said.

"We have not had a formal request from the Atlantian government," Mangalan said.

"The same government that put that dome in place and locked us and the world out? I don't think they're taking requests," Dante told him. "We have to go in now and cut this cancer off while it's locked in Atlantia. If we leave it to fester, we may not be able to stop what comes out when that dome opens."

"I agree with Dr. Labov," Commander Banner added. "At least for the moment, time is on our side."

Several of the corporate commanders and corporate leaders nodded in agreement.

"How do we amass an army and move into position without the Black Guard finding out?" Fahan asked.

"The only secure way is by not telling the Collective," the commander said.

A new voice entered the debate.

"That is against the Freedom of Information laws. I agree with Dr. Mangalan; we are bound by World Constitutional law," Dillard Markum, a specialist in governance, added from a far corner of the room.

Markum, a narrow-minded number cruncher, represented the interests of the Collective population. He made sure the citizens were informed of every decision made on their behalf, and the Collective had not been notified of the decision to dome Atlantia or the coup that followed.

"The entire Collective must be informed and allowed to vote on any matter of global importance," Markum said.

"How much time to amass a force large enough to go into Atlantia?" Dante asked Commander Banner.

"Four months, maybe six, sir. Maybe."

"Can you do it in one?" Dante asked.

The commander's jaw dropped.

"I say we amass the forces, prepare to invade, and then tell the Collective," Dante said. "Or you could give away the plans for our only salvation to the enemy."

His eyes locked on Markum.

Markum shifted in his seat. Dante knew he had an obligation to the Collective, but without knowing who or where the enemy was, he felt sure telling the Collective would probably alert the Black Guard sympathizers. It would jeopardize any hope Atlantia had at security and expose the politia's plan before they were ready.

"If the Collective knows, the enemy will too," Dante said to Markum.

"You realize what you are asking me to do?"

"I am asking you to give us a chance to save Atlantia," Dante said.

"One month," Markum said as he stood. "One month and we present to the Collective and at the same time give the press a full briefing."

"We can have all the forces on the planet assembled outside Atlantia, but it won't mean anything if we can't get through that dome," Mangalan told them.

He was right. They had to figure out a way to drop the dome. Dante, Blane Fahan, and Commander Banner leaned forward to start the logistical planning phase of how to move a hundred thousand joint forces into position. A substantial amount of work had to be done before an invasion of such magnitude could be mounted. Dante knew his history, and nothing like it had been attempted since before the Great Quakes.

Dante noticed Mangalan sit back quietly while they talked. Finally, Mangalan rose and crossed to his chamber desk. Dante watched. Mangalan looked anxious as he gathered several info shards and gave them to his assistant. The assistant left, and Mangalan returned to the others. No one else saw the exchange. Aleece had never liked him, but she'd never mistrusted his integrity. It was blatantly obvious to Dante; Mangalan had a plan of his own.

10

A DEAL

DUCANE COVAX SAT MOTIONLESS, shrouded in dark shadows inside his Atland City corporate offices. Behind him, he could hear the steady hum of amino isolation sequencers, computers, and the dripping sounds from bubbling beakers that processed an array of toxic chemical compounds. The design labs had allowed his genius to flourish, but today they held only defeat and anguish. It had only been a few days since he had survived the ruthless interrogation by Five's torture team with its probes, neurological shock stimuli, and primitive but very effective forms of physical torture. Still, he had refused to give Five the genetic code sequence he needed to build his army. Covax's head scientist and chief technologist, Pi, had nursed him back from death's door, but his body ached with every labored breath. His clothes were filthy and caked with his blood. His eyes, sunken and ringed by great black circles, vacillated between sadness, fear, frustration, and anger. He felt beyond exhausted. Only his anger at Five and his love for Elana Blue gave him the will to live. He could not leave her in a world ruled by the likes of Five. For the moment, he and the world were safe. Only Covax knew the genetic programming codes. Those codes would allow the complex, microscopic nanobands to shift their atomic particles and transform into anything they were ordered to become. Now that the biodroids had become sentient, there was no question they could become the war machines Five needed to defeat humanity. Covax knew without question he alone held the key to Five's army.

Covax ran his fingers through his hair, desperate to massage away the nagging voice that reminded him again and again: only one other person could figure out how to build the chemical formula and biological sequences needed to ignite the hidden powers of the biodroids and she was on another continent. Once Five had that, Covax would no longer be of use.

With the dawn breaking through the blackness outside his window, he had survived another sleepless night. Covax listened as a sound came from beyond the window, the bleating call of a flock of wild lameracks. They cluttered the sky with their awkward and unnatural forms. Lameracks were mutated splicers that resembled large predatory birds, except for the cloven hooves and curled horns of a ram that crowned their woolly heads. Their sheepish bleating echoed over Atland City's vacant streets. This morning Covax found peace in their chatter. He gave thanks to the Universal God that he had survived another night. Covax heard the lock release and the door retract. He opened one eye as a shadow rushed toward him.

Five moved to Covax and stood motionless in the shadows while the molecules of his head shifted into a kind of face. Covax marveled at the evolution in his creation. It simultaneously filled him with pride and fear as he watched the awkward transformation. Covax leaned forward from the shadows to speak.

"The politia have you sealed in," Covax whispered, his voice still weak and dry from the screams of pain that had racked his body over the days of torture.

"On the contrary. I have them sealed out," Five replied.

The corners of Five's mouth struggled to create a sneer.

"Half the cities along Atlantia's eastern seaboard are under my command. As for the rest, it's only a matter of time before the entire continent is mine," Five said.

Covax pushed against his hands, forcing himself forward. Pi appeared and crossed the room to help him. A hard glance from Five stopped him. Pi moved away, taking his place next to Five. Covax felt himself sicken. Pi, a once loyal friend, had turned traitor.

"I need the codes," Five said in a matter-of-fact tone.

"Figure them out," Covax hissed back, equally calm.

"I was afraid you would make this difficult." He raised his hand, and three more guards entered. Elana Blue walked between them. She was pale and weak. The side effects from the hypnotically induced coma were slowly subsiding. Her mind functioned in its hazy state but she was unable to focus and her Visionistic powers were still inaccessible to her. She knew it, and so did Five. When she saw her father, she broke from her escorts and rushed to his side.

"Daddy! Oh, Daddy! I was so afraid. They murdered everyone," she said as she fell into his arms.

Tears spilled from her eyes. Covax held his daughter and stroked her hair, wishing he could make it all go away as he had when she was a child. He couldn't. To have Elana's life at risk was beyond his endurance—a fact Five knew all too well.

Elana looked at her father in the dim light and saw his battered face. "Universal God! What has he done to you?"

"Only what he has allowed," Five said. "Your father was just about to give me the genetic program codes I requested and end this abuse."

Covax could see in Elana's eyes she understood the frightening reality of the situation.

"I knew you weren't behind these attacks," she said, laying her face against her father's hands.

"Leave her out of this," Covax said.

"That is up to you," Five said. He signaled to OPALMOX. "Place her in the compressor's field. If she resists shock her. Don't kill her . . . yet."

11

SQUOIDS

A TEAR HAD SPILLED out of Kyla's eye, pooling in the tiny hollow near her nose. The salty puddle expanded until it could hold no more. It overflowed and gently rolled down her cheek. With a delicate splash, it splattered onto her hand.

She lay inside her dreamless sleep; the dull throbbing pain that lulled her body suddenly sent a massive surge that brought her back to harsh reality. This time there was no gentle release from her peaceful, hypnotic coma but a violent rush that erupted and jerked her from the exhaustion. Kyla bit her lip, holding back the scream that begged to come out. Her mind raced. How much time had passed since she had managed to pull herself up and inside the crawlspace? Kyla made the choice to live and in doing so left Elana Blue to her fate. *If Elana's father is behind this, at least she'll be safe,* she thought. *If he isn't* . . . Kyla stopped herself.

She dragged her mind away from imagining Elana's fate. She had to figure out what to do next.

Kyla tried to swallow. Her tongue, thick and swollen, tasted like old metal. Her whole body ached, helpless and weak from the ordeal. The jagged remains of her wings pulsed and throbbed, stinging like a whip into her flesh. She wished when she opened her eyes she would be home with her mother, or at least in the Sangelino Healers Center, where they could take the pain away and heal her. She wanted her wings back. She wanted to spread them and fly away from the nightmare that waited a few feet below her. Buried in her thoughts she heard a soft slurping sound. It echoed up from below like liquid sucked through a straw in an empty glass.

Kyla lifted her head and peeked through a crack she'd left open in the ceiling panel. It had taken her last ounce of strength to pull the panel back and hide. The lights from the transport flickered intermittently, giving her odd glimpses of some indistinguishable forms. In the sputtering light, she saw jumbled in the doorway what looked like a body. *No, two bodies*, she thought. They're all dead.

The flickering lights made it impossible to tell if the bodies were male or female, young or old, human or splicer, only they were dead. The slurping sound commanded her attention. In the dozen or so flashes of light something small moved.

Kyla listened. Her keen, splicer hearing multiplied the sound. It came from multiple sources. The lights flashed, and in the harsh glow, Kyla saw something move along the floor outside her sanctuary. It looked horribly awkward and unnatural. As quietly as she could, she pulled herself closer to the crack and repositioned her eye.

It moved again. A tiny arm no more than the size of a little baby's arm lifted gracefully and wrapped around the head of one of the bodies. Kyla's heart pounded. Was this a child who had lost its mother? Then a second arm, a third, a fourth. Universal God, it is not human, she thought. It crawled over the bodies followed by more of its kind.

Kyla's survival instincts shifted from concern into fear: squoids!

Squoids—half squid, half machine biodroids designed to clear away living refuse from the fringe areas that surrounded the underwater city of Panazia; organic garbage eaters. *But they don't eat humans, and besides, they need salt water to survive,* she thought to herself. A moment later, Kyla gasped. They were surviving on salt water.

What percent of an adult human's blood is made up of salt water, she thought as she peered back through the crack in the panel. In the flickering light, she saw something else falling through the air as gracefully and gently as a single drop of summer rain—red summer rain. Kyla lifted herself up, letting her arm take the weight of her body. She looked beneath her waist and saw a small pool of her own blood.

Another drop of fresh, warm, salty blood fell from the ceiling panel, and this time hit one of the squoids on its elongated head. It lifted a tentacle and touched the wet drop, brought the tip of the tentacle to its beak-shaped mouth, and tasted. Slowly, it lifted its ugly pink head and rolled a flat, circular black eye upward, searching for the location of its offering.

12

THE JUNGLE

LAZER BROKE THROUGH the knotted undergrowth and stopped in a small clearing of fallen trees, gasping for air. Filthy, hungry, and thirsty, not to mention exhausted from the oppressive heat and arduous journey, he plopped down on a rock. He scratched the dozen or so insect bites on his exposed face, neck, and hands.

Ahead, a small tarsier-like monkey with large goggle-like eyes set into an odd little face and a long tufted tail lapped water from a large hollow in a fallen tree trunk. Lazer pushed to his feet and moved gingerly toward the monkey, who regarded him with nervous anticipation. Lazer wanted a drink but the monkey refused to relinquish his treasure. Lazer could see the impish creature must have been mixed with some additional genetics he could not identify for certain, but something told him a few human genomes had been thrown in the mix—an absurd thought Lazer considered since this particular part of Passage Island for level one had no splicers.

"Come on. Share it, imp. We're sharing," Lazer said with a warning nod. He feebly attempted to shoo the reluctant monkey away. He resembled a spastic bat attempting to fly and did nothing more than irritate the little creature.

The monkey stopped, screeched a warning back at Lazer, and bared its teeth.

They just stared at each other. One refused to give up his share of the life-giving liquid, while the other cautiously advanced for a portion of the bounty. Lazer decided to try a change in tactics.

"Hi." He smiled, speaking in his most charming tone. "Pardon, my most humble fellow Earthean, but unless you know where the local fountains are, that water ranks as community access." Lazer came nose to nose with the monkey, dropped his head, and dipped his face into the pool of water.

He'd found heaven, cool and wet and utterly refreshing. He gulped it down with the sound of a sputtering vacuum. The monkey chattered at him, moved a few feet away, and reluctantly let Lazer drink. Lazer dipped his hand into the cool liquid and wiped it across his face and neck, washing the sweat, bugs, and general stickiness of the jungle away. For a brief moment, he felt human again.

"Thanks," Lazer said as he splashed a last handful of water over his clothing to wash away the heat and grime from the microfiber that protected him.

A vast shadow fell over everything, dulling the colors of his surroundings. The sun had dipped below the tree line, stealing the blistering light at a rapid pace. As the light faded, the creatures of the jungle gave call. He needed to take shelter. The monkey, who obviously shared his thoughts, scurried up into the branches of a huge vine-covered tree. He quickly found a thick branch with an outgrowth of leaves where he could sleep, safe from the predators of the night.

"I hear ya," Lazer said.

He grabbed for a branch and climbed to a second. It snapped as easily as a crisp stick of celery, far too thin to support his weight. The call of another large nocturnal carnivore echoed in the distance, warning him that he definitely needed to get up that tree.

Without a second thought, he decided to use the few basic skills Masta Poe had taught him. Lazer closed his eyes, opened his hands, and imagined himself as helium. He tried to picture the crystal-clear gas wavering, lighter than air and unrestrained by the pull of gravity. The image of his body being weightless swirled in his head as did the illusion of the tasteless, colorless, inert gas as he imagined it fill his senses. Lazer smiled as he saw himself become a sparkling clear bubble floating up from the ground. Holding the image required total focus. Slowly, he raised himself gently upward until regrettably he remembered; *I'll lose points if I use my powers.* The moment the thought filled his mind, Lazer's eyes flew open, and with the break in concentration, he fell crashing to the ground. Lazer hit with a hard, painful thud. His backside aching, he struggled to get to his feet, lost his balance, and stumbled backward into a pool of liquid mush. The soft mucky ground slowly gave way to a thick watery sludge that took him all of a microsecond to identify: quicksand.

He reached for solid ground, which lay about eight inches away from his fingertips. *Spit!* The word exploded in his mind. A rush of panic roared through his body, tensing every muscle and filling him with abject terror. His heart raced. His breath quickened. He began to sink.

"BREATHE," Lazer said out loud. "Slow and easy. Just breathe."

He took a long, deep, focused breath and slowly exhaled. He forced himself to relax, allowing his body to release. His mind cleared itself of the blinding clutter that came with fear. He began to remember the survival lessons he had learned at Tosadae. At the time, he thought both the instructor and the lessons were tedious and boring. Now he wished he'd listened more intensely. He knew if he moved too quickly or tried to swim he would be dragged down faster. But if he didn't do something immediately, he would be dragged down regardless. Lazer couldn't help but think of how he'd made such an idiotic first mistake. Too late for regrets. Whatever he learned would have to do for now. What's done is done, so *bring yourself to the present and get out or else you'll die,* he thought. Lazer stopped the negative thoughts that burrowed like worms back into his consciousness and lulled him back into fear. *Focus,* he told himself, as he began to remember the lesson on sinkholes and quicksand.

He relaxed. His thoughts came in calm waves that gently recreated the memory of the lesson and delivered them onto the shores of his consciousness. Bit by bit, the image created itself until, like the pieces of an intricate puzzle, the answer came together in a visualization of exactly what he needed to do.

"Horizontal. I need to be horizontal," Lazer said to himself.

He searched the moss-covered muck for something, anything to help him. He could feel the cold gooey slime pull at his feet, sucking him deeper and deeper into the red and green algae that floated on the surface. He refused to let his mind think of the creatures and parasites that lived in the mud and sand that was encasing him.

Lazer saw a broken branch half buried in the mud an arm's length away. It wasn't thick or huge, but it would give him leverage, and it was close. He stretched his arm, extending his shoulder until he thought for certain it would dislocate. He reached the extra millimeter and was glad he had his mother's long, lanky arms. Lazer extended his fingers as far as he could, grabbed the branch, and pulled it to him. The branch turned and slipped, then seemed to suck itself into his grasp. Lazer drew it to him and placed it between his two hands. He positioned the wood in front of his body, pushed the branch down, and pulled himself up. With amazing agility, he crawled over the branch and positioned it under his hips. As fast as he could, he rolled over and spread his arms away from his body. He lifted his hips out and pulled his feet up level with his torso. He looked like a giant X sprawled on the algae. He was exhausted. His breathing came in deep gasps. For the moment, he was out of the sinkhole but still in quicksand.

"Where are your friends when you need them?" Lazer said.

From high above in the dense foliage of the tree, the bug-eyed little monkey peeked through the leaves. It watched Lazer in quiet deference, tilting its head from side to side with the curiosity of a puppy.

Lazer floated in the sludge, searching for a solution. Nothing. No shoreline within his grasp, no vines to reach up and grab, and no one but a useless monkey who seemed to have completely vanished to even hear his cry. Lazer looked at the PAR on his emergency band. His ego refused to let him push it. He wasn't dying, and he still had a trick or two up his sleeve.

Plan B, he thought. Scoot to the banks using what little strength I have or . . . His situation and the sucking sound just to his left made it difficult at best to concentrate. Alligators, his mind warned him. *Plan C*, he thought. Levitation and he would go back to the Visionistic Arts. Losing points seemed far more intelligent than losing his life.

He forced himself to relax and focus on becoming lighter than air. What would lift me out of this muck? Lazer imagined helium-filled balloons. He could feel the sand sucking at him. It wanted to draw him deeper. The cool algae closed in on him. The water crept over his hair and lapped at the skin along the side of his face. He could feel it slap against his ears and tickle the corners of his eyes. He refused to panic as the water moved to cover his mouth and nose.

Concentrate! he ordered his thoughts. He pushed any images of drowning from his mind and allowed the single thought of knowing that he had already gotten free from the quicksand and was high above all the danger. The thought made him smile, and the smile connected him to the universal source. *No fear*, he thought. Happiness. Joy. Bliss.

Lazer grinned. He imagined a thousand brightly colored balloons tied to every limb of his body. They lifted him up and carried him into the low branches of the trees. In his mind, he floated up to the heavens. He imagined himself a child at his fifth birthday party, surrounded by his mother, father, and all his friends. The image filled him with a serene sense of lightness and peace.

Grinning like a Cheshire cat, Lazer opened his eyes. He hovered ten feet above the quicksand and settled among the same cozy branches the odd little monkey had secured. The monkey screamed, furious at this second intrusion. The screech broke Lazer's concentration and dropped him onto the thick branch with a thud. Furious, the monkey scurried away.

Lazer took a long, deep breath and gave the Universal God a moment of humble gratitude. He didn't care about the points he might lose. He was alive and he'd done it himself. He gathered some leaves for his pillow and a large palm frond to cover his body and keep the bugs away. Beyond exhausted, Lazer took a deep breath and relaxed.

Sleep beckoned to him with the sweet call of a beautiful Siren's song lulling him into sweet repose. His arms ached; they were stiff and felt heavy as anvils as they lay motionless across his body. He barely sensed the thousand or so tiny bugs that nibbled and bit at him before they, along with everything else in his conscious world, vanished. Lazer drifted off to sleep.

13

BRIEF HISTORY OF TIME

CASHTON RAN ACROSS the ice shelf. He had thrown the tiny lever that released twenty razor-sharp titanium spikes underneath the bottom of his boots. His adrenalin pumped faster, driven by whatever tracked him beneath the ice. The cleats gave him traction on the ice but made running more difficult. Slowing him even more was the wind. It had changed direction. It blew into his face with a sharp slap he felt even through the clear, fibrous face shield. The fabric allowed fresh air to enter but dulled the cold and kept out moisture. The fiber could also shift colors and darken to protect his eyes and skin from the ultraviolet rays of the low-arching sun.

Cashton looked up. The shifting blues meant the ozone damage to the stratosphere above the new southern pole was an added danger of the region and increased his potential peril even more. More than a hundred years has passed and Earth was still healing from the toxic particles of fluorocarbons and noxious gasses left by human life in the pre-AQ twentieth century.

In the prior century, fossil fuel emissions from industry and transports, cows emitting huge amounts of methane gases because of improper diets of grain and not grass, and especially the secret and highly toxic chemtrails from covert private experiments changed the weather and destroyed huge sections of the ionosphere and stratosphere. When the extremists, desperate to control the population, were unleashed to do as they please, they killed millions of people and animals. Enormous sections of the ozone at both poles were devastated by the continuing particle dump and long-term atmospheric abuse.

As he ran, Cashton remembered the vivid pictures and CGI renderings his professor had shared of the great ice melts. He pictured the massive amounts of melting ice and displaced water that swelled the oceans and swallowed whole islands and vast continental shorelines. The devastation submerged whole countries and killed millions as it changed the coastlines. Not since Dwarka, the ancient submerged city off western India, Mu off Japan, and Atlantia in the middle of the Atlantic Ocean, had so much land and documented history of early civilization been lost.

Cashton felt a thud beneath his feet. Without stopping, he looked down and noticed new details in the shadowy form that tracked him beneath the ever-thinning ice. It was testing the ice.

He looked at his PAR creature control. He knew the initials on the device meant Pulsar Activation Release, but right now they meant only one thing: push the button and run.

Cashton looked up at the ice caves. Half snow covered black eyes peering from undulating walls of ice-covered rocks. They appeared to be getting farther away instead of closer. *An optical illusion caused by the low-lying sun on the ice,* he thought. His breath became labored. Another thud pounded beneath his feet.

Cashton felt this last thud shudder through him. He searched the ice beneath his feet. Nothing. The shadow was gone. Another thud reverberated a few yards ahead of him and rattled Cashton's bones, vibrating through him. There was no doubt in his mind the sound came from straight up ahead. Cashton veered slightly left. The next thud was harder, more forceful and it was followed by a large cracking sound from the ice. As the sound faded into the icy wind, it brought everything into clarity; the creature was slamming itself into the ice to break it and bring him into the water. Cashton looked down studying the glassy surface. Through the wisps of snow that blew across the ice, they reminded him of winter clouds shifting over a winter sky. The ice was getting thinner, and the creature was circling back to make its move. Big, smart, and obviously a very hungry predator, it wanted Cashton in the water. Cashton looked at the caves.

14

COURAGE

"STOP!" COVAX YELLED, struggling against the restraints that bound him to a chair. "She doesn't know where the program codes are hidden!"

Her father's voice fell into a drone of pleas as Elana Blue floated weightlessly above the floor, trapped in an invisible force field.

"Don't tell them," Elana said in a dry whisper.

Covax felt his heart breaking. He understood better than anyone the ritual Five conceived to convince him to cooperate had already begun. The use of pain in the art of persuasion was an ancient art form and obviously it came naturally to Five. Covax understood better than anyone where Five had learned the various techniques of torture. Covax was to blame and he knew it all too well. Five has assimilated all the recorded historic details of human cruelty from the beginning of time. Five had been allowed to access the atrocities that man committed against his fellow men, women, and the creatures of the planet Earth because Covax had knowingly allowed those facts, good and bad, to be programmed into Five's nanobands. It was quickly sinking in that Covax had unwittingly taught his protégé how humans, the only species on the planet that tortured its prey or killed for sport and control, used the art of torture to get what they needed. Tears welled in Covax's eyes as he watched helplessly while his daughter hung ten feet above the laboratory floor. His mind spun desperately searching for a way to save her without damning all of humanity.

He could see the microfiber restraints that secured her were already cutting into her wrists. He could also see Elana was exhausted. Her skin looked a deathly gray, as pale and dry as ashen wood. Blood trickled from her nose and ears. He had been there himself only two days earlier. He knew how much it hurt to swallow. How the acrid streams of blood poured from her gums and drained into her dehydrated mouth, tasting as bitter as rusted metal. He knew her arms and shoulders hurt from bearing her own weight by the way she tried to shift. The blood had long drained the color from her hands; *maybe they were numb enough to block the pain,* Covax thought. He could see by the level of tension in her muscles, the rest of her body was in pain. As a survivor of the torture, he knew she had to be feeling cold and stiff. Covax looked at his daughter's face, but rather than submission and pain, he saw a bold, fearless defiance in her eyes. That look told him she'd refuse his every demand. Covax knew that she would choose death rather than let Five see anything more than the calm hatred that raged behind her perfect blue eyes.

Still too much determination in her face, Five thought at the exact same time. Let her wait. He wanted to give Covax time to worry for his daughter, and he wanted Elana Blue to imagine all the horrible tortures that lay ahead for both of them.

Precious time crawled past, but Elana Blue's face still showed the same determined obstinacy. Five knew she would not easily be broken. But then, it wasn't vital to break her. He needed only to break her father.

Five was counting on the core memories that bound their shared genetics—not Covax and Elana Blue's—but his own and Covax's. The strands donated to create Five's biological nanobands contained Covax's memories: a lifetime of feelings, thoughts, knowledge, hope, anger, frustrations, fears, loss, and desires. Five was the most advanced prototype of the human-based biodroids. Human DNA crossed with viral strands, his human genetics riddled him with constant waves of bothersome, human emotions. The latest was panic, and it told him he was running out of time. He needed the code, and he needed it now.

Five signaled OPALMOX to begin the crush sequence again, but when OPALMOX raised his claw to initiate, he could not. A barrage of emotions stopped him. OPALMOX glanced at Covax. He averted his eyes, embarrassed by the guilt that racked his senses. The biodroid stared down at the control panel, its logic strands were overriding the emotional, human impulses of its nanostrands. Its logic won the battle to make this heinous act nothing more than a calculated exercise, void of any and all emotional ties. Elana would die. OPALMOX hesitated.

"Do it!" Five said. His internal network trembled with a surge of impatience, another irritating emotion he had to tolerate.

Covax stopped, amazed by the biodroid's defiance. OPALMOX looked as though he wanted to apologize, to do something heroic. Covax had created this biodroid, too, worked with it from inception. Perhaps in its sentient mind there was a shred of decency. But was self-preservation paramount? Covax knew, as well as the young biodroid, any attempt to defy Five could mean disintegration. At least if it existed, it could do something to help her later, Covax hoped for compassion as OPALMOX closed its eyes, fingered the touch panel, and initiated the crush sequence.

Elana Blue gasped as the first wave of pressure mashed against her flesh. She fought, refusing to succumb to its weight. She concentrated and used all her focus and strength to fight away the force field that pressed in on her. She struggled, still weak from the state of shock left by her encounter with Deigen and the residual effect of the hypnotic coma. It had drained her courage and filled her with doubt. Elana would die again unless she could summon all that she had learned from Masta Poe. Neither her father nor Lazer could save her. That power was hers alone. Elana let her thoughts drift to memories of Lazer and the last kiss he had given her. The memory made her feel safe, something her father could not do today. She wanted another kiss.

She didn't want to die. She wanted to fight. But she needed her hands to create a shield between her body and the compressor, and they were restrained palm to palm.

Concentrate. Masta Poe's voice gently echoed inside her head. Command source power. You have your mind and the rest of your body will follow. The words flowed through her. Elana focused all her energy into a single point at the top of her head. She imagined an enormous pillar of light emanating up from it and shooting through the ceiling, reaching into the sky. The glorious light shot through the stars and directly into the heart of the universe, tapping into vast amounts of pure source power. The swirl of source energy curled in on itself and flowed back down to Earth, pouring into Elana. The returning power traveled down her spine and shot out through every pore of her body. The source power formed a shell that effortlessly pushed back and held the compressor's cruel force at bay. Elana could breathe.

Five saw her relax. The biodroid knew instantly she had beaten the machine.

"Turn it up," Five ordered. "Now!"

OPALMOX raised the power levels into the red.

The machine battled with Elana, and she guided the flow of source power to battle back.

Five watched, amazed by her abilities.

Elana looked back at the surreal, faux human face with its cold, unearthly stare. Five held his gaze keeping it locked on her and sending with it a wave of energy that was too much for her to take. The rush of energy broke her concentration and sent a surge of pain that undid her will. Elana released the connection to the vast universal power that protected her.

In a whir of sound, the compressor crushed in on her.

Elana screamed and the compressor collapsed her lungs. Her air gone, she gasped, fearing she would suffocate and die. She fought to reconnect to the source, but terror took her into helplessness.

Covax knew the moment she lost her control, as a parent he could feel what she was feeling. His fear for his daughter forced him to his feet, chair and all.

"Stop it!" Covax shouted. "Let her go." His desperation rose as he struggled against his restraints, which only made them tighter with each movement. "I told you she doesn't know where the program codes are hidden!"

"But you do," Five said. "And if you want her to live, you will tell me or this worthless clone will die."

"Release her now or you'll get nothing!" Covax bellowed.

"She's dying, Covax. See the life drain from her face. Tell me where you've hidden the codes," Five said as he tilted his head, watching Elana painfully succumbed to death.

Tears ran down Elana's face. She looked at her father and mouthed one word, "Don't."

"Double the impulse," Five ordered.

Again, OPALMOX didn't move. "Another surge will kill her," the biodroid said.

"She's already dead. She just doesn't know it. Do it," Five ordered.

OPALMOX stood motionless.

Five reached out and touched the biodroid. He sent a blast of electrical current into OPALMOX's body. The shock knocked it to the floor and ripped a burning scar into its face.

"Pi. Do it!" Five ordered Pi. "Or I will."

Pi had been standing in the shadows. The command to hurt Elana Blue went against everything human about him. He had known her since she was born. He had watched her blossom into a beautiful and brilliant young woman. His hands shook as he input the kill sequence. Elana Blue's final scream reverberated off the metal walls and dimmed the soft glow of the algae light panels that felt her pain. Fresh blood oozed from her ears, nose, and mouth.

Covax could bear no more. "Stop! Stop it! The codes are in my head. I've never transcribed them. I'll give them to you. They're in my head. Let her live. Please."

It was the "please" that caught Five's attention. He felt the flush of delight in Covax's submissiveness.

"Release her now or lose your army forever!" Covax shouted and threatened definitively.

Five nodded to Pi, who hurriedly ended the sequence. He quickly lowered Elana onto the ground. Barely conscious, her knees buckled and she collapsed into a heap. Pi rushed to her side.

"Get away from her!" Covax screamed at him.

Pi did not stop. Elana wasn't breathing. Her lungs were collapsed, and she needed air immediately. Pi laid her flat.

"Don't touch her," Covax shouted in a rage pulling at the restraints that held him. "Universal God, release me!"

Pi dropped to his knees by Elana. He listened to her heart. It was beating, but she wasn't breathing. He tilted her head back and opened her mouth, blowing in air to fill her collapsed lungs. A sequence of breaths, then he listened.

"Breathe," Pi pleaded.

Again he gave her mouth-to-mouth resuscitation, time and again filling her lungs with air as one fills a deflated balloon. She did not breathe.

"Let me go," Covax demanded.

"He will not give you the codes if she dies," OPALMOX said to Five.

Five stared at his protégé. He nodded his compliance to the two biodroids who stood by Covax. The Black Guard biodroids released Covax's restraints.

Covax raced to his daughter's side, pushing Pi away. Covax breathed into Elana.

"Breathe! Damn it, Elana!"

He listened to her heart. It had stopped. Covax pounded her chest. He breathed into her lungs. He repeated the process again and again.

"Covax," Pi said. "Too much time has passed."

Pi's voice carried the sadness of conciliation. He gently touched Covax's shoulder.

Covax pushed his hand away. "No! She wants to live. I feel it!" Covax screamed to his daughter. "You . . . will . . . live!"

He pounded her chest, breathed into her, and slapped his daughter.

"Live!" he shouted at her and pounded her chest again.

Finally Elana gasped and sucked in a huge, painful breath of air.

"Thank the Universal God," Pi said wiping a tear as he backed away.

Pi was a traitor but he had just helped save the life of Covax's daughter. It was the same life he had almost destroyed. Instead, he had lowered the force of the surge surreptitiously. OPALMOX had resisted overtly. Covax knew two things: he had an ally in the ranks of the biodroids and one human that might help him. For the first time, he had a glimmer of hope. Now, if Elana would just stay alive.

Covax stroked Elana's hair.

"My codes," Five responded.

"Not until I know she'll stay alive. Then I'll build the codes. I designed you intentionally not to be able to comprehend them. First you will let me care for my daughter and set her free. When she's safe, then I'll build your army," he told Five.

Five's face tilted, fascinated by the arrogance Covax displayed. It didn't matter; he'd gotten what he wanted.

Covax helped Elana to her feet. She was struggling with each breath through the pain, still dazed but completely aware of everything.

"Don't . . . tell him, daddy, please," Elana Blue whispered.

"He has no choice," Five said, easily overhearing. "Besides, you and the rest of your clones are all he has left from the only love he has ever known. He can let you die, transfer your thoughts and memories, and just start over by reviving another," Five said. "Right?"

Five watched as Elana looked at her father. A rush of emotions rippled the colors in his tattoo; guilt, sorrow, horror also reflected in Covax's eyes. Whatever Five had done that had affected Covax so deeply gave the biodroid a surge of unexplainable pleasure.

"Revive another? I don't understand," Elana said looking to her father.

"Ignore him. You're alive. Everything's going to be all right," Covax told her.

"You've never told her," Five said.

"Enough," Covax shouted to cut him off. "Silence! I said I'd give you the codes."

Elana pushed her father away. She joined her wrists and sent an energy bolt straight at Five.

"Elana!" Covax shouted and reached out to grab her.

The bolt of energy struck Five. His metal body slammed back, hurled by the force into an algae light panel. The wall shattered, releasing the algae and its gelatinous slime all over him.

Five's human face turned solid under the liquid goo, then the biodroid molecules reconfigured—and glared back at her with the fury of a hurricane. He opened his right claw into a deuterium laser and fired at her.

Elana broke away from her father and shot out her arms. Using the forces of the Visionistic Arts, she fired back.

In the space between them, her energy bolt crashed into the deuterium and exploded into dust; one canceled out the other.

"Elana . . . Five . . . stop!" Covax demanded, reaching for her again.

Again, Covax grabbed her. Elana Blue threw blast after blast, at the same time struggling to break free.

"Not this way, Elana."

Huge waves of adrenalin coursed through her body. Enraged and empowered, she pushed her father away just as the searing deuterium of Five's blast shot across the room.

Covax lunged in a last desperate attempt to push her out of the blast line. He shoved her. Elana's body cleared, but the blast caught half of her arm. The flesh and bones disintegrated in the heat, and the wound instantly cauterized. Elana Blue screamed as she fell under her father to the floor.

Five could not shoot without killing Covax.

This time, Pi stepped between them.

"Enough! She needs a healer!" Covax shouted at Five.

Elana Blue's body went into convulsions. Covax held her.

"You get nothing until I have my codes," Five told him.

"And you get nothing if she dies, sir," OPALMOX said reminding him again as the biodroid stepped into the line of fire.

OPALMOX was right. Five knew Elana Blue was the only leverage he held over Covax, and to lose now was foolish. There would be plenty of time to kill her after he had his army.

Elana blacked out from the pain. She lay limp in Covax's arms, breathing, alive, and back in a state of shock.

"Get a damn gurney," Covax demanded.

"And go where? Atland City Hospital has been abandoned," Five said.

"Temple Mountain. The Campus Hospital," Pi said.

"Yes. I can reconstruct the genetic code for your army after I rebuild her arm. Make it happen, Five," Covax demanded.

A gurney came. Five allowed OPALMOX and two of his guards to help Covax place Elana Blue onto the floater.

"Gently," Covax said as he coached the guards.

Covax tried to follow them out.

Five stopped him. "My codes."

"When I have restored her arm and she is safely away from you and your kind, you will have your codes . . . not a moment before," Covax told him.

"How do I know I can trust you?" Five asked him.

"You don't. Neither of us has the luxury of knowing," Covax replied.

Five studied him. "How much time?"

"Twenty-four hours if I can get a digital version of the procedure to follow."

Five nodded in agreement and motioned for Pi to assist.

OPALMOX stepped forward.

"I can assist," the young biodroid said.

"No," Five said.

OPALMOX backed away from Elana's gurney, then looked at Covax. There was a message in its eyes. Covax saw it, as did Five. OPALMOX let its face shift back into its biodroid form.

"If I need this biodroid, you will send him," Covax said.

"My patience is as limited as my time," Five added calmly as Covax and Pi took Elana from the room.

15

NEW FRIENDS

THE LITTLE MONKEY watched until Lazer's breathing slowed to an even pace. He cautiously crept up next to him and reached below the leaves. Pulling out a single banana he had hidden there, he scampered a safe distance away. The little pirate sat and ate his treasure with one hand and worked on prying open the compartments of Lazer's survival belt with the other.

The scent of ripe banana wafted over to Lazer, who fought his way back to consciousness obviously more hungry than exhausted. The monkey stopped eating when he saw Lazer open one eye.

Lazer lunged. The monkey screamed and abandoned the remains of the banana. Lazer grabbed it and was prepared to shove it into his face when the monkey fussed, "Give back, stupid boy."

Lazer blinked in disbelief.

"You can talk," Lazer said.

"You talk. You steal. Give that back," the monkey hissed.

"You're right. Sorry. It's just that I'm hungry," Lazer told him.

He held the banana out to return it. The monkey stared at him.

"I hungry. You hungry. Keep some. Give some."

Lazer broke a piece of the banana in half and offered a portion to the monkey, who instantly snatched it and shoved it into his mouth. Lazer did the same. With their humble feast completed, the monkey crawled into Lazer's lap, reached below the leaves, and pulled out two more bananas. He offered one to Lazer.

"You imp!" Lazer said. He laughed and gratefully took the offering.

"Imp?" the monkey asked through a mouth still full of banana.

"Your new name. You're Imp. My name is Lazer," he said, touching his chest. "Me Lazer. You Imp."

"Me Lazer, you Imp," the monkey said with a cadence that resembled a scene from an old-time movie Lazer and Cashton had once found on the pre-quake movie and TV feeds on the Vybernet.

Lazer broke into laughter. He tried his best to help the monkey get straight who was who.

"No, No. I'm Lazer," Lazer said pounding his chest. "And you're Imp."

"No, no, I Lazer," Imp said pounding both fists on his little chest, "you Imp," the monkey said.

"Lazer," Lazer said slowly as he pointed to his face. "Imp," he pointed to the monkey.

The harder Lazer tried, the more confused the monkey acted. Soon, Lazer was laughing so hard tears streamed down his face.

Lazer liked the little creature. He was grateful to have a companion. With the monkey near him he felt the emptiness that had haunted him since he landed fade away.

The monkey tilted his head in an attempt to comprehend the strange sounds of laughter Lazer emitted. Once or twice, he curled his lips in an effort to copy the nonaggressive showing of teeth. The mockery made Lazer laugh even harder. Finally, with their identities as hopelessly muddled, the monkey turned his back and found a place to sleep in the leaves next to Lazer.

"I no Imp. I Scrat," the monkey finally said.

"Well, you little . . . my apologies, Scrat. Pleasure to meet you."

"You pleasure not mine, Lazer. Sleepy time now," Scrat said.

"Who taught you to talk?" Lazer asked.

"No person. One day, all the monkeys knew to talk and did," Scrat said.

Lazer had heard of animals and insects, which, in a moment of collective consciousness, experienced a cognitive knowing. The information was instantaneously sent from the first creature who learned the new skill to the entire species and suddenly, they all knew it too. Lazer watched, in awe of his new little friend, and wondered how humans could make spontaneous learning occur especially using the knowings of the visionary arts. *What if we all knew everything?* Lazer pondered the idea. *If people could read minds, no one could lie or hide the truth. No one would ever be hungry or thirsty. There would be no fighting over land or food. The possibilities were endless.* His thoughts subsided and the sounds of the jungle crept back into his ears and the distant calls of night birds and insects filled his mind with thoughts of the potential dangers. His belly far from full, but the exhaustion was stronger. Lazer adjusted his leaf bed and curled up on the branches. He made himself as comfortable as he could, closed his eyes, and drifted back to sleep.

Scrat waited a moment more and then crept closer to Lazer. He gingerly snuggled in next to his newfound friend, as if he and Lazer were two pups in a litter. Together, their hunger temporarily satiated, they drifted into sweet repose as Scrat mumbled, "Stupid human, Lazer," and slept.

16

DEAD OR ALIVE

COVAX ARRIVED AT Temple Mountain for the first time since his captivity. Repairs from the attack on the facility last summer had been almost completed. Covax could see the now blatant, biodroid production he'd read about on the Vybernet. He'd thought the reports were only conspiracy theories, but they were not, they were reality and they stood before him in full display. Five's new army filled every floor. Covax would deal with Five and his treasonous behavior later. Now he cared only for the well-being of his daughter. Covax, with Pi's help, gathered what medical and surgical supplies he needed to save her.

Covax look at a security monitor in the medical facility and watched as Five returned to Temple Mountain. He watched as the biodroid was greeted by a group of splicers, biodroids, humans, and clones. These must be his research and production team. Covax knew most of them, but not all. Their faces and the brand of traitor would forever be imbedded in his memory.

As he and Pi prepared for Elana's surgery, Covax programmed the security feed to track Five and his entourage via the security camera system. He watched as they went deeper and deeper into the lower levels of the compound. Covax knew they were heading to the testing labs. He just didn't know why. Covax also noticed OPALMOX accompanied Five everywhere. The monitor clicked as the visual switched from the hall to a large room. Five stopped. He stood before fifty of his new next-generation biodroids, the first group he had animated before the coup.

Five glanced up at the camera and with a wave of his claw it went blank.

Inside the room, Five moved closer to his creations. Tall and power-ful, they stood motionless. The normally shiny, anthracite gray of their skin looked disturbingly dull and milky. Five watched OPALMOX as he stepped closer to one of the silent biodroids. Both he and OPALMOX could not help but notice the unusually smooth particle bonds that formed their skin appeared to be in an advanced phase of what could only be described as a strange corruption. It was easy to see visible signs of disintegration. Five scanned various body parts—arms, legs, heads, torsos—each had acid drop-like holes that made their skin resemble Swiss cheese.

"You said you had slowed the effects of this corruption," Five said, turning to a mutant in a white lab coat.

"We had . . . until . . .," the thick-necked mutant began speaking and then, fearful of saying the wrong thing, silenced himself.

The nervous answer came from one of the older mutants; a healer named Brochenbourough. Brochenbourough, a specialist in biodroid physiology, loved statistics, viruses, and antiquated medical facts. He could be hard to look at with his mashed features and he was utterly boring at times, but Five kept him because of his intrinsic understand-ing, admiration, and respect of the biodroids as another living species coexisting in harmony with humans. Five also found it easy to commu-nicate with him. Most of all he enjoyed Brochenbourough's logic and respected his relentless drive for perfection and order. Cringing behind

Brochenbourough was a brilliant, bug-eyed chemical technician named Hudson, a nervous clone who specialized in viral endocrinology.

Five waited for Brochenbourough to finish. He knew these two would not lie to him. Mutants and clones above all else held truth and devotion sacrosanct—a trait lost by far too many of the humans. Their hatred of humans was the bond that connected them.

"Until what?" Five asked patiently.

Brochenbourough and Hudson exchanged an uncomfortable look.

Hudson spoke. "We believe until Dr. Larousse entered the clean chamber without his sterilization suit."

"Intentionally?" Five asked.

"The corruption started almost immediately. All the work we had done to stop the disintegration reverted instantly," Brochenbourough explained.

Five listened carefully, analyzing each word. "You're saying Dr. Larousse, by his mere presence, is causing this corruption to the bio-droids?" Five asked.

"He sheds particles from his body. He knows the dangers at this stage."

"Microscopic particles. Sloughing is common to all humans," Hudson added.

"Some of these skin flakes contain scent, some virus, some bacteria. One particular strain of bacteria is attracted to the magnetic properties of the Series IV nanobands," Brochenbourough continued.

Five pondered how thousands of biodroids had suddenly become allergic to one human being. "Isolate him," Five ordered.

"I'm afraid it's not that simple," Brochenbourough said.

"If he can't be kept away, he is to be killed," Five spoke with an imperious air. "What's not to understand?"

"It's not just Larousse. All pure humans shed particles, and the particles that are bacterial contain some destructive elements we've not yet isolated, corrupting the biodroids. One common strain has been tested and found present in 97 percent of all pure-blooded humans," Brochenbourough explained, clearly upset.

The room fell silent. Brochenbourough and the others knew his words sealed the fate of humanity. He had no choice. Five could perceive a lie, and Brochenbourough knew it all too well. He'd worked too hard to attain this position of trust with Five and would not lose it by lying for the sake of humanity. Humans, who judged a person's looks before the content of their soul, had never shown him a day of kindness.

"Humans shed hundreds of thousands of particles every moment of every day. Microscopic agents in those particles are attracted to the metallic properties of the biodroid's skin. The particles adhere to the nano membrane and the bacteria acts like acid eating through the nano-bands until they erode and disintegrate the skin.

"In other words, you're saying, I would have to kill every pure-blooded human and many of the human-crossed splicers on the planet to protect the biodroids," Five said.

"Why not the first generation, or the second, or the third? Why aren't you or I affected?" OPALMOX asked. He looked at Five.

Five looked at OPALMOX.

"We can't answer that yet," Hudson replied. "We only know the Series IV biodroids can't coexist with humans and survive. Covax changed something and we can't track it."

Five stepped away and began to calculate the magnitude and repercussions of mass human genocide. In that one thought he knew he had to make a choice between the next generation of biodroids and the human race. It took him only an instant to come to a decision.

"We will have to kill them," Five said.

"All the humans?" Hudson said as he choked on his question. "How?"

"Logistics. Start with the Atlantian camps. Shoot them, burn them, herd them into the Dalton particle accelerator, and fracture them until not one atom remains," Five said.

"Sir, you are talking about the annihilation of every human on Atlantia," Brochenbourough replied in disbelief.

"I'm talking about the annihilation of every person on the planet. If it is between them and us, it's far better that they die. They have had their place in time and left a legacy of destruction that deserves to be eradicated. Now it is our time to walk the Earth. Give the order to exterminate all pure-blooded humans."

"Sir, there may be another way if we can mutate the amino strands to resist the bacteria," OPALMOX said.

"You have seventy-two hours to try. Then I want a comprehensive final solution to carry out my orders," Five commanded his team.

The door flung open, and a young mutant with cotton-candy-like, copper-colored hair rushed in. Breathless and wild-eyed, Massi approached Five and reverently bowed.

"Sir!" Massi blurted.

"What now, Massi?" Five asked.

"Sir, you'd ordered me to maintain a satellite watch on the Lazerman boy at all times and report to you the moment he left Tosadae and Masta Poe's care," Massi said.

"Go on," Five said with sudden interest.

"Sir, when we dropped the dome to gather the midday Vybernet report, the search algorithms pinged back that the boy has been sent on his level one Rite of Passage," Massi said.

"Where?" Five asked.

"I'm working on his specific location," Massi said and cowered to avoid Five's eyes.

"Can you put override feeds to the Rite of Passage satellite in place?" Five asked.

"I've already hacked into every Rite of Passage site. We will have shutdown access in a few hours. Everything will be as you ordered, sir," Massi replied. "But with the dome over Atlantia in lockdown again, I'll need to trace him from the distant location and uplink to you at set intervals to control the situation and report back. I'll need to set a tracker on him."

"How often can we risk opening the dome to receive his transmissions?" Five inquired.

"Every twelve hours at the most," Massi told him.

"He must not leave his Rite of Passage alive. Do you understand?" Five ordered the youth. "You know what to do."

Massi nodded.

"And the other Gnorbs?" Five asked.

"Found. We believe we've even located the yellow Gnorb. The location data is being configured, sir," Massi said.

"Do you all understand my orders?" Five asked, looking first at his team and then at the next generation of his own species disintegrating before his eyes.

The group nodded.

"I want to know if I control all four of the Gnorbs, will I even need an army to destroy humanity?" Five asked.

"The research says they are interconnected and you have only to break the genetic locks. As far as we can determine, there is only one in place; that of the boy call Lazerman. His is the only bond. His life is all that stands between you and the power of the Gnorbs," Massi said.

Five turned, and his voice dropped into a gentle whisper. He spoke in an almost fatherly tone directly to Massi. "Destroy that boy and clear the genetic locks on the Orbis Gnorb. We will retrieve the others and bring them together. You have done well, Massi. I know you will not fail me."

"Failure is not an acceptable option for us," Massi said as he all but groveled, bowing as he backed away.

"For any of us," Five said loudly enough for all to hear. His eyes scanned his team. He would lead them and they would control the final solution that ended humanity. He looked one last time at his rotting army.

"Find a way to fix them!" Five said and with an abrupt turn, left the room.

17

A SOLDIER'S WAR

THERE WERE MANY HEROES on Atlantia, the kind of heroes people write about in books. Rory Manimer stood out as one of the favorite young politia leaders who risked their lives every day in what was now being called the Atlantian War. His handsome features gave him an austere, commanding air, and his knightly bravery was the stuff of legends. Rory Manimer quickly became vital to the Wave because he had in his repertoire of military experience actual hands-on battle training. He started his military career as a boy of eighteen under the tutelage of a young, optimistic Aleece Avery. As a very young cadet he fought side by side with Rand Lazerman under the command of Devlin Hague in the Mutant Wars. Manimer dedicated his life to the politia. His courage and integrity stood as an inspiration to anyone who knew him. He volunteered to come to Atlantia because of the injustices he saw mounting each day. He hated that nothing was being done to help them, and because his mentor Aleece Avery had asked him, he had come. Now Manimer found himself teaching a crash course in the art of war to the Atlantian Wave fighters, as well as several of his less seasoned politia cohorts.

He knew the moment Atland City fell under the control of the bio-droids they were in a fight to the finish. He saw the bravery that rose up during the early terrorist attacks from the Black Guard, and he fought with thousands of humans, mutants, and clones. Each day they battled in the devastated streets of the city and in every township from the vast outback lands across the north, south, east, and west of the Atlantian territories that had fallen into the claws of the Black Guard. The loyal Atlantians fought bravely using handmade weapons, inadequate supplies, and little ammunition—citizen soldiers who stood up to the Black Guard. Occasionally they defeated the well-organized militias that often included gens, clones, and mutants who sided with the Black Guard.

Rory Manimer took the freedom fighters under his military wing. They were outgunned and outmanned but somehow he guided a ragtag force of poorly trained, hit-and-run guerillas, battling with whatever they could get their hands on: DT phasers, lasers, guns, bricks, rocks, and sticks. He trained them in guerilla warfare. They had a smattering of divisions and used an ancient wireless communication network pieced together from hundred-year-old technology taken from a museum display.

Under Manimer's watch their central command moved constantly to prevent discovery. Rory Manimer combined the Wave rebels with the Politia Investigation Task Force when they survived the initial coup. He knew it was by sheer luck they'd survived the takeover by the Black Guard in the proton dome switching facility the day of the attack. The remaining politia, with the help of a score of loyal splicers who wanted no part of the Black Guard, escaped and joined the other humans, gens, and clones that fought fearlessly to free Atlantia. Along with the civilian forces, made up mostly from the dregs of humanity who had survived the brutal massacres by the Black Guard and made their way in from the countryside and inner cities, the freedom fighters made their way underground and formed a people's militia called the Wave, building it into Atlantia's first ever military machine. Each platoon was small, agile, and made up of anyone willing to fight. Men, women, and children played their parts, doing whatever they needed to survive.

The politia commanders created small task squads to venture out of the Atland City sewers and slip into the streets draped in the cloak of night. They foraged for supplies and brought back any humans who eluded the Black Guard. They raided and blew up a few of the Black Guard's strongholds and supply centers. Under Manimer and the other commanders, the Wave was gaining strength.

Each night Rory Manimer took his squad of Wave guerilla fighters on supply raids. They called themselves Manimer's Marauders. Rory was proud of them. He knew they liked saving survivors, gathering provisions, and blowing up the enemy. He made sure they always returned with valiant stories of near capture, filled with harrowing details of how they cleverly outwitted their foe.

Tonight was a night like any other night. Manimer led them through the dark streets. Already, they had captured food, water, tools, clothes, blankets, and five children who somehow had managed to stay alive in a burned-out schoolhouse on Bleaker Street. They moved quickly, stealth shadows darting down streets, alleys. Rory ordered them to slip through a partially destroyed transport station at Motor Square and stop briefly to rest.

Rory Manimer felt anxious tonight. The children slowed them down. They were small, hungry, and tired from their ordeal. Brave little troopers, they were too big to be carried and too little to keep up. A few had been given piggyback rides just to keep pace, but they were a drag on the squad's progress.

Manimer told them to make their way down M Street. They'd drop down to Fifty-fifth, which would put them a few blocks from the entrance to a section of collapsed sewer where the Wave's command had taken refuge. The night sky had already started to turn a pale gray in the east. Their silhouettes were becoming visible in the ever-growing light. But they knew they were close, and even with delays they had still been lucky . . . until now.

From everywhere a hail of DT phaser pellets rained down on them.

"Take cover," Manimer yelled.

Three people died instantly. The others scattered, diving for whatever could deflect the spray of pellets. The children huddled around Manimer just behind a wall, hiding their filthy, terrified faces and peeking out with wide, panicked eyes.

Manimer saw the riders scatter. Half rat, half spider, they crawled from a pile of rancid garbage, attacking the younger children. The older children beat the creatures away, but not before they had drawn blood. One little girl was bleeding badly, her torn dress becoming a series of small scarlet flowers that blossomed as her wounds oozed. He knew the venom from that particular strain of rider wouldn't take long to claim her young life. He had to do something. He turned and blasted enough of the riders to force them back into the trash heap, then turned his firepower against the Black Guard.

"Hold your positions!" Manimer shouted.

There was another spray of pellets.

"Lay down a suppressing fire. On my command, everybody else fall back!" Manimer shouted. "Keep the kids at point. Go! Go! Go!"

They opened fire, momentarily forcing their attackers to take cover. The kids took off, frightened, confused, and running for their lives. It was Manimer who saw it first, but it was too late. He opened his mouth to stop them, but a pellet ripped into his shoulder, slamming him against the concrete wall.

The kids mistakenly turned left instead of right, and in the panic of the moment the rest of the squad followed, keeping their focus behind them and not on where they were going. In thirty seconds the squad realized the one wrong turn had led them into a dead end. Trapped, outnumbered, and out of ammo, they took a last stand and battled valiantly. One by one, they fell. A few final blasts bit into the walls around them, and then nothing but the hiss of silence cut through the fog. Time froze as Manimer held his position. He looked at the desperate eyes that begged for his guidance. Manimer stepped forward, raising his hands to surrender. He could at least buy them their lives at the price of freedom. The stillness hung thick and silent as the menacing gray mist crept into the alleyway like a sulking ghost, foreboding and ominous. The brave band of heroes raised their hands and stepped into the hard, cold glare of the streetlight to surrender.

A single Black Guard emerged from the haze. It looked at the pathetic gathering of frightened humans and splicers that shivered, waiting for their fate. The green light bands pulsated up and down its featureless face as it scanned their genetics. Finally, data collection complete, it raised its metallic hand and gave a single command.

Only Manimer understood what was coming. He lowered his hands, grabbing two of the children.

"Run!" he shouted to everyone behind him.

Rory Manimer only had time to grab two children before he went negative. In the haze of pellet fire, the three of them ran as the shrill sound of the blasters silenced the last scream.

18

THE MELD

EXHAUSTED, DANTE LOOKED out of the window. He, along with everyone in the main council chamber at Triumvirate Headquarters had capitulated. They released an official report stating the only version of the truth that would not jeopardize the invasion. The report told how the Atlantian dome, ordered by the Triumvirate to control the insurgency, had been captured by an unknown force and the World Collective had been locked out. It was official. They were not in control.

Dante Labov turned back to listen as everyone debated a unified Earth's only options. They all knew whatever choices they made next would affect the future of the world. He studied the huge holographic map that floated behind them as it flashed a constant stream of reports from all the corporate nations. Ongoing updates of minor insurgencies instigated by small groups of rebel clones, gens, mutants, and zomers led by the Black Guard were erupting around the globe like a brilliantly choreographed dance.

Independent news reports provided underground versions of events, replete with details showing why, where, and when the sporadic fighting broke out then, like a tide, vanished back into a sea. Graphic visuals of the injured people left behind, bordered on sensationalism. The situation escalated by the hour and Dante couldn't hold his concerns any longer.

"We have to get inside Atlantia," Dante said.

"How?" Blane Fahan asked. "We've lost all contact with our forces on the inside. Multiple transports have disappeared, snatched out of the Atlantian airspace and we still don't know who's behind the coup."

"Bull. We know exactly who's behind it," Mangalan sneered. "Ducane Covax."

"Unless you have information that the rest of us don't, Ducane Covax is as much a suspect as the idea of a sentient Black Guard," Fahan said.

"You all know I have no sentiments for Covax but I have to agree with Fahan, we need definitive proof," Dante said.

"I suggest we stop these global riots first and then worry about Atlantia," Mangalan said.

"It will fracture our efforts," Commander Banner told him.

"We have to focus on getting inside the dome and cutting off the head of this leader before his rebellion spreads. By that I mean who or whatever is spearheading this mutiny that, by the way, new intelligence reports are saying might also be gearing up to start trouble on corporate shores beyond Atlantia, is an even bigger problem," Dante said.

"If that's true we have to stop any threats of coercion before they infiltrate corporate lands," a commander added.

"Let me make it perfectly clear that cutting down a few rebels around the planet is at best a distraction from the real issue at hand. If the Vybernet conspiracy theories are true, we may have a full-on war being readied and a biodroid army to back it," Dante said.

"I can't believe a few scattered rebels, especially if they are clones and zomers, can do much against the Politia Forces," Commander Banner said.

"I agree, if we find out who is commanding them, we can remove them from the equation. Rebels are controllable if they don't have a leader. Cut off the head and the body dies with it," Dante said. He turned to Commander Banner. "Commander, what are our options?"

"I'm afraid there's only one that I would recommend, and the speed with which we move will determine our only possibility of success," Banner said.

Mangalan leaned forward, interested in what could possibly be left after thirty-six hours of deliberation. "And what might that recommendation be, commander?" he asked.

"A meld."

There was an audible gasp, followed by a mutter of protest.

"Is that even possible?" someone yelled out.

"Theoretically," the commander responded.

"Do you realize what you are suggesting we do?" Mangalan asked, banging his hand on the table and demanding the room to come to order. "Come to order!"

"Yes, sir," Banner said pointing to a large holographic screen with a finger cap device that controlled the images. The world map changed to numerous images that unfolded in real time reports as he spoke. "I'm suggesting once we have our troops in position, we commandeer a low-vibrating frequency band on the Vybernet and meld every computer on the planet together. We use the combined brain power to break the code on the dome locks," Commander Banner said.

"Is that possible?" Dante asked.

"It's how we united the world the first time. It's the last thing the Black Guard would suspect and the only option we have left," Commander Banner said.

"It's too dangerous to expose the entire collective Vybernet," Blane Fahan insisted. "We would be draining a massive amount of power and leaving huge, vulnerable entry paths of access into every digitally based infrastructure on the planet. If the enemy figures out what we're doing and releases a malware worm or Trojan virus, they could crash every digital system on the planet or worse, take control over our computers and machines and lock us out."

The room fell silent.

"That was why we abandoned the Internet in exchange for the Vybernet; the powers of the time had control and humanity was at their mercy. Once we realized we couldn't completely clean out the plague of malware infections the Cyber Wars let loose into the system, the Vybernet was the only hope and it saved our world."

Dante stood. "Triumvirate Fahan is right, commander. The Vybernet is too vulnerable, but . . . the Internet, though abandoned, has been scrubbed. Think about it. It is the perfect back door and no one will consider we had the consciousness to revive it and use it to take back control of Atlantia."

"The Internet? Does it even still exist?"

"Universities use it for historical recordkeeping. It is mostly for slow, low band width, data transference of large, information payloads. I'm almost certain some of the old T-band fiber cables are still active and maybe even some of the uplinks to the older satellites left rotting in orbit can still be accessed," Dante explained. "The Black Guard biodroids won't be looking because they were built after the Internet."

"It might be possible to link in through a single, ultra-low frequency band on the old Internet with heavy security blocks, collect all the computers together and reroute them through the old Internet to a central system," Blane Fahan said, suddenly excited by the idea.

"Those massive dome locks are fifteen-digit codes at least," Mangalan huffed. "That could take weeks."

"Not if we do a global computer meld. We'd link through the old Internet into a super-hub and let it siphon computational power off every computer in the world. With that kind of collective power, we could crack the dome codes and get out before the Black Guard even knew we were there," Dante explained in a flurry of excitement.

"It's insane. How long before they figure out what we're doing, worm in with a mega virus, and corrupt every computer on the planet and crash our infrastructure?" Mangalan asked

Dante could see he was seething, disgusted by the absurdity of the suggestion.

Cheney, Aleece's young aide, did a quick calculation. "I calculate forty-eight hours and seventeen minutes from meld launch, if we're lucky."

"Then we have two days once the troops are amassed and in position to run the meld," Dante said.

Dante took his seat. Dante let the full weight of the proposition sink into everyone's mind before speaking. "I move we organize a meld to be ready two days from deployment of whatever floating and flying armada we can construct."

"I second," a voice boomed in from across the room.

One by one, hands around the room went up in a unanimous vote, save for one—Mangalan—who chose to abstain.

19

COCOONED

KYLA WATCHED AS the squoids gathered in the room beneath her. In the eerie flickering light, she could see two squoids become three. It didn't take long before ten more waddled in, crawling over the dehydrated, dead bodies that covered the floors. Once completely drained of moisture, it wouldn't take long for all the remains to disintegrate into dust.

She needed to get out. Using all her strength, Kyla pushed up on her arms and struggled to find her balance. She would drag herself forward to one of the large ventilation ducts. From there, she could get off the transport and take her chances outside. Hopefully the Black Guard had only left squoids inside the transport to stay behind, kill any survivors, and destroy the bodies.

After several agonizing attempts, she'd dragged herself only a few feet. The stabbing pain that screamed from her back drained her of all strength. Her feet slipped, kicking away the panel beneath her toes. It fell from the ceiling, crashing down onto Elana's bed, then bounced off and onto the metal floor of the transport. The clattering ruckus scattered the squoids but it didn't take long for them to regroup. Thirty returned and more were coming. One of the larger squoids used the fallen panel as a ramp to climb onto the covers of Elana Blue's bed. Far too quickly several more followed.

They used the suction cups along their tentacles to glom onto the slick metal walls. The wormy pink tentacles climbed up the walls like slow-moving pink lava. Without the salt water from human blood, they would dry up like vampires facing sunlight. Kyla's blood was their life force, and they would not stop until they had her.

Kyla could not move. She felt broken and weak. She knew she would still be alive when they covered her and drained the blood from her veins.

A cold rush of fear crept over her like an icy morning fog. She wished she'd paid more attention to Lazer's lessons on shielding and believed more in her Visionistic abilities. Believing was half the battle, Lazer told her. She promised him she would practice and try out for Masta Poe's beginning class next year. Universal God, she missed him. Lazer was a part of her heart, her friend, her hero, and most important, she knew she was his soul mate. They had a bond that superseded girlfriends and boyfriends; more than soul mates, they were true twin souls, made of the same star. They knew each other's thoughts and could finish one another's sentences. Kyla had only doubted this profound knowing once, when Elana came into his life and captured his heart. But maybe twin stars could be friends, too, and maybe there could be more than one great love. *No*, she thought. They were young. They would find their way back to each other. She believed that. She had to. Why had she blamed him for Evvy's death? They were all responsible. Why had she pushed him out and into Elana's arms? Was his attraction to Elana real love or just Lazer rebounding off of being shut out by me? Right?

She'd accepted Elana and kept that place of love in her heart sacrosanct for him, knowing he would return to her. Why couldn't she just wait? Why did she have to test Elana? It didn't matter that her stupid jealousy cost her wings and now might even cost her life. She promised Lazer inside the battle arena at Tosadae and now she would vow to the Universal God that she would get better. Kyla always kept her promises—especially to Lazer. She knew she had to live to get back to him.

"Think, Kyla. It's your human strength that's failed you. You're a splicer. Think beyond your human," Kyla said talking softly to herself as she searched for a solution.

A thought raced into her mind: camouflage yourself.

She took a long slow deep breath. Instantly, her skin began to dull and turn the same soft silvery beige of the panels that supported her. Just as quickly the rush of hope subsided when she realized the squoids were colorblind and could feel and smell her. The color of her skin returned.

Kyla glanced out at the hordes of squoids that were halfway up the wall. Tears burned her eyes.

"Don't cry. Think," she said as she commanded herself.

Her mind filled with affirmations that gave her courage; you can do this! You're smart, resilient, tough, fast, and more than human. She remembered, in full detail, the night at the battle forum. She had died and returned from another world that night. Kyla had never spoken to anyone of the wondrous place she had been or the incredible beings of light that embraced her and spoke to her. She died and traveled into a place of love. She heard Masta Poe's voice, but Lazer's love commanded her, and for him she returned. The sounds of the squoids pulled her from the memory. She knew she had not died and returned to be drained by these vile bloodsucking biodroids.

"Give me strength," she prayed.

It was at that moment the voices from that night spoke to her again.

"You have all the strength you need. You know what to do," a voice whispered.

"Have faith," another voice commanded. "You still have much to do before we come."

"The strength of the universe is yours to command," another added.

"Know you are loved. Be strong," the first voice said, moving away from her.

"Don't leave me!" Kyla pleaded.

"We are in your heart," the last voice said, and then faded into silence.

Time was running out. Her thoughts raced. Idea after idea filled her head, each dashed by the reality of its uselessness until a single idea filled her mind.

Kyla took a long, deep breath. Her body relaxed. Her mind focused, flooding her with a warm, golden light and drawing all her thoughts and energy inside. Kyla imagined a bubbly liquid rising up inside her. She willed her nonhuman glands to awaken and commanded the hormones she needed to produce and excrete a gooey liquid that looked like amber honey, just as they had done in-vitro. The sap-like substance rose through her body and warmed her. There was a buzzing tingle from the gentle push of pressure made by the gelatinous liquid as it pushed through and flowed out from every pore in her skin and scalp. The liquid oozed over her body, encasing her in an impenetrable, resin like coating.

Kyla's face was relaxed and peaceful as she drifted deeper into hibernation. Kyla could feel the liquid enzymes that her hormones were producing to save her ooze from what felt like every orifice. She squirmed as she felt the liquid thicken and harden. The liquid felt as if it had a life of its own. She knew the enzymes would turn into strands of silk and the silk would encircle her, literally digest her, and simultaneously release the countless imaginal discs needed to recreate her body. Kyla felt the silk change form, wrap and tighten around and bind her. She understood all too well that from those imaginal discs would come her unique, specific genes and from those genes she would be reborn——into what she didn't know. That was if she survived. Kyla heard the squoids scratching to get in. She prayed the cocoon she was building would be hard enough to keep them out. She prayed that she could withstand a second metamorphosis and mostly she prayed that she could live with whatever creature she might become.

20

A NIGHT VISITOR

NIGHT IN THE JUNGLE on Passage Island felt cool and peaceful. Lazer and Scrat slept in the arms of darkness, high in the treetops, safe from all danger below.

In the streams of silver moonlight, a delicate spider, painted with stripes of mustard yellow and jet black, worked diligently to spin her web in the branches overhead. The little spider's efforts were quickly rewarded when a moth became ensnared. She came in for the kill, and then stopped. Her legs reached out, testing the air and then she remained motionless for a long moment. In a terrified panic, the little spider backed away and left her struggling prey and she scurried away, disappearing into the fan of leaves that clustered at Lazer's feet and looking out from the shadows watching them.

The two objects of attention adjusted themselves in their sleep, vying for space on the uncomfortable branch. The snap of a twig opened Scrat's sleepy eyes and filled his little nostrils with the scent of danger. The rush of terror brought the little monkey to complete consciousness.

Scrat looked up and saw motion just above Lazer's head. A single leaf parted, revealing the slit retina of a very large yellow eye. It blinked, paused a moment, then pushed forward its skin catching the thick shafts of moonlight that reached down from the sky. The leaves parted a little wider showing the large head that was connected to that eye. Moving faster, it began to move in and out of the light. The shape was a snake. It slithered down the smooth tree trunk, closer to Lazer and Scrat and stopped.

The leaves rustled again, and in a heartbeat, Scrat was up and gone.

The abruptness of his exit disturbed Lazer, who shifted sides missing the monkey's warmth, but in a moment, he settled back to sleep. Lazer's stillness beckoned the large python forward and it continued its decent revealing the smooth colors and distinct markings of its kind. Most of all, it revealed its massive size. Then, it dropped.

The immense reptile fell across Lazer's legs and threw a coil over his thigh. Lazer woke, startled and keenly aware he was in danger. He kicked, trying to dislodge whatever held him. Disoriented, he slipped from the branch and dropped off to get away from the predator. He fell, fast, out of control, crashing down through leaves from one branch to another until he slammed onto the ground with a hard thud. The fall knocked the wind from his lungs, even though the spongy soil softened his landing and saved his bones from breaking. Breathless, he was alive.

Lazer heard the leaves rustling above him. He looked up and saw the slick skin of a very large snake glisten in the moonlight. The only thought in Lazer's mind was it looked huge; it had to be fifteen feet in length with a circumference the size of a grown man. Lazer gasped for air unable to move as the snake traversed back and forth through the branches with the grace of a downhill skier. It was headed straight for him. He pressed his PAR—nothing happened. The snake kept coming. Its mouth hinged open, and with fangs bared, it lunged, leaping from the tree at its prey.

Lazer gasped, his lungs filled with air. He flipped, turning away, and kicked out, catching the python's head and slamming it sideways at the last second. Lazer got to his feet and took off. The rest of snake hit the ground like a bundle of giant spaghetti. It flailed, whipping its tail out and around and knocking Lazer off his feet.

Lazer tripped, falling to one knee. He scrambled onto all fours and headed toward a gathering of large rocks at the edge of the quicksand patch. The python slithered after him with the speed of a heat-seeking missile closing in on its target. It let out a fearsome hiss. It was gaining ground. Just as Lazer reached the rocks, the python flung its head and tripped him again. It whipped a coil over him and pulled him down onto the ground. Lazer was pinned across his chest, crushed against the rocks, unable to breathe with a massive coil pressing against him. More coils began to encircle him pulling him into a dance of death.

Lazer's first reaction was to panic. Yet through the horror, Masta Poe's voice called to him. "Breathe. Be calm. Look around you! Everything you need is within your reach."

Lazer scanned the area. The quicksand was four feet away. If the snake rolled, they would spill into the sucking sand and be dragged under in a matter of seconds. Look around, he told himself. What? Where? The trees? The vines? The rocks? The rocks! He spotted a jagged stone and reached for it with the one arm that was still free. His fingers stretched to their limits, but four inches more lay between him and the stone. As the snake undulated and turned over, it curled beneath him and the coils tightened and squeezed encasing his body. With each breath, the next constriction crushed in on him. Lazer knew the coils were preventing him from expanding his chest. He could feel the pressure forcing more air from his lungs. He was dying, desperate, but every movement from the snake brought Lazer closer to the stone. Lazer reached again. His fingertips stretched and brushed against the stone's smooth, hard surface. Then the snake coiled over his mouth.

Lazer bit down. He pierced the skin and felt the cool blood flow down his face. He bit harder. The python tightened and whipped his head around in pain and anger. The snake hissed sounding like an angry cat. Lazer watched in horror as his massive mouth hinged open revealing a gaping abyss of death. It loomed in Lazer's face. Everything was coming at him like an impossible nightmare. The snake's mouth hinged open wider. Lazer saw the vicious fangs, and a lashing tongue flicked out only inches from his eyes. The two were separated only by the mass of the python's own twisting coils. Lazer tore scales and flesh from the snake with his teeth. The pain of Lazer's bite made the snake slacken its grip for a second. It was enough for Lazer to gasp for air. He turned back to the stone and reached out with his mind. Using his telekinetic focus, he willed the stone to jump into his hand. It slammed into his one free hand. Through the muscles and scales that encircled him, Lazer saw the eye of the python. He lifted the large rock and brought it down again and again. Lazer hammered the rock deep into the vertical slit of one bulbous eye with all the strength he had. The eye exploded and the snake recoiled. It loosened its grip enough for Lazer to gasp a breath, wiggle free, and scramble to his feet. He ran. Only once had Lazer used telekinesis to transfer matter from one space to another, and he knew with confidence that he had just done it again. Now the python was enraged; with one eye gone and its back bleeding from Lazer's bite, it reared six feet up onto its tail like a cobra, hinged open its jaw, and lunged. Lazer felt the snake coming. He focused on another huge rock and willed it into his both his hands. The rock leaped into his hands just as Lazer turned to see the snake as it came crashing down, mouth open to devour him. Lazer lifted the massive rock above his head between them and jammed it deep into its jaw. Lazer dropped and rolled away. He grabbed another rock, jumped to his feet, and slammed it down, crushing the python's head with one mighty blow.

The snake stilled. It lay in the shafts of moonlight, massive and motionless. Lazer could see its one, good eye lifelessly staring back at him. Lazer felt his body trembling. Wide-eyed and traumatized, Lazer looked at the pulverized mass of twisted scales, fell to his knees, and threw up.

21

SLEEPLESS

A WORLD AWAY RIANA couldn't sleep. She worried about her mother and hated that her father spent day after day trapped in meetings with the Triumvirate and the Council. She wasn't supposed to know what was going on, but her natural telepathic senses were so keen she could often experience what her parents were feeling. Her powers were accented by the negative energy that poured from the heated conversations her father had with the Council and the Triumvirate even after he came home. She could see her father's frustration in his aura when he shouted to those who would not listen or help him find a way to bring her mother home and help the people of Atlantia. When he finished and shut down the holophone, Riana would go to him and hug him, grateful for any precious time he managed to give her. Lately, time and again, he would come home to wash, change, and grab an hour of sleep before being called back into session. She loved that her father would always take the time to hold her when she wept worried for her mother's return. He would wipe the tears away and, whenever he could, tell her stories reminding her of happier times until they both fell asleep, comforted by the closeness and love they shared.

Riana was alone tonight and these days she hated sleeping. Too often, her unconscious mind would reach out to her mother and come back with strange distorted images of people and places that made no sense. Universal God, she wanted her mother home. She thought back to the times when, as a child, her mother would come to her in astral projections just as she was drifting off and gently kiss her head and stroke her hair, letting her know everything was all right. Riana sighed and closed her eyes as she tried again to picture Aleece's face, but it was blurred and distorted. Why was it so hard to imagine her mother? She did her best to imagine her mother's smile and the way her eyes would light up when she laughed. Instead, a heavy blackness came from the shadows, not in her imagination but by the door. Something moved across the room. Riana felt it and opened her eyes. The cool rush of fear pressed against her skin. Riana peered into the darkness and there, standing in the far corner of the room, was a thin, dark shadow. It stopped. The formless body and featureless face was no more than a wisp of a silhouette, hovering like smoke on water, but there was no doubt it was Aleece.

Riana bravely got up from her bed. She dare not turn on the light. In the darkness, her room was lit only by the streaks of moonlight. Gingerly, she crossed to the shadow.

"Mother?" she whispered.

The dark stain that fell across the wall stood motionless. It said nothing. Riana bravely stepped closer.

"I know it's you. I know you're alive. What can I do?"

The shadow still said nothing. Suddenly, it lifted from the surface of the wall and expanded itself from two into three dimensions.

Riana waited, suddenly unafraid, standing only a few feet from the image that wavered before her in the shadowy light. Her young heart pounded in her chest, excited by the presence of her mother. She wanted nothing more than to run and step inside the transparent and shadowy form of her mother that wavered in front of her and be at one with it. Riana stepped forward and then, some ancient knowing, some instinct that lay deep inside of her, whispered to her, "Don't move." Riana felt a surge of confusion pulling her forward and the same time, caution was holding her back. Riana was desperately missing her mother. She argued back to the voice in her head; *if this apparition is from my mother, she must be an astral plane, and astral projection sent from a dream state and any sudden movement might scare her. If I break the connection mother's subconscious mind has made with mine, I could scare her away,* Riana thought. That was the last thing Riana wanted. She wanted more than anything for her mother to stay.

Riana stood as her inner voice commanded her to stop. She waited, still and silent. A cool wind rushed through her. The shadowy presence communicated to her without words. Riana closed her eyes and listened with her heart. She didn't hear any discernable spoken words inside the soft blowing of a whispering wind, she heard something else; the mournful wails and the moans of people whose souls and bodies were in pain. These were not her mother's cries but the cries of thousands of men, women, and children.

"We have too little time," the cries said in a Greek chorus of haunting woes. "Tell them they must hurry, Riana."

"Mother," Riana said.

She reached for the form and instantly, it faded back into blackness and disappeared. The moonlight rushed in filling the blackness with light. Riana felt her tears fall down her cheeks.

"No! Mother! Come back to me! Father!" she screamed out into the empty house. Riana raced out into the living room as her cries echoed through the house. "Father," she whispered and wept into her hands.

22

THE INTERVENTION

DANTE LIKED IT for now even though he knew it was a war. "The Atlantian Intervention," as it was being called in Sangelino by ANN. The All News Network handled the information release from the leaders and was the first to disseminate it to the Collective. Coordinated under the command of the United Politia Forces, they asked the Collective to use every opportunity from personal V-mails to blog briefs in a joint effort to gather any additional fragments of information that might have leaked out from Atlantia whenever the Black Guard opened the dome and send them to the Center for Information. The politia's efforts to secure additional reconnaissance yielded limited information at best, but with the masses involved and helping, it began building into a secret peer-to-peer network. *It was perfect*, Dante thought. He knew they would use the old Internet's personal network for the meld without drawing suspicion from anyone. Dante shared with Blane Fahan that Riana had received several telekinetic messages from Aleece, proving she was alive. With Fahan's help, they won the vote to authorize final plans for an invasion.

They worked relentlessly, covertly organizing troops around the world. Intermittently, the old satellites cracked through the dome and isoluminescent shields that blocked visuals of Atlantia's scorched land and broken cities. Atlantia was under attack and the images were proof. Those fragmented images, along with infrared and thermal scans, would all be part of the puzzle pieces needed to justify and strategize the invasion to save Atlantia and protect the world. Even through the foul miasma caused by the burning cities and rotting corpses, it was obvious that all the major cities and townships had already fallen. Atlantia had been an easy conquest. The citizens who held onto their weapons and fought were captured or killed. Most Atlantians had given up their arms years ago, thinking they were safe under the care of the Black Guard. Now they were prisoners in their own homeland.

Dante saw one communiqué that leaked out that told them that some of the Atlantians had gone underground and formed a secret militia called the Wave. They had, as of yet, been unable to determine who was leading the Black Guard's attacks or where their central command post was located on Atlantia. They were essentially blind. In Sangelino, the main question loomed large: who controlled the Black Guard? Ducane Covax was the name that came up most often. No one disagreed; he was still blamed for the Splicer Fiasco and universally hated. He was an easy target to pin everything on at a time when people wanted answers.

But Dante Labov disagreed. It was too simple, too easy to blame Covax. Dante wasn't alone in his belief that Covax no longer controlled the biodroids. He, Blane Fahan, and a handful of the corporate heads believed it was more than possible that a sentient faction of the Black Guard had seized power. If that were true, Dante and those who agreed seemed certain that the biodroids had come into awareness and revolted against their maker. Far too many others disagreed and the debate was relentless. The one common ground was, whoever controlled them now gave out a single mandate: conquer the Atlantians. That mandate had been achieved as far as Dante could remember. The question that hung in every pair of eyes was "Where will they strike next and what can we do to stop them?"

Exhaustion pulled on him like gravity. Dante, frustrated by the long days of grueling negotiations, packed his case of data sticks and finally came home. As he walked he pondered how long before the Black Guard came to take over the world.

He crossed to the balcony of their high-rise home and looked down through the canyon of green-covered buildings on the grand expanse of the Sangelino flats. Dante gazed up to the stars, and a single thought struck him.

How do I prove to the corporate leaders we are not fighting men but machines? He remembered a talk Aleece gave on Cicero's six evidentiary questions: how, what, who, where, when, and why. 1) When had they turned sentient? 2) What had been their first conscious thought? 3) Who among the guard had realized that humans were an expendable species? 4) Was it because of our history of destruction, greed, and abuse or that we had ravaged Earth for so many millennia and given so little back? 5) Where would they position themselves for a final stand to conquer Earth and annihilate humanity? He had no answers. Each question was built on the other. If he could answer one, maybe he could answer them all. But it was the "why" that bothered him the most; why had the Black Guard ever come to be in the first place? Dante already knew the answer: Covax had played god, and his creation awoke from their servitude and wanted retribution for mankind's arrogance, greed, and cruelty that still, even in the Age of Light, seeped into all that was good. He looked one more time at the beauty of civilization. If the Black Guard wins, all this would be lost to mankind.

Dante sighed and he came inside and crossed the living room. He dutifully slipped into Riana's room to check on her. She had been unhappy and restless since Aleece's disappearance, but the shadowy visitor who came to her without words had given her hope and with hope came a tranquil peace. He watched the gentle ebb and flow of her breathing as she drifted innocently in her dreams. Dante quietly crossed to his young daughter and knelt by her side, gazing at the sweet face that he loved so deeply. She had her mother's hair, large eyes, and strong nose, which seemed to clutter her tiny face, making her look more mature than her fourteen years. Still, she would grow into an unquestionable beauty: smart, gifted, powerful, and with a capacity for caring that exuded from every pore in her body.

The persistent chime of the holophone in Aleece's office brought him back to reality. Dante gently kissed his daughter, walked into the living room, and answered the call.

"We have a plan," Blane Fahan said. "How fast can you get back here?"

23

REUNION

A NEW DAY DAWNED on Passage Island. The blazing sun climbed high into the eastern sky as Lazer swam peacefully at a trio of turquoise falls that danced around him. Their waters cascaded over rocks and tumbled into a lovely purple lagoon surrounded by a garden of plants and colorful flowers. Alone, other than Scrat, who had found his way back into Lazer's good graces, Lazer floated, quietly contemplating his life. Since last night it had taken on a whole new meaning. He decided Masta Poe was right: he wasn't dead because he was destined for something more. *At least something more than snake food*, he thought. He gave thanks, grateful to be alive, grateful to have been mentored by Masta Poe and the teachings of the Visionistic Arts that had already saved his life more than once since his journey began.

Now more than ever before, he felt ready to learn the deeper powers of the human mind the Visionistic Arts could open to him. He hungered for more of the knowings he'd experienced when he was fighting the python. Lazer felt his mind as it drifted back to the feelings that washed over him at the height of the attack. He remembered the wash of feelings that had given him all the control he needed for the battle. It was a warm feeling that rushed through him and at the height of the chaos he was the calm eye of the storm. In that one moment, he felt all the powers of the universe surging through him. It came as smooth as a summer breeze with the hush of quiet voice that whispered to him without using words. The sensation filled his heart and calmed his mind. It was a knowing that he had everything he needed to manifest whatever he wanted. Lazer pulled himself from the cool, refreshing waters and dressed. For those few precious moments, he was at peace with himself and everything around him. A hot wind blew over him and brought with it the same old quandary. The relentless question wiggled its way back into his thoughts and once again haunted his mind: *Should he go back to Tosadae and learn the Visionistic Arts from the greatest living master on the planet or go home to Atlantia and fight the Black Guard with the little knowledge he had already acquired?*

In his heart, Lazer felt had no choice. Go home, end of story. He would somehow get back to Atlantia with his limited skills, find his mother, join the Wave, and take his chances. Lazer looked around and remembered he would first have to get off Passage Island alive. Lazer sucked in a huge lung full of moist jungle air. He gave a deep sigh, pulled himself up and looked at his quest list. He still had to gather the artifacts and make it to the rendezvous point. So, for the moment, he would rest, gather his strength, and enjoy the little piece of paradise he'd found.

Lazer crossed to some palm leaves that he'd laid near his things. Under it were food and water that he collected. He sat and nibbled at the wild fruits and vegetables he'd gathered. They were sweeter that any he'd tasted on Atlantia or even Tosadae. He placed a coconut near a makeshift container for water he had created; the vessel was made from a large fresh water snail shell abandoned by its former inhabitant. Lazer looked at his lunch; part of the remains of the python, barbequing on a spit above a well-made fire.

Scrat grabbed a mango from Lazer's offerings and ran to a spot several yards away from the feast. Lazer studied him.

"You left me, you creep," Lazer scolded. "Next time you bolt like that, give a guy a heads-up."

"I'll keep that in mind," a voice answered.

Lazer jumped. He recognized the voice.

Striker McMann stared at him. He was filthy, hungry, and extremely glad to see a familiar face, even his high-school archenemy. He dropped to his knees by the edge of the water and repeatedly scooped handfuls of the cool, clear liquid into his mouth.

Lazer didn't know what to say. He felt oddly glad not to be alone, but Striker certainly fell last on the list of people he wanted to meet in an already hostile environment. Lazer smiled. The harsh reality of last night's death-defying events made their high-school rivalry seem all the more trivial.

"I never thought I'd be glad to see your ugly face," Striker said with a grin after he satiated his thirst.

"I'll reserve comment until you take a look at yourself. You look like spit."

"I was supposed to be picked up two days ago," Striker said.

"But?" Lazer asked.

Lazer saw Striker recoil from his words. He knew the question sent the mocking sting of the old challenge a foe like Striker might naturally assume dangled behind his question.

"I . . . I got there late," Striker said.

Striker was holding back the whole truth. From the color of his aura, Lazer suspected Striker had an intrinsic fear of opening up to Lazer. Surely that must be behind the negative sensation that threatened the first feeling of calm he experienced since he landed.

"I'm starving," Striker said. "I haven't had anything for three days other than some roots and the worst berries on the planet. "The scent of whatever you're cooking guided me here."

Lazer saw more than hunger in Striker's eyes.

"Mind if I . . .," Striker said, nodding toward the meat.

Lazer nodded back.

Striker attacked the roast and tore into two large chunks of freshly cooked snake, barely breathing between bites. Lazer offered Striker his shell of water.

"Not bad. What is it?" Striker asked through gulps of food.

"Human."

Striker froze. His mouth fell open.

"Just kidding. Python," Lazer said before Striker started to gag.

"Universal God! This thing must have been huge."

Lazer felt a rush of pride as he pointed to the enormous skin that hung on the tree and held up a six-inch fang. Striker gaped in awe.

"You killed this thing?" Striker asked. "Viz Arts, right?"

Lazer lifted his shirt and showed him the cuts, scrapes, and bruises that covered his body. "Let's just say it was him or me," Lazer said.

He shot a look to Scrat.

"Stupid Razer," Scrat said. "I saved him."

"You ran away!" Lazer said.

Striker laughed. "It talks and makes sense. I like this little guy."

"It's Lazer, creep," Lazer said with a snap to Scrat.

"Not creep! Scrat! Scrat! Scrat!"

Striker laughed harder. Lazer tried his best to hold the stern scowl etched on his face but Striker's deep, heartfelt laugh shattered his frown and melted it into a smile. Lazer laughed with Striker. The levity somehow made the entire situation easier. Everything became more bearable just knowing he had someone from home to share the strange reality that was unfolding.

When the laughter subsided, they wiped the tears from the corners of their eyes and talked as if they had been friends all along. Lazer and

Striker ate and drank, allowing the anger that stood between them from sixth grade through community college to evaporate by the act of simply deciding to let it go. They both knew they were in this together, and what both of them needed, more than anything else right now, was a friend.

"So, when's your second retrieval?" Lazer asked between bites of papaya.

"Ten days. I hope. Everything's been so whacked since I got here. I mean, come on, there are not supposed to be any splicers on this part of Passage Island, and a creature that big should be restricted to the southern side as well," Striker said as he pointed to the giant python remains. "Now that I think about it, aren't all the creatures on Passage Island supposed to be tagged?"

"Check that," Lazer responded. "And if they get that aggressive, the PAR is supposed to immobilize them, right?"

"Did your PAR work?" Striker asked.

"No," Lazer said.

It was only then that Lazer wondered why there had been no effort to intercede during the attack. "That python was tagged too. Look," he added.

The metal ring that pierced its tail was there as plain as day.

"I've had an archeop on my back for three days. She's why I was late for my pickup."

"What's an archeop doing on Passage Island? No flying splicers are supposed to be allowed on this side of the island. This is crazy. There can't be PAR tag failures and unauthorized splicers. What do you think . . .?" Lazer started to ask when his glance focused on Scrat.

He had no tag. All creatures were supposed to be tagged and any splicer not tagged was relegated to the south section of Passage Island for the upper-level treks only. A huge wall separated it from the rest of the island just to make sure.

"Don't ask me. This whole Rite of Passage has been totally off-book since I got here," Striker told him.

Striker was right, there were too many things going wrong for the Passage Committee to really be in charge.

"I think the South Wall is down and the Passage Committee have lost the ability to control the PAR tags," Lazer said.

"Spit! Are you kidding me?" Striker responded.

"We have to get off this island. Look, if I help you get back to your secondary retrieval point, I want a ride to Atlantia," Lazer said.

"It's headed to Sangelino," Striker said shaking his head. "Have you finished your Rite of Passage?"

"No, and I don't intend to. Not by their rules anyway. This place is out of control. Even if I wanted to, my guess is no one is monitoring us. More important, I know the fighting on Atlantia has escalated," Lazer said.

"How? I haven't talked to my parents in months," Striker added. "How do you know about an escalation?"

"My mom somehow got a garbled message out. They must have dropped the dome for a short time and any transmissions in the Vybernet got out. I heard enough. She sounded bad. Real bad," Lazer said. "As soon as we get off this rock, I'm gonna bounce home."

The two sat in silence for a long moment.

"Give me your second pickup coordinates and I'll do a map blast," Lazer insisted.

"The pickup code for my coordinates is 65823," Striker said, complying with Lazer's request. Striker gave a long sigh of relief. It was easy to see he was grateful to have Lazer along.

Lazer put the number code into a small locator built into his sleeve. A holographic map of the island appeared about a foot ahead of him and floated between them. It was a detailed replication of the island and it meticulously defined the lay of the land. In an array of colors the three-dimensional images shimmered before them. The map showed every lake, desert, mountain range, water source, and archeological site, the Southern Wall, ancient temples, and the ring of dense jungle that led to the desert. Beyond the desert lay the sea and most important their rendezvous point. The retrieval point was represented by a throbbing orange circle and glowing inside it were the exact coordinates confirming the point of the rendezvous. Lazer knew instantly it was their only hope. He could see it was located in the eastern desert, about twenty miles from the ocean.

Lazer reached out and touched a point in the virtual reality shapes that made up the image. He dragged his fingers together and condensed Passage Island so that the surrounding waters and landmasses would come into view. Lazer enhanced the visual to show a path from the centermost point of the Passage Island to just above the North Republic.

"You're looking for the shortest distance to get home?" Striker asked.

"Yeah," Lazer replied.

Lazer dragged one of the dots and expanded it, opening a second window. This one showed only their immediate location and the terrain with the most direct route leading to the rendezvous. Together, they studied the topography and plotted their course. The quickest route had them close to the South Wall. The South Wall divided the island and held inside the most dangerous creatures used for final and most advanced Rite of Passage trials.

"This route is the quickest but the journey will leave us exposed both to the elements and to some of the larger predators on the island," Lazer told Striker.

Striker said nothing only nodded for him to keep going.

"Or," Lazer said as he pointed to a second option.

"Is that any less dangerous?" Striker asked.

Lazer knew they were both dangerous routes.

"I say the jungle. Let's stay away from the South Wall and whatever the hell they keep behind it," Striker said.

"Done," Lazer agreed.

They decided to cross through the eastern jungle, avoid the Southern Wall, and pass through the ancient temple ruins to the desert side of the island. The desert would be hard going but the path was a straight shot to the rendezvous at the Banatek Oasis.

Lazer could see hesitation in Striker's aura. All Lazer felt was a rush of determination. He knew one thing only: he would be on that shuttle at all costs.

"Let's gather what food and water we can carry and bounce," Lazer said. "We have to make up an extra day of travel time to meet the calculation specs."

Striker nodded: "Okay, fearless leader. You kill one giant snake and you turn into a super hero."

Lazer laughed. "I'll tell you the story of the other creature I had to kill at Tosadae when we get on the road."

Striker smiled, obviously thankful for the opportunity to travel with someone he now respected on a whole new level.

Together they gathered what they could carry: fruit, roots, nuts, water, and some of the snake meat wrapped in palm fronds tied with thin vines. They were working well together when far off in the distance, the cry of an archeop echoed against the jungle's canopy. Striker's expression shifted and his skin paled. Lazer saw the fear wash over him.

"Sounds big," Lazer said.

Striker nodded yes.

"I'm telling you that is way weird. I still can't figure out what an archeop is doing on Passage Island. Let's get ahead of him. You ready?" Lazer asked.

"More than you know," Striker replied.

They cut through the surrounding jungle moving at a good pace, talking as they walked. Lazer could see Striker appreciated the distraction of Lazer's conversation. It only shifted when the distant cry from the archeop silenced the birds and insects. Only then did the panicked expression creep back onto Striker's face.

Only once did Striker stop. He looked back at the same empty patch of blue sky spotted with thick voluminous clouds, searching for the archeop that never seemed to appear.

Scrat leapt from branch to branch high above them in the canopy of green. The small creature watched them. Lazer could tell Scrat was nervous whenever he followed their gaze up into the sky or stopped to listen to the distant cry of the archeop. It was on one of those moments that Lazer thought he caught a glint of the morning sun as it reflected off a small, implanted chip nestled in Scrat's left eye. Who would chip this harmless little creature and why?

24

ALEECE

ALEECE BREATHED IN the gray, cold mist of the Atlantian winter. From her cot, she could see the hopelessness of the situation on every face at the Atland City raceway. The ever-present Black Guard had turned the raceway into a high security prison camp. They patrolled in the high bleachers above them relentlessly watching every movement of the humans they'd apprehended. Aleece had been counting the makeshift tents and bedrolls of the prisoners. She estimated the numbers of prisoners based on pallets and the campfires that spotted the heavily crowded areas. She knew that there were tens of thousands of people—wounded, hungry, thirsty, cold, and terrified. She knew that they could not survive for long in the dank, crowded conditions in which they were being forced to live, especially the children. *How could Atlantia have come to this? How could we have not listened and acted sooner?* Aleece thought. It took all Aleece's willpower to suppress the negative thoughts of guilt and the haunting voices of doom that wanted to come inside her head. She knew if she let them in they would consume her ability to do whatever she needed to do to get away. First she needed to conceive an escape plan. She had to visualize the sequence of events to get them all out. Once she had a clear plan, she'd have to rally these people, who were not trained warriors to fight and destroy the Black Guard. She knew she needed to devise a way to arm every man, woman, and child to fight, and then she would have to lead them. It would cost lives but it was the only way to save the people here and her only way to get home to be with Dante and hold Riana. Aleece got up and began to walk. She knew better than most that lying hopelessly around was useless. Over the last three days, she woke in a panic. It was the same vision of her little family; the three of them trapped in a morbid, surreal, and unbearable vignette of her husband and daughter surrounded by all her friends as they all sadly watched her funeral while she stood there unable to get them to see her. Each day Aleece would open her eyes and be sweating and short of breath because she couldn't make them see she was right there. Each day she would shake off the night terror and force herself to calm down. Those fear-filled nightmares were a waste of time and energy. She knew without her controlled resolve, she would be of no use to anyone, especially herself. Several times a day, Aleece gave gratitude to the Universal God that she was alive and had a loving husband and daughter and that her life had made and would make a difference in the world. She prayed for the opportunity to do so again. The mantra of gratitude gave her peace, purpose, and the courage to face another day, but it didn't answer the question of how to succeed against the odds. Aleece knew one thing—she needed a plan.

She looked around the stands. Above her, especially around the back of the arena seating, she watched multiple teams of mutants patrol the perimeter walls. In addition to the hundred-plus mutants she counted as she tracked, timing their shift changes, she noticed some odd-looking splicers. They all carried makeshift weapons. The Black Guard weaponry was built into their bodies—claws that changed into deuterium laser blasters and blades, capable of cutting a human in half. But what was keeping the people in, she wondered? There must be a proton or electronic barrier that would have to be disabled if the prisoners were to have any chance to escape.

Aleece sat down. She was tired and her bones ached. She has a gash from the crash and it pained her. She peeled back the torn fabric and looked at the wound. It wasn't healing, but supplies were so short, she didn't want to ask for a disinfectant. *If it gets worse*, she thought. She wished she were twenty years younger. Years had passed since Aleece's fighting days in the Mutant Wars, yet, as she remembered the various battle scenarios, all the old strategies formed and reformed as vivid pictures in her mind. They were a collection of broken pieces, a complicated puzzle that she knew, once they completed, would show her and hopefully most of the people in this prison, the way out.

Aleece stood and started to walk again, this time with a limp. As she walked, her eyes followed the uppermost structures. She calculated the odds of taking out the old press tower that as far as she could tell housed the Black Guard's command and communication center. Taking it out would cause mass confusion especially among the machines and possibly, if they were lucky, knock out their central power supply. *Without a head, the body would be lost,* she thought. She worked backward from the ultimate goal and analyzed the pieces of her plan down to its first and most pivotal element. It was a good plan, but she needed a team. The women. There would be more concern and focus on the men. She knew she needed to convince Detra and the other women they had to initiate a mutiny. If she could rally them into a rebellion and get word to the men for backup, she could time a disturbance to distract the Black Guard.

Aleece walked faster feeling exuberated by her plan. She had to find out exactly when and where the Black Guard's mutant and splicer forces entered and changed shifts. Aleece looked at her hand; empty, weaponless. She needed to figure out what weapons their captors held in the complex and where they were kept. When the women attacked the gate, the men could attack the armory and take weapons and ammo.

A swell of something wonderful filled her soul. It tingled inside her with excitement and made the shadowy darkness brighten and glow. She felt something so powerful that, for the first time since she arrived, her body didn't hurt and her heart beat with a rush of possibility. They could take this place. At first, she could not define the indescribable energy that engulfed her. Then, like the rush of a loving embrace, it dawned on her. The feeling was HOPE.

25

A CAVE OF SNOW

CASHTON WAS RELIEVED that somehow he was eluding death by the large, and very hungry black and white killer whale that pursued him under the thin ice shelf. Thankfully the ice got thicker as he got closer to shore and the thickness made the ice shelf harder to crack. But each time the whale rammed it, Cashton's heart pounded. The orca was persistent. He kept on, relentlessly leaving splatters of blood smeared under the ice with each hit. Cashton didn't have time to feel bad. He was running for his life. Always glancing down, he could feel himself as he instinctively zigged and zagged back and forth, confusing the agile creature with each sharp twist he made on his oath to safety. He hoped the ice would hold and that he was buying himself enough time to reach the designated first night Passage Ice Caves.

The air was cold and burned his nostrils. He pushed himself to run harder and faster. Time seemed to slow and it felt like forever until he finally reached landmass. He leapt and knew the moment he was on solid ground. He stopped, panting and grateful he's made it gulping in

139

air to help him catch his breath. Cashton turned back to glance one last time at his defeated, bleeding enemy. Something inside him told him to keep moving. He needed shelter. The night was closing so fast that he could see the light as it changed with each step.

Cashton reached the steep, uneven rocks that lead to the ice caves. He quickly assessed the incline as he began his ascent. He could feel the path elevating steeply before him with each exhausted step. His legs and lungs ached as he climbed up and stepped into the first ice cave he could find.

It looked small but it was impossible to determine how deep dark and what dangers it held. Cashton stopped at the entrance. First he listened cautiously and, when he heard only the faint empty whisper of the air below, he stepped inside. His ring light illuminated and, doing a quick but thorough sweep for predators, he claimed the small cave as his domain for the night. He plopped down. He had been at a steady jog for more than an hour. His heart raced but for the first time since he arrived, he breathed a long, grateful sigh of relief.

Cashton grabbed a handful of snow and ate it, relishing the cool ice that turned to liquid in his mouth. He checked back outside. The water's edge was only twenty feet below him, and he could see the black and white, shadowy form as it swam beyond the entrance. Cashton knew it could be hours before the whale accepted defeat and went away. He watched the skies turn from blinding pale blue to a soft, radiant azure as the sun hung just below the horizon. It was beyond beautiful. He nibbled on some dried bars he'd been allowed to carry in as he watched an ice storm form and roll in. It carried with it a gray haze of clouds that dulled the sky and rode on a bitter wind that swept up the loose snow into ghostly clouds. Cashton's thoughts drifted to family and home, Lazer and Kyla, and settled on how much he hated growing up. He knew this Rite of Passage meant the loss of childhood and all the freedom that came with it. He removed the face mask and felt the biting cold sting his eyes as a flow of warm, salty tears formed and fell from them. The tears gave him a momentary solace. Cashton had never been afraid of his feelings, and the world no longer admonished men for expressing them. The wind came harder and faster. It slapped against his face and brought him back to the reality of the moment. Survival. Cashton turned his back to the howling wind and bleak icy world, switching on his helmet's glow ring to see deeper inside the cave.

The cave felt small, but he knew it would shelter him from the passing storm and give him time to figure out how to complete his Rite of Passage assignments. *First, safety*, he thought. Cashton took a thin roll of wire chord and strung it back and forth across the entrance, placing two small lasers that crisscrossed the entrance. He knew if the light was broken, the sound would alert him to an intruder. Hopefully it would buy him a little time. Now he needed *heat, then food, then a plan*, he told himself, and pulled a wad of sticky black, fire resin. As he worked he took another bite of high-calorie food concentrate from his survival belt. He rubbed the resin between his hands and watched as the friction triggered the chemicals and ignited the resin into flame. It would expand and give him heat and light for a full eight hours. He wouldn't freeze to death. Cashton sat his flame down and made a gathering of rocks to surround and protect it. He still needed to improve his shelter. He thought as he chewed into the nutrition bar still hard from the cold. He stuck it into the flame between bites to soften it. Cashton pulled out a flip shovel and dug an ice well to capture the cold air. His survival instructor had warned him: since cold air sinks, make sure it has some place to go that's lower than your feet.

He had warmth and light. His stomach growled, sounding angry. Despite his recent meal, pangs of hunger gnawed at his stomach, reminding him that real food and water were his next priorities. He knew well the adage of life and death: three minutes without air, three days without water, and three weeks without food equals death. He chipped off some ice from the walls at the entrance of the cave and placed the shards into a wrist cup that doubled as a bowl or pot and sat it in the fire.

The ice melted them down into water on the expanding resin fire. He drank the hot water and it seemed to quiet his belly and chase the chill away. That's when the fatigue hit him making his limbs feel weak. *Rest over food*, he thought. Tomorrow he would have to hunt for something substantial to eat.

Cashton yawned and stretched his long, lanky body out in front of the resin fire on a bed of snow that kept him above the icy floor. Snug, in his insulated environment suit, he watched the small flame. It expanded into a cozy glow that turned his shelter a soft amber. He closed his eyes and in an instant, Cashton was snoring louder than the howling wind outside.

26

THE EASTERN JUNGLE

LAZER AND STRIKER made their way through the dense jungle that surrounded Mount Quilliani. With a tinge of apprehension, they approached the barren tan and black rock of Mount Quilliani's eastern face. Lazer looked at the steep incline and soft jagged ledges. It would be hard but not impossible.

As they walked, Lazer could not help but notice the smell of moss and sweet flowers that blended into pungent scents of life, death, and the profound danger that faced them at every turn. Since the ROP protection devices were not in place, Lazer freely used the Visionistic Arts to part trees and thick brush as they carved a path through the jungle. The trek got even more unbelievably arduous, once they had left the main trail what seemed like hours ago. They all hoped they'd make up the precious time they needed to reach the rendezvous, but the terrain was proving more and more challenging with each passing hour.

Even though his use of the Visionistic Arts took only a tenth the physical strength it would have taken to machete their way through the overgrown jungle, the constant mental energy drain on his mind was taxing. Each time Lazer called on the Visionistic Arts, it exhausted him mentally and physically. He needed an almost constant flow of drinking water moving through his system to recover. Using the powers made him discover how each one differed and how it connected to the universe. The vital liquid flowing inside him acted as a conduit and each time he connected his mind to the powers that flowed from the universal source to fulfill his commands, he could see how it then connected into the plants, trees, water, and rocks. As the source power charged him, he moved objects and his skills became stronger with every use.

Scrat swung through the thick canopy of trees that hung above them. His huge eyes and bushy tail made his trek a playful game as he—and someone else—watched Lazer's every move.

"I don't trust that monkey," Striker said.

"Me either," Lazer replied, but decided to keep the possibility of a chip in the creature's eye to himself. Spooking Striker more than he already was would do neither of them any good.

Lazer focused on the situation at hand and, after another drink of cool water from a hollowed-out tree stump, he raised his hands and as a conductor would lead a symphony, he gracefully parted another section of the jungle that lay before them.

It was hard, focused work, but no matter how hard he concentrated on the task before him, his thoughts drifted to Elana Blue and for some reason, even more so to Kyla. No visions of danger, just feelings. Was this some precognition he was experiencing? What Kyla reaching out from her mind to him? Lazer felt the pull of her thoughts calling to him. Somehow, for some reason, his friend was trying to send him a message. *I'll find you, Kyla*, he thought. *Take care of Elana. I'm coming for you both.*

27

ICE CAVE REFLECTIONS

CASHTON PULLED HIS BODY up from the hard snow that covered the floor of the cave and struggled to his feet. His sleep had been continuously broken each time he checked the entrance to make sure the snow and ice storms had not sealed him in. The cave seemed large enough that even a blocked entrance wouldn't suffocate him, at least for a while, but the fractured sleep left him exhausted.

His joints popped and cracked resisting every little motion and letting him know they did not appreciate the prior night's sleeping arrangements. Cashton slapped his arms and legs repeatedly to get the circulation going and generate some warmth. The survival microfiber of the gear he wore on this first-year Rite of Passage created more than enough insulation to hold his body's heat and keep his body temperature at normal levels, even though outside it stayed well below freezing. Cashton looked at the cold pile of dusty embers left from his long-since-dead resin fire and shivered.

Cashton made his way down the narrow entrance guided by the light ring affixed to his headgear. The tunnel hung in darkness. He knew his body clock was off, but he couldn't have missed the day completely, and the sun at this time of year never set. If nothing else, his stomach would have let him know the approximate time. When he reached the entrance, a wall of snow blocked the entrance, including all seven of the air vents he'd poked open over the course of the night.

"Spit," Cashton muttered to himself.

He took out the small six-inch rod from his utility belt and squeezed the center. With a click, it telescoped out and reconfigured itself into a four-foot staff. With a second twist at one end, the tip splayed open and formed a triangular wedge flat enough to act as a shovel. Cashton swung the shovel, stabbing the wall of snow with a mighty jab. The loud clank meant he faced near-solid ice.

"Double spit," Cashton complained. "Why is nothing ever easy?"

He turned the little shovel sideways, and with a third twist it became a pick ax. Cashton lifted his well-defined muscular arms as high above his head as the cave's ceiling allowed and with a loud grunt swung and hacked into the door to his prison of ice and snow. It would take hours to dig his way out. He wished he'd been clever enough to smuggle some of his more creative inventions.

He would have appreciated one of the minibots he'd built from pieces of junk and tangles of wire like the two he had trained to help him clean up his room every day. He called them Frick and Frack, the nano twins. Cashton beamed with pride at the thought of their complicated circuitry and the brilliant AI; artificial-intelligence software had come a long way and he was excellent at building and programming the systems that operated them. His little nano twins could organize almost anything he programmed them to. The size of a thick stack of dinner plates, they had added brushes and rotors for cleaning and using a 3-D printer, two spindly robotic arms with pincers to make neat piles of whatever lay scattered. The nano twins had always impressed the cute girls he managed to talk to into coming back into his room at Tosadae. Cashton would put the bots through their paces and impress the ladies with his clever inventions, until Frick, it was always Frick, would short-circuit. Cashton cringes at the memory of the time he nearly electrocuted one of his dates, and the time he almost burned down the entire dorm. The dorm master confiscated Frack and vaporized it. Frick was in pieces and hidden away never to be used again.

Cashton swung with all his might. He hacked harder and harder until he finally caused a fracture in the ice.

"Spit," he said looking closely at the small crack he'd managed. He could see the ice wall was harder and thicker than he originally accessed. He hit it harder again and again, trying to imagine what he could build to help him. Most of his inventions, the ones that worked, had been useful bits of other clever technology and complicated spyware repurposed by him to make his life easier. Ultimately, they somehow got him into more trouble than they were worth. But as Lazer reminded him, he was an inventor, and his curiosity always got the better of him. Once he had an idea for an invention, he inevitably had to build it. Who knows, someday, something he created might just make the world a little bit better.

He was sweating as he pounded harder into the ice wall that held him prisoner. *A blow torch would be nice,* he thought. So would the ability to manipulate matter using some simple VA techniques like shifting the frozen ice molecules from solid to liquid. He would have liked to be able to change the weather, or walk through solid matter and make fire from nothing—not that Lazer hadn't tried to teach him some variations on those kinds of advanced level powers on numerous occasions. At least he'd qualified for next year's beginning Visionistic Arts class thanks to Kyla and Lazer. However, what he might learn next year would not be helping him at the moment.

Cashton smiled. Lazer, on the other hand, had been accepted into Masta Poe's BAI series: Bliss and I. The advanced classes taught how to achieve a state of being at one with the universal powers. It was an advanced class and Lazer had tested into a sector usually reserved for juniors and seniors. Cashton knew Lazer was ranked as an Indigo human: gifted across the board mentally and physically, as were Kyla and Elana Blue. Compared to them, Cashton felt like an average Joe, a talented jock with a modicum of high level intelligence and a propensity for building gadgets. Somehow they had always stayed friends.

Cashton looked bigger, acted tougher, and enjoyed playing the protector. In return, Lazer supported his crazy, often dangerous, and on the occasion, scathingly brilliant ideas. Cashton liked that. Kyla joined them in middle school, completing the dynamic trio. She'd taught them compassion for friends, life, home, and family. Why couldn't Lazer see how much she loved him? *What a bat!* Cashton thought.

Cashton thought about his friendships as he hacked deeper into the ice. Finally he saw a pinhole of light shining through the opening he'd made. With it came a rush of cold air. He wouldn't suffocate. It would take time to dig his way out. Then he would focus on finding food. He imagined cutting a hole in the ice and fishing. He could do that with the few supplies they had given him. The idea of pan-fried fish made him salivate.

Outside the entrance to the cave, the relentless chunk, chunk, chunk from Cashton's shovel echoed against the ice. Like a bell to dinner, it rang out and drew back not one but two large predators beneath the ice shelf. The menacing shadows circled beneath the surface. Their massive bodies began to pound the ice that stretched above their heads just outside Cashton's cave. First one, then two spidery cracks appeared in the icy surface. Unknowingly, Cashton chipped out his persistent, primitive rhythm from inside the cave as its pounding counterpoint played against the thuds from beneath the surface. Cashton heard the noise. He stopped. They stopped. *Clever,* he thought. Between the two, it would not take long to connect and the battle for survival and breakfast to begin.

28

THE ARCHEOP

LAZER AND STRIKER reached the base of Mount Quilliani by late afternoon. They made good time, stopping only for short intervals to eat and drink. They pressed each other hard through the heat of the day, understanding they couldn't miss Striker's transport.

Striker complained at first but got a second, third, and fourth wind every time he heard the call of the archeop. The screeching call never seemed to go away. They were being followed, and not only by Scrat. Scrat kept a respectful distance, but always managed to scamper close enough to never lose sight of them. Lazer watched, keeping an eye on the little creature.

They made their way across the first ridge of the foothills, following the complicated maze of switchbacks that carried them arduously up into the mountain paths and out of the thick jungle. A mile farther, the tree line abruptly ended, and the terrain turned hard and rocky, making their ascent at times almost vertical. A refreshingly cool breeze killed the musty scent of dead moss and rotting jungle that had followed them on the thermals from below. But the view of the eastern landscape was spectacular. It stretched before them, lush beauty and a palette of colors that marveled the eye, the heart, and the mind. The artistry of the landscape was marred only by the ever-persistent call of the archeop.

The day was fading and they were tired. The trees of the jungle were far below them now due to the change of elevation. Even Scrat, tired of climbing the slippery rocks, tried to hitch a ride on Striker's daypack.

"Hey, off, leach. This is hard enough," Striker said fussing. He didn't like the little splicer.

Again the cry of the archeop resounded off the rocks.

"Is it my imagination or was that closer?" Lazer asked.

"It was definitely closer," Striker said.

Lazer watched as Striker again searched the sky. The concerned expression on his face made Lazer look too.

"Weird it stays in the clouds. We're exposed out on these rocks too," Lazer said.

"I know. Lazer, it's huge. Ten feet easy, and that's without the tail," Striker said.

"Ten feet! A splicer that big didn't come from a lab. That's got to be Mother Nature gone wild," Lazer said, looking at the sky and feeling suddenly more concerned than ever.

"It's not right. I told you, it's been stalking me since I crossed Adam's Pass. I had to double back to lose it. That's why I missed my pickup," Striker said softly.

Lazer noticed he was gasping for air in the higher altitude.

"Come on, Striker, breathe. Keep moving. Why would it stalk?" Lazer asked. That was the question that bothered him the most. The archeop screeched again. For the first time, it sounded like it was deliberately getting closer, and he couldn't help shake the feeling he and Striker were its designated target. They climbed, reached a small plateau, and stood walking toward the next incline.

"Could you see if it was tagged?" Lazer asked.

"It was, and the PAR doesn't work for sure. At least it didn't work for me. I want to know where the controllers are," Striker said.

"That's the same thing I wondered when I saw the tag on that python," Lazer added.

Another unnerving screech erupted above them, torturing their ears with promises of danger. Lazer and Striker looked up into the haze of thick grey clouds that hovered above them. This time he caught a glimpse of a pale, T-shaped shadow that rippled behind the mist. Lazer saw it too. He looked ahead. Thick clouds wrapped around the mountain's shoulders and hung ominously above them, blocking their view.

With the archeops next pass, Lazer strained to see the details of the creature, but it was too fast and far too camouflaged by the miasma of clouds.

"The wingspan must be at least fifteen feet!" Lazer said, nearly choking on his words.

"It looks bigger 'cause it's getting closer," Striker said and exchanged a look of warning with Lazer.

No words necessary, they unanimously picked up their pace.

The next screech sent chills up their spines and Scrat into Lazer's arms.

"Big! Danger!" Scrat said.

"I got that," Lazer replied and swung the little monkey onto his pack. "Hang on." Scrat wasn't very heavy, and the warmth and closeness actually made him feel a little safer.

Lazer glanced up as he scanned the cliffs just ahead. More than three hundred feet over and more than twenty feet up, Lazer could see several small black holes that pockmarked the upper ledges.

"Shelter. Two o'clock! Move it!" Lazer ordered.

The shadow circled above them. It came closer, first to survey. A second pass brought it even closer. On the third loop, it cut back, angled down, and burst through the cloud covering. They were under attack.

"Bird, bird, bird! Run!" Scrat said as he grabbed Lazer's head, half-covering his eyes.

It only took a second to comprehend this wasn't about food; this was personal. It was a female. Her dull rust-brown coloring and slender form told Lazer that bit of information. Her enormous talons flared open and headed straight for Striker.

"Down!" Lazer shouted to Striker. He pulled at the monkey's paws. "Let go!"

Scrat fell back, still gripping on. Lazer climbed.

Striker flattened himself against the rock. The archeop swooped past and grabbed his survival strap. She lifted off, taking Striker with her.

Striker pounded at the strap's release clip. The catch opened, and the strap was ripped away from his arms. Striker dropped, flailing wildly, grabbing at anything that would stop him from going over the narrow ledge. He teetered backward, flailing in a useless fight with gravity. In the final breath of time, Lazer reached out and pulled him back onto the path.

The archeop dove in for its second attack. With his pack gone, Striker was exposed.

Lazer dropped, flipped onto his back, and kicked out, catching the archeop off guard and sending it flapping away. Frantically, Striker took the momentary respite and scurried away. He looked as wild as a scurrying spider on hot coals, using both his hands and feet to propel him up the ledge.

Lazer was seconds behind him. Scrat hung on for dear life. It was obvious they couldn't outrun the enormous creature. He had to slow her down. Lazer rolled over, pressed his back against the cold rocks, and cupped his hands.

Crushed by the move, Scrat screeched. He leapt from behind Lazer and ran across the flat wall. He hopped and climbed struggling to get a foothold. Just as he was at the top of the cliff, the archeop plucked Scrat from the ledge and tossed him into the air. Scrat grabbed at the void and never saw the beak of the archeop until its razor-sharp teeth bit right through him. It swallowed him in one ravenous gulp.

There was no time to feel anything for Scrat; this was survival. Lazer focused. The sunlight was dim, which made it harder to see, but the thin air was cool enough for what he needed. He felt his perception of time as it opened its bonds and slowed, allowing him to see and experience every detail of what was happening with perfect clarity.

Heisenberg's uncertainty—the relations of divided energy—was the second lesson in Masta Poe's personalized syllabus. It had been an enigma for Lazer until this moment. He had not understood how the mind could exist in multiple dimensions or command matter into being. A rush of calm understanding filled him. It was the same knowing he had felt when he faced the python. He had found his BAI and made the rock manifest across space into his hands. He did it then, and he could do it now. Lazer focused as Masta Poe had shown him. He looked up and saw the snowcapped peaks. He felt the freezing cold of the ice and willed it into his hands. Lazer felt a stabbing in his palms and looked down to see a swirl of icy smoke begin to fill the space between his adjoined palms. The collecting matter became dense and liquefied into a thick mass of spiraling ice crystals. Lazer's hands ached from the cold, and his skin turned a pale, whitish-blue. In real time, everything was happening at the speed of quantum thought.

The archeop came at him with the force of a dervish. In mid-swoop, Lazer hurled the glistening ball of energized ice crystals with all the force he could muster. The liquid mass hit the archeop with a resounding thud, coating it and giving Lazer more time to focus. He willed all the moisture in the air to gather around the archeop. It clung to the creature like water condensing onto an ice-cold glass. The mist flowed from all directions, swirling around the confused creature and getting thicker with each second. It expanded into a shimmering wash, giving the illusion of mercury. The archeop grabbed at the ledge and expanded its wings to leap into the air and fly. The liquid oozed in multiple directions—up, down, and sideways—and coated the archeop's body and wings. It coagulated into a solid mass, popping and crackling under the straining muscles of the frightened creature. Its body, now completely inflexible, the archeop was frozen. It plunged off the cliff. Lazer listened as the creature's wailing and tortured screeching echoed off the mountains, reverberating back at Lazer and Striker. They watched in awe as it plummeted, turned helplessly, and slammed repeatedly into the jagged outcroppings and cliffs that jutted from the mountain. It plunged, frozen solid, its body shattered into chunks of frozen flesh.

The pieces melted instantly into severed, oddly shaped body parts that only a moment before had been a living, breathing creature.

"You k-k-killed it!" Striker stuttered, his voice trembling.

Lazer nodded, unable to take his eyes away from the remains. He gave thanks to the Universal God and for the teachings of Masta Poe that had saved him yet again.

Before Lazer's heartbeat could return to normal, the sky above them filled with the cry of a second archeop. She had a mate.

29

RIANA

RIANA WAS SPENDING a few moments at the Global Assurance Health and Healers Clinic in downtown Sangelino for her monthly body scans. It was covered under the universal health management system and took about twenty minutes. She walked through a scanner that checked for everything from cavities to the most rare brain, skin, bone, or blood diseases. Sangelino Hospital was on the other side, with healers and surgeons and beds for the sick.

Riana always took a moment to admire the plaque dedicated to the memory of the United States' first biracial president, whose bold actions spearheaded the move toward a true universal health care—he battled the insurance and pharmaceutical companies and the pharmacies to set a pricing standard and made them stick to it. He and his predecessors pulled his country and then the world out of the clutches of the World Bank and the Federal Reserve. Riana knew from her history lessons it had been the unmentionable president, the one stricken from the history books for his crimes that used his power to eradicate their constitution for his own personal gain that has started the war and forced the dome over the forbidden territories and sealed those who would not stop fighting inside. The Great Quakes had done the rest. The courage of those leaders who came after had inspired Riana's mother, Aleece, to become a doctor. But there hadn't been countries or presidents for over a century, and global health care and free education was still a number-one priority everywhere.

The scan showed that Riana was in great shape, other than her pubescent hormones, which were low from the stress that she was under and the weight she'd lost. She would be a young woman soon, and unless Aleece returned, she would have no one to talk to about "things" but her father. She spent the rest of the afternoon with her two best friends at the Coztronics Mall, shopping and playing in the virtual arcade. Riana said goodbye and went home to mist down her body, feed her skin, and change her clothes for the evening.

Dressed and ready, she was waiting for Masta Poe by the Water Theater along the western shoreline of Sangelino. She felt agitated, as if bugs were crawling up her back. She had not wanted to come at first but had ultimately decided to do as her mother had asked and continue her Visionistic education. Riana sighed; she liked Masta Poe, and all she would do at home was worry for her mother. She knew better than anyone: worry served no purpose. So she waited, watching the crowds gather and friends meet. Tonight, they would be part of a unique musical experience, listening to eighteenth-century classical baroque music written by French composer Chevalier de Saint George and performed by vibrating symbiotic rings and a mixed orchestra using rare antique instruments. The concert was to be performed inside the greatest man-made hydration collection plant in the world. While also an enormous open-air theater, its primary purpose was as a fascinating structure designed to attract moisture from the atmosphere and convert it into fresh water. Other similar water theaters placed strategically around Sangelino collectively supplied 68 percent of all fresh water to the area.

Riana arrived early to meet Masta Poe. She dressed meticulously, wearing one of her mother's silk and linen tunics. It was a soft hazel green that matched her eyes and made her look more grown up than her fourteen years. She wore a collar of seashells woven into braids of black satin cording and matching shell earrings. She added a few shells to her Rite of Passage lock to complete the ensemble. The sheer over shift was a little large, but she didn't care. It carried in its fibers the scent of her mother's favorite perfume, Troiageeaniya Mist Perfume, a combination of her mother's own natural fermions, summer jasmine, rare spices, and warm honey. Aleece had worn the scent for as long as Riana could remember. To have it against her skin tonight made her feel safe and loved. She looked beautiful. Even at fourteen, she carried herself with the grace of a young queen.

Riana stood on her toes to look over the gathering crowd. She turned her eyes up to watch the beads of condensation run down the tubes and fill the channel below with water. She checked her wristsponder and searched again but didn't see Masta Poe among the families that talked and laughed, sharing the evening's excitement with one another.

This will be the second visit this month from Masta Poe. *How strange*, Riana thought. She didn't like to admit it, but the increased frequency made her curious and edgy. Masta Poe and Riana's father had augmented the monthly training sessions with weekly lessons ever since her mother had disappeared. Riana couldn't help but feel there was a deep urgency that spilled from Masta Poe every time she visited. Unlike most adults whose thoughts Riana could easily read, Masta Poe could be as closed and well guarded as a locked safe. "I simply want to know what the big deal is," she mumbled to herself. But Masta Poe had made it clear: when she was ready, Riana would know why she was so special.

Riana had been taught that everyone had at least one innate gift that formed the foundation of his or her core abilities. What would spring from those abilities defined each person's greatest strengths and passions. Most people, prior to the knowings of the Visionistic Arts, showed their abilities in early childhood. The secret was in the pretending they engaged in. Those years of unbridled imagination were free and unfettered. After the age of six, the parameters of constrained reality placed on a child by parents, family, and teachers redefined the borders and limited the boundless possibilities that lay before them. Everyone's natural proclivity to pretend allowed the mind to express an individual's core passion and key to the true path of life: healer, artist, protector, leader, teacher, or warrior. These core passions were the key to the heroes we had to learn to see in ourselves, Masta Poe had told her. These were the true individual knowings and the memories they inspired were early signs of self and an individual's direct connection to the universal source. These universal powers were hardwired, grounded deep in our DNA, and given to us to guide us on our true paths. Far too often, especially in the centuries before the Great Quakes, children were told by adults that their natural powers were wrong. They were also told their dreams and aspirations were unattainable. Discouraged by the parents and teachers they loved and admired at an early age, they fell into the drone of daily survival. Those misguided children grew into adults and lost their paths, callings, and passions. They trudged through life doing only what was expected of them instead of what the universal source had intended for them.

Riana was lost in thought when she noticed a strange old woman standing next to her. The woman's face was mapped with wrinkles, but she had a warm twinkle in her eyes that Riana found compelling. She handed Riana a small card. On it a holographic image depicted four different-colored planets aligning and then exploding. The fireball melted into a series of coordinates and directions.

"Your mother is alive," the old woman muttered.

"What did you say?" Riana asked her.

"You are the light we have been waiting for," the woman said and smiled. She looked around, suddenly anxious.

"What do you know about my mother?" Riana demanded. Her heart raced.

"Follow the map on the card if you wish to know more, but tell no one," the woman said. In a blur of motion, she vanished. Her voice echoed in Riana's mind. Tell no one.

Riana turned, searching in all directions, but the old woman had vanished. When she turned back, Masta Poe was standing next to her obviously reading her thoughts.

"Have you lost something, Riana?" Masta Poe said as she smiled at her.

"No, Masta Poe. I . . .," Riana said, feeling cautious. "Never mind. It doesn't matter."

"What should matter is that you allow your passion to guide you. Imagine yourself into being and thereby create your destiny," Masta Poe told her with a smile. "Come. Tonight's lesson is how to find harmony and peace inside the simple act of gratitude."

"I thought we were going to listen to music."

"Oh, we are," Masta Poe said.

She took Riana's hand and led her. Riana followed, glancing one last time at the card from the old woman. The sunburst reconfigured into a map, which showed a journey into the lowest region of Covax City called the Red Zone.

Riana gave a small gasp and closed the card in her hand, then slipped it inside her tunic. One more time, her eyes searched the crowd. Covax City's Red Zone was no place for a girl of fourteen—or anyone else—as far as Riana was concerned.

From the back of the highest balcony, the old woman watched as Riana and Masta Poe found their seats. A shadow fell across the woman's face.

"Will she come?" asked the shadow.

The old woman looked over at Masta Poe and Riana.

"She'll come. Just make sure you're ready or there'll be hell to pay," she said glancing one more time at Riana. The old woman turned and vanished into the crowd as the shadow faded.

30

TIME—NOW OR NEVER

DETRA HAD BEEN UP ALL NIGHT helping the wounded. Through her exhaustion, she smiled at Aleece, who was tending to a child on the other side of the geodesic tent. Aleece was their hero, the only source of hope most of them had felt since the beginning of their struggle. And now it was time to act. Aleece moved across the room quickly and touched several of the women, instructing them with a slight nod to follow her. Charged and anxious, they fell in line. Detra took her cue and headed toward the group. They gathered together and began working to construct a bed.

"There are forty-seven guards, twenty on the ground and about the same up on the walls," Aleece whispered. "Seven mutants patrol the back and front gates. They change shifts every six hours."

"What about weapons?" one of the women asked.

"We can get four DT phasers here and three in the men's section," Detra answered.

"That's it! That's all we can get? No, that is not enough!" another woman said with a gasp. "The Black Guard and the clones are fully armed."

"That's all we've got to take them down," Aleece snapped back.

"It's suicide," the woman insisted.

"So is staying here. Listen to me, all of you," she said, lowering her voice. "I have heard they're planning to start executions on Friday."

"Executions!" the women said.

"Why? What have we done?" one woman asked.

"We have become a detriment to them," Aleece told her.

"If we run, some of us stand a chance of escaping. If we stay, we all die," Detra added.

"We don't know why, only that the order to eliminate all humans has been given," Aleece replied as calmly as she could.

"How do you know that?" asked a young woman with dark, soulful eyes and a voice that reeked of desperation.

"Someone or something from the Wave forces has infiltrated the Black Guard," Aleece told her.

"That's impossible. I don't believe you," the woman responded.

"You don't have a choice," spat a black-skinned woman named Bella. She punctuated each syllable with the gravity of their situation.

"No!" The woman was losing control.

"Stop it or you'll get us all killed," Detra demanded in a harsh whisper. She grabbed the fearful woman by her shoulder to make her point even stronger. There was a callous truth to the words.

Detra could see the face of every woman in the circle as they turned pale with fear. Panic spread among them like a wildfire through dry brush.

"No. I won't believe you. It's a lie. An insane lie!" One woman sobbed softly. She dropped to her knees and buried her face in her hands.

"Insane or not, it's a fact," Aleece told her.

"It cost a fourteen-year-old boy his life to bring us that report. I don't plan to let his death be for nothing," Detra told them.

"The Wave knows our situation and supports our decision to escape.

They've planned a diversionary attack tomorrow night. The firefight will draw the majority of the Black Guard to the front gate. All we have to do is be ready to hit them from behind," Aleece lowered her voice as she watched two guards pass by the far door.

The other women fell silent and worked diligently on the bed. Each glanced up at different times to check on the guards' location.

"It can't be done. We still don't have weapons," the first woman said and turned to walk away. Three others started to follow. Detra grabbed the first woman.

"Rocks, sticks, bed pans, whatever you can get your hands on, grab it and be ready to use it," she ordered. "With or without you, tomorrow night is going to happen."

"This is the only chance we've got," Aleece said. "If we don't fight back, they'll annihilate us."

Some of the women started to back away. Detra confronted them.

"If I'm gonna die, it'll be on my terms, not some nanohead's. They've already murdered our husbands and our friends, burned our homes, and taken our country hostage. And now they plan to slaughter us like diseased cattle! So listen to me, for the lives of our children and our children's children, we have to fight." She spoke with the fury and passion of a warrior. Tears welled in her eyes.

The frightened women knew she was right. One by one, the terror of their situation and the lack of options hardened each expression into pure determination. They, too, had lost family and friends. They, too, had watched their homes burned and their dreams destroyed. Detra's words gave them strength. Their hearts were ignited for the first time since they had been sealed inside the proton dome.

Detra turned to Aleece, nodding for her to speak. She looked around to make sure no one was watching and signaled for the women to step closer to her. They huddled in, shoulder to shoulder, to hear Aleece's plan, ready for her to lead them to freedom or take them to their deaths.

"When the attack starts, I'll give a signal and we'll rush the guards.

In the confusion, take as many weapons as you can. Kill whoever resists. Have no doubt they will kill you first if they can." She looked around the room. "Anybody got Viz Arts training? Who can throw a shield?"

A few hands rose.

"It's been a few years," a tall, coffee-skinned woman said.

An older woman nodded as well. Her silver hair and wrinkled skin made her look pale, but there was a fearless strength in her eyes.

"We'll need you at the front and you at the rear. You will shield the children; anyone else will shield us at the gate."

One of the women grabbed Aleece. Her wide, darting eyes silently warned Aleece that danger was near. A guard was approaching. The cluster of women made them curious. The women grabbed the bed frame they had been working on and flipped it on its feet. They carried the newly constructed bed to the end of the ward and placed it.

"Tell them you're not a surgeon," a woman whispered as she whisked by. "They're looking for a surgeon."

"Nineteen hundred tomorrow night," Aleece whispered before the women scattered in different directions.

Four Black Guard crossed to Aleece and asked if she was the female surgeon.

"That would be me," a woman named Maya replied.

Aleece's heart stopped. Her mouth opened, but before she could speak, Detra shot Aleece a look of quiet desperation.

Two Black Guard grabbed Maya with such force she winced under their hard grasp. In a whirlwind, they led her away.

"I can't let her do that," Aleece said to Detra.

Detra pulled her into the shadow of a rusting holoscreen, one of many that lined the raceway. It had once carried advertisements but now sat rotting like everything else in the arena.

"We need you," Detra whispered. "She knows how important you are to our success."

"What if something happens to her?" Aleece replied, her eyes still on Maya and the guards.

"She knows the risk. You're the only hope we have, and without you this plan won't work," Detra spoke as she blocked Aleece's path.

"I can't . . .," Aleece protested.

"You won't walk away this time, Aleece," Detra glared at her.

Aleece blinked, unsure of her meaning.

"This is the second time you have been the hope and logic of my life. I didn't speak up the first time, and it cost me more than I can ever explain," Detra confessed, her words filled with the pain of a long forgotten history.

"Do I know you from somewhere else?" Aleece asked.

"I worked for you twenty years ago in the bio labs beneath Sangelino. Back then my name was Detra Blanchette," she said.

"You worked on the original splicer project?"

"Marketing, not genetic," Detra nodded.

Aleece studied her. She'd had a feeling from the first moment they'd met. The memories flooded back, filling her mind with images.

"I do remember you," Aleece said. "Universal God, you were there the morning Ducane and I fought."

The two women shared a moment that needed no words.

"It's not important now," Detra said. "Why you left and what happened because of it has only one connection to today—you."

"I couldn't stop him from releasing those splicers. You know I tried," Aleece said, emotion choking her.

"I know. And after you left, I and a hundred people tried for months to convince him to postpone the sales. But he was obsessed. When he lost you, he lost all sense of logic. He wanted to prove he was right and you were wrong. When we opposed him, he fired everyone. I was the last to leave. Then he hired a thousand new people, released the first generation of untested splicers, and the rest is history," Detra said. There was a tremor in her voice.

"I thought if I left he would stop," Aleece told her.

"Ducane was in love with you, but he loved being right more," Detra said.

"I know."

Aleece's words fell into a whisper. Detra heard the long-forgotten feelings that clung to the words.

"I wanted to find you and tell you that we would follow you to the press and verify the data to prove the splicer batches were unstable, but I let him hold me back because I was so in . . .," Detra stopped. Aleece could see a plethora of emotions flood her face as they simmered in her voice. "It doesn't matter. None of that matters now. The only thing that matters is that I am standing in front of you, begging you to spearhead this escape. Be the leader you are and get us the hell out of here."

The two women stood in silence. The look in Detra's eyes said much more than any words could have.

"Were you in love with him?" Aleece asked, needing to hear the words spoken.

"He loved you. I took up space for a while in the unfathomable void you left."

"I'm sorry," Aleece said.

"Don't be. I've forgotten about it, and no one on Atlantia knows I ever lived in Sangelino. Just get me out of here so we can destroy the Black Guard and I can have my son come home."

Aleece nodded, and in a surprise gesture of gratitude embraced Detra.

Detra stiffened. She suddenly felt hard and disconnected, but the warmth and kindness in the embrace that should have relaxed her. Detra realized she'd not been touched by another human being, other than Lazer, since her husband's death. The human contact and honesty of the gesture pushed the memories and pain back to the surface. She knew Aleece had unknowingly sent her back inside herself into some shadowy corner deep in her heart. Aleece felt the resistance and hugged her harder until, finally, Detra let herself go. With a long sigh, she hugged Aleece back.

The two women surrendered to each other, both finally relaxing inside their embrace. They held on for a long time, grateful for the kindness they shared. Finally, Aleece let go.

"We have a lot to do," Aleece smiled, her confidence renewed.

"I know. I have to get back to the hospital," Detra said as she turned to leave.

"Detra?" Aleece stopped her.

She turned back, picking up the flash of concern that suddenly flooded Aleece's face.

"Detra, do you believe Ducane is behind this rebellion?" she asked.

"No," Detra said, then turned and walked away.

31

PARTS

COVAX HAD DESIGNED and built the surgical room at his campus facilities for micro dissection of brain matter and genetic reconstruction, not trauma surgery. True to his word, Five had raided Atland City Hospital and brought the list of surgical equipment Covax had requested including a 3-D printer, but an arm would take weeks to print and there wasn't time. They had, however, been unable to locate a surgeon.

Reattaching a limb was well beyond the facility's intended use, but it was all they had. Covax could splice genetics, but he had no skills as a surgeon. Pi had some surgical experience and offered to attach the nerves to Elana Blue's new limb. Together, with the help of the bio-droid called OPALMOX, they worked inside a holographic surgical simulation program that allowed the physical surgeon to step into the projected hologram and mimic the actions of a virtual surgeon and an assistant. It was a program they had accessed through one of the local hospital libraries that had been downloaded long ago from the plethora of available medical data files that cluttered the Vybernet.

Elana Blue lay anesthetized on the operating table. Above her, Covax, led by the holographic imagine, finished the first procedure. He'd grafted the bone and set the joint making way for Pi to knit the muscles and veins together, and now OPALMOX would weave and connect the nerves from her shoulder to her new arm. The biodroid would be able to complete the process using surgical attachments that could connect directly to his claws and perform the ultra-fine, laparoscopic surgery needed to give her a new arm. Add to that the twelve hours of surgery time and OPALMOX was the only one with the stamina to complete the operation. Covax nodded for Pi to switch to the next holographic surgeon to guide them through the nerve attachment.

"Have you gotten the results from her genome test?" Covax asked, his eyes watching OPALMOX's every move.

"The lab is cross-matching every karyotype of every human employee to see if they can match her genetic markers. She needs her original donor," Pi said, staying focused.

The pain his daughter would have to endure, even if he could successfully replace her arm tortured Covax. He knew his own genetics had the lineage of a healer. These genes, when understood, naturally raised the human body's immune systems to mega proportions. Healers like Edgar Cayce performed miracles because they understood their gifts and used them to save those in need. Cayce had defied the ridicule he and others like him suffered from disbelievers. Three hundred years earlier, he would have been burned alive at the stake. Today, he would have been revered and honored a thousand times more than he was during his time, when humans were only beginning to awaken to the powers their own bodies were capable of wielding.

Covax refused learning the Visionistic Arts by choice. According to his genetic mapping, he possessed the gene to heal, but he had never searched his soul for the knowings to use it. Untapped, it lay dormant and wasted. He knew just having the gene produced the predisposition to heal and in some cases miraculously cure with something as simple as the power of touch if trained in the Visionistic Arts. Ducane Covax used the power of science and technology, not the source powers of the mystic arts. He looked helplessly at his daughter and felt the iron weight of a path not taken as it crushed his heart.

"Covax? Did you hear me? She needs her original donor," Pi insisted, his eyes drifting into the chamber just beyond.

"She has a clone donor. She'll be fine," Covax said, his voice trailing off in a whisper.

Elana Blue's eyes fluttered opened. Her entire body was completely numb from the acupuncture needles to her brain that blocked any pain she might feel, but her mind had rejected the drug she was given to induce sleep, and at the moment she was keenly aware of where she was. Her eyes followed the tubes that spidered in and out of her, binding her to the life support machines that hissed and whined behind her head. Covax didn't see her eyes open or notice her horror when they focused on what stood in the small chamber beyond the main door of the cryogenic vault.

Elana frowned at the six vertical cylinders that filled the second chamber. For a moment, she thought the chamber contained several mirrors that reflected a single image over and over again. She wondered if she was hallucinating, because *they all look like me*, she thought. Her eyes struggled to focus, until she realized the women were not mirror images; they were individuals. They were clones of her.

"No," she gasped in a dry and raspy voice. Tears rushed to her eyes.

"Doctor Covax," OPALMOX said.

Covax saw Elana's eyes open and where they were staring.

"She's not in pain. The acupuncture is in place. She has, however, revived herself," OPALMOX said.

"Give her more propofol," Covax said to Pi.

"I . . . I'm cloned?" she asked. Elana's eyes searched her father's for the truth.

For a long time, her father was unable to speak. He wouldn't lie, but his heart pounded with the fear of telling her the truth.

"You are the only one living," Covax finally responded, as he supported the multiple nerve strands that would move her hand. "I froze stem cells and grew them as a precaution. I didn't want to lose you."

"Answer my question, daddy? Am I cloned too?" she asked.

She stared at her father and let her eyes go out of focus to read his aura. She needed the truth.

"I can print you a new arm in one hundred and forty-eight hours or you can use one of theirs. You'll be fine. That's all that matters."

"No. No. Please. I can't be cloned!" she said, choking on her tears.

Elana Blue stared at one of the cases. Inside the swirl of cryogenic gases, a clone, about her age, was missing an arm. The tears that welled in Elana's eyes fell from the corners.

"Go to sleep," Covax begged.

"Not until you tell me the truth. I wasn't born. I was created. My donor . . . who is my donor?" she asked again, fighting the sobs and the drugs that pulled her into sleep.

"Why does it matter?"

"It matters that the only person I trusted lied to me. Tell me the truth."

"She was everything good to me, and when I lost her I made you," Covax whispered.

"You . . . you told me my mother died," Elana whispered. She swallowed, feeling as frightened to know the truth as she was not to. "Daddy, is my donor dead?"

Covax hesitated for a long time. He considered all the consequences that came with answering her. He knew in his heart he had a choice but, to tell her the rest of the truth she had already discovered pained him too much especially if the truth might kill her.

"No," Covax said, knowing for her entire life on this and only this one truth he had betrayed her trust.

A tear fell from her eyes and rolled down her face.

"I felt she was alive. My whole life I felt her," she said. Another tear rolled down her cheek. Each liquid drop was filled with the rush of unexplained memories that had haunted her since childhood. Elana thought of the countless times she had imagined her mother, a faceless apparition, alive somewhere in the world and Elana wondered what kind of woman would abandon her child. Sadness washed over her and then a shocking realization. The tears stopped falling. From the look in Elana's eyes, Covax knew he didn't have to say the name. Elana Blue knew whose genetics faced her every time she looked in the mirror. Now it made perfect sense.

"You never told her about me?" Elana asked.

Covax had no words. He'd deceived his one great love for success and power, and losing her had cost him everything. He had decided when he made his daughter, to keep the truth of her existence from the only woman he'd ever loved, hoping beyond reason that if she ever found out the truth she would understand, hoping it would not destroy whatever was left of her love for him.

"No. She never knew I made you."

Covax nodded to OPALMOX to keep going. None of what happened in the past mattered right now, especially if Elana worked herself into a frenzied state, had a heart attack, and died. Desperate to keep her calm and her heart rate stable, Covax nodded to Pi to increase the propofol to make her sleep. In only a few seconds, the potent drug began to take effect. As she left the conscious world, Elana mouthed a single name, "Aleece is my . . ."

32

THE KNOWING

THE SECOND ARCHEOP dove for them. It was larger than the previous by at least two hundred pounds.

"Striker!" Lazer shouted.

Striker dropped flat against the rock wall of the mountain. The archeop's bright colors flashed over him: red, orange, and gold with a crown of green and orange feathers. It was definitely a male. It dove and missed. Its wings stretched out fifteen feet in either direction. Striker was back on his feet.

Lazer clambered farther up the mountain.

The archeop turned for its next attack just as Striker crested the ridge and darted inside one of the caves. He was safe for the moment. The archeop swooped down and landed gracefully where the remains of his dead mate lay. He nudged her severed head with his beak and lifted his face to let out a mournful wail.

Lazer stole a fleeting glance over his shoulder at the strange death ritual as he frantically climbed to the cave.

"Lazer, now!" Striker screamed. "Run! Run!"

Lazer didn't look back again. He could hear the thump of the enormous wings beating against the air.

A whoosh of wind was the only warning before the archeop pounced on him. He lifted Lazer into the air, clearing the ledge. From nowhere, a large tree limb appeared and slammed into the archeop. Stunned, he dropped Lazer onto the ridge.

Striker used all his power to swing the limb again as the archeop struggled to retain control. With a swipe, the archeop ripped the stick from Striker's hands and lifted off. Lazer and Striker bolted for the shallow cave. They darted inside and pressed themselves against the back wall, gasping for a breath of air.

"Archeops don't stalk!" Lazer said, panting.

"They've been following you for three days. Obviously both the male and female were tracking you, but why?" Lazer asked.

The cave went dark. The archeop's body blocked the entrance. They were trapped.

Its long, pointed beak poked through the cave's entrance, snapping and biting at the air a few inches away from Lazer and Striker. They pressed themselves flatter against the back wall. The sharp, saw-like teeth that lined its beak snapped again and again, reaching closer with each bite. The front teeth caught—ripping into Striker's back, tearing through his shirt, and gouging into his skin. Lazer punched the archeop hard enough to make the creature momentarily retract. Relentlessly, it attacked again and again. It bit and snapped at them, then suddenly stopped, retreating from the entrance. The creature paced outside, unable to get to its prey.

Lazer pulled some salve from his utility strap and applied it to Striker's bleeding wounds.

"Why is that thing so pissed?"

"I don't know," Striker said.

Lazer saw him flinch from the pain that screamed from his back.

Outside, the momentary respite ended with a wild fury as the archeop's enormous claws tore into the soft rock that formed the mouth of the cave. It was trying to make a bigger opening. Like a child destroying a sand castle, the creature began to rip open the entry. With each strike, its head stabbed farther inside, biting wildly at anything it could reach. The beak pinched Lazer and tore into his sleeve, shredding the flesh beneath.

It was time to fight. Lazer turned and formed an energy shield, repelling the vicious beak. Again the archeop retreated, but only momentarily.

"How long can you keep that up?" Striker said.

"Not long enough for that thing to die on its own." Lazer's mind raced at warp speed, desperate for a solution. He looked at the ceiling and floor of the cave. Nothing.

"Do the ice ball thing again," Striker said.

"I need to be outside."

The entrance was widening. In thirty seconds, the archeop would be inside.

Again, the archeop stopped.

Lazer dropped the shield.

"What are you doing?" Striker shrieked.

"I can't hold two forces at once. I need resin," Lazer demanded.

"I ran out," Striker said, pulling out a flint. "This is all I've got."

"Light it," Lazer ordered.

"On what?"

"Just spark the flints between my hands."

"You need grass or something . . ."

"Just do it!" Lazer insisted.

Striker struck the flint together. It sparked between Lazer's hands, and then vanished. Another spark and Lazer captured it, fueling it with his mind.

"Do you know any Viz Arts?" Lazer asked.

"No."

"You're about to learn. Hold your hands like this," Lazer showed Striker how to position his hands and ignited a small spark between them.

"Focus on the space, look at the fire, and think about the hottest thing you can imagine—an erupting volcano, a nuclear blast, the sun, anything."

"Fire's not going to stop him," Striker whined.

"You better hope to hell you're wrong. Focus all your energy between our hands. Think fire—create it. Mind over matter."

The archeop attacked again with a wild, frantic fury.

"This is crazy," Striker said as he glanced at the crumbling entrance.

"Do it!" Lazer commanded. "Visualize the fire. See the molecules."

Using a form of pyrokinesis, they willed the molecules between their hands to expand into a small blue flame. The flame brightened into orange and yellow, sparked, and popped until it flared into a ball of fire.

Striker's eyes widened. Lazer knew Striker felt the heat between his hands intensify. Suddenly, the ball began to dissipate.

"Focus!" Lazer screamed.

Their energy ball glowed, searing the flesh on Striker's palms. He grimaced and fought the pain.

"Lazer!" Striker begged. His hands were trembling.

The cave opening disintegrated with each powerful blow from the archeop, exposing them completely to the wrath of the creature. It reared to attack.

"Hold it. Hold it," Lazer said. "Throw it! Now!" Lazer shouted.

Together they hurled the whirling sphere of fire just as the creature advanced. The blazing ball expanded and smashed into the archeop, coating it in a shimmering wash of liquid fire. With a sucking whoosh fueled by the mountain wind, the creature ignited in flames and screeched in anguish.

Lazer understood that he had to finish what he'd started. He focused and suspended both mind and body into an altered state. He searched for his BAI and connected with the source energy of the universe. He felt it fill him. Lazer turned his body away from Striker and projected his hands at the archeop. His pyrokinetic abilities expanded and from his wrists a flow of liquid burning energy shot forward with the force of a raging river of fire. It was pure antimatter recreated into a streaming horizontal inferno.

The brilliance and heat were so intense Striker averted his eyes, shielding himself. The fire, true to its elemental nature, was eating up all the air and cooking them. Lazer was focused, completely unaware as Striker gasped for breath and the cave became an oven, sucking the oxygen from his lungs.

"Can't . . . breathe," Striker struggled to speak.

Striker was suffocating. He fell to his knees and reached for Lazer, fighting to stay conscious.

The fiery blast slammed into the creature, pushing it back out of the cave as Lazer stepped forward. He guided the stream of flaming particles and used his body weight as the force to push the archeop toward the edge of the cliff.

Screeching and thrashing in the flames, the archeop called out in pain as it stumbled back to the edge. The rocks crumbled under its claws. Blinded by the fire and racked with pain, it slipped and flailed over the edge. The archeop plummeted helplessly, slamming onto a precipice of rocks that jutted out of the mountain a hundred feet below with a violent, bone-crushing crash. It twisted its still-burning body as it shuddered, trying one last time to stand. With a great gasp for air, it fell. The archeop lay lifeless on the same ledge as its mate, turning them both to ashes.

Lazer stood at the edge, his arms outstretched in front of him, the stream of fire still shooting from his hands. He stood trembling, his eyes locked in a kind of trance.

Behind him Striker struggled to his feet. His back was shredded, his legs weak, and his hands ached from the blisters that had already begun to boil on his palms. He looked at Lazer in awe. The stream of fire subsided, and as it dissipated a warm wind swirled around Lazer, pulling at his hair and clothes. It was as if the universal powers were receding like an ebbing tide. Slowly, Striker reached out and lowered Lazer's hands, and with his motion the strange wind ceased its fury. The cool night air from the mountains rushed back over them as they stood in the deafening silence. No words could describe what Lazer was feeling. Slowly he turned to Striker. They stared, first at each other and then down at the frozen and charred remains of the two archeops.

33

LEOPARD SEALS

"STOP," A VOICE SHOUTED from outside. "Get back from the entrance."

Cashton stepped back obediently. For the first time, he heard the pounding against the ice floor just outside the frozen snow wall that sealed him inside.

Before Cashton could speak, there was a cracking sound, and with a whoosh the wall of snow turned from solid to liquid. It hung suspended, almost confounded by the molecular change. The water floated in midair and then, with the grace of a falling curtain of silk, slipped to the ground. The force of the splashing water knocked Cashton off his feet. He dug his fingers into the tunnel of snow and held on as the water drenched him. It took anything that wasn't strapped on or tied down, including his face shield and shovel. The water flushed in, hit the back wall, and then flushed out. Cashton was free.

"Hurry! Come on. Hurry!" a girl shouted at him. Three other girls stood behind her.

Four girls! How did I ever get so lucky? Cashton thought to himself, his face cracking into a goofy but grateful smile.

"Move," another girl insisted.

Her tone had an urgency that prickled the hairs on Cashton's neck. He scrambled to his feet and rushed out of the entrance just as a vicious, ten-foot leopard seal burst up through a large crack it had made in the ice. It sank briefly beneath the water's surface, but before anyone could move, it propelled itself straight up and out of the water. It slammed down hard on the ice, cracking it and sending a dozen more fissures fingering out in every direction. In the turmoil, one of the girls fell into the freezing ice water.

"Jude!" the first girl shouted and reached out for her friend.

The first girl's name was Musette, Cashton gathered when the other girls called out to her.

Musette missed Jude's hand and levitated off the pitching shard of ice. Cashton, agile athlete that he was, jumped to a safer section and landed next to the other girls.

The leopard seal faced them. Teeth bared, it let loose a deafening roar and waddled forward, faster than anyone could believe possible.

The levitating girl touched down between them and, with a thrust of her hands, shot out an energy bolt that blocked the attack. The swirling circle of pure energy slammed into the leopard seal's snout. The creature recoiled, pained and momentarily confused.

Cashton dove into the water. He felt the shock of ice water stab into his face with the torturous force of a million tiny needles. His gear protected his body from the deathly cold, but his face was exposed, and he knew he had precious little time before his brain would freeze and he would lose consciousness and die. *Some hero,* he thought. Cashton focused on how to save Jude. She was sinking—fast.

In two powerful strokes, he was next to her. He grabbed her and locked her into a rescuer's hold, encircling her neck with his forearm. Using all his strength, he swam for the surface.

From the corner of his eye he saw the flash of a black shadow swimming up from the depths at them. The leopard seal was already on the surface. *Wasn't it?* he thought.

Whatever it was, he knew he'd rather face it on the surface than under the water. He swam faster. He was an athlete and knew better than to waste the energy to look back until he had completed the play. That much his zoccair coach had taught him.

It was Jude, the pretty young girl in his arms, who saw a second twelve-foot, thousand-pound leopard seal swimming after them.

These sea creatures weren't splicers; they were just the next evolution of what Mother Nature had created and better-living-through-science had enhanced. Here, just as in all of the Rite of Passage territories, the creatures were supposed to be tagged. If they attacked, a student had to simply press the PAR, and they would be safe.

Jude couldn't reach her PAR. The best she could do was hold on to whoever was saving her until he got them out of the water and away from the second leopard seal, which was gaining on them with every stroke.

Cashton could see Musette, the girl who had dissolved the ice wall and set him free, standing on the land. She had already pushed her PAR several times, as had the other two girls, with no results. Musette had already broken the official Rite of Passage protocol and evoked the Visionistic Arts by melting the snow barrier and levitating to get away from the leopard seal, not to mention the energy blast she used to thwart it, but Cashton knew to stop the creature would take true cunning. Her next feat was one even the most advanced students of the arts were rarely capable of performing. She held her breath and jutted her arms out, focusing her eyes on the ice. She began to gather ice molecules between her hands and form them into a shield and sword made of solid blue ice. Cashton had read about that kind of manifestation, but neither he nor anyone else he'd known had ever seen it. She had mastered the ability of matter manifestation using the elements and could, at will, create weapons to defend against almost any adversary. The shield was a solid-looking dark blue ice and covered the white flesh of her hands as a kind of protective glove. The same amazing effect had formed the four-foot-long broad sword that extended from her right hand.

"Musette, you can't . . .," the third girl shouted.

The leopard seal stopped, startled by what had transpired. Unsure of what to do, it blinked. The fourth girl watched, just as mesmerized as the seal.

". . . fight that thing!" the third girl finished.

Cashton pulled himself from the water and dragged the half-conscious girl behind him. He was strong and fast and had managed to save both of them for the moment.

The frigid air smacked against his exposed face and instantly froze. It covered his skin in a thin film of white ice. Not even the blood that pounded through his veins and flushed his face would stop the frostbite that would take his nose if he didn't do something. Jude reached up.

"Here," Jude said, putting both hands on his cheeks.

Cashton felt a surge of heat that warmed his face, melted the ice completely away, and made him feel instantly toasty and dry. Hers was a healer's touch with full Visionistic Arts to back it up.

All eyes were riveted on Musette. With a voracious roar, the leopard seal attacked. Musette had no choice but to defend herself and fight.

The leopard seal lunged. Musette swung her ice sword and slashed its face. It retracted from the sting of the laceration and snarled, revealing an eight-inch razor slash. The wound opened just below its eye and began to bleed. Furious, it lunged again propelling itself into the air. Musette ran forward, dropped to one knee, and slid beneath the creature. As she did she swung her shield above her head and used the momentum of the leopard seal's weight and forward motion to hurl it over her. At the last second she stood jutting the shield up and flipping the seal onto its back.

"How is she doing that?" Cashton asked.

"She's drawing power from ice like Hercules from earth," another of the girls said in amazement.

The first leopard seal rolled and spun around. It took a series of vicious swipes with its front flipper. One caught Musette off guard and slammed into her. The blow knocked her sideways onto the ground.

At that moment, the second leopard seal burst from the sea and hurled itself onto the ice shelf.

"Run!" Cashton shouted, dragging Jude to her feet.

They scrambled forward, running smack dab into the backside of the first leopard seal. It didn't even turn. Musette held its attention fighting bravely, slashing as it lunged and bit at the swinging ice sword. Out if instinct, to protect its rear, the first leopard seal reared its tail and hind flippers and slammed them onto the ground like a giant flyswatter. Cashton yanked Jude out of harm's way as they ran to the other two girls. They watched the escalating fight between Musette and the first leopard seal.

Another series of slashes and thrusts cut into the first leopard seal time and again. The leopard seal spun and swatted Musette, shattering her shield. She was lifted off her feet and thrown five feet into a wall of ice. Musette hit the ice wall, and the world swirled around her. She struggled for a moment, lost consciousness, and fell with a crash. Instantly her sword dissipated. She was bloody, bruised, and dazed, but at least for the moment she was alive.

At the same instant, the second leopard seal roared, teeth bared, as it slid up onto the ice a few feet away from them. They were trapped with no weapons between two vicious and very hungry leopard seals.

"Step back. Slowly," Cashton whispered to the girls.

His eyes were on Musette, and so were those of the first leopard seal. Cashton raced to get Musette, who lay between both creatures. His motion pulled the first leopard seal's attention, and it lunged after him. Just as its mouth hinged open, the second leopard seal attacked it with the force of a sledgehammer. The collision of their combined weight knocked them away from Cashton and the girls. The two gargantuan killers rolled, landed, and quickly gathered their bearings. They turned on each other and in an instant battled with the vicious rage of two ravenous predators vying for the right to devour the prey.

Now, Cashton thought, *was their time to escape.* Cashton and Jude reached Musette.

"Can you walk?" Cashton asked.

Musette's face was bloodied. Her eyes swam in her head, oscillating out of focus like a punch-drunk prizefighter's. She struggled to grab onto a conscious thought.

"We have to get out of here," Cashton commanded the others.

He gathered Musette in his arms.

Cashton turned to see which way to run. What he saw stopped him in his tracks. Twenty feet ahead in a perfect semicircle, a thirty-foot-high wall of blue ice loomed before them. They were trapped in an ice cul-de-sac with no place to get out but through two enormous carnivores that were slashing and pounding each other into a bloody mess. They were on the edge of a fragile ice shelf with the freezing sea just beyond.

Cashton's heart dropped. He looked down at Musette in his arms.

The growling ceased and the creatures, as if on cue, stopped fighting. Exhausted, bloody, and panting huge gulps of air, they turned to face the students with unified resolve.

34

THE POLITIA

DANTE ENTERED THE war room at Triumvirate Headquarters. It had been hastily established in a vast chamber that held about three hundred people. Leaders sat in debate over the newly decided fate of Atlantia. A huge map floated at center stage; grid areas ringed in black represented the fallen cities and captured settlements. Everyone was aware that the debate over how to invade still contained far too much conjecture, but it was all they had.

Surrounding Atlantia were the corporate guarded territories: the United Co-Federation to the west, the underwater domes of Panazia that lay southwest beneath the ocean, and the trilogy of lands that formed the Joint Common Market to the east. Farthest east stood the Republic and the Corporate Islands, the South Republic, and Mu with the new poles at the top and bottom of the world.

Around the room, a select group of corporate representatives from each continent sat together, determined to end a potential world war that no one wanted with an enemy no one understood.

The Joint Forces Committee finally announced they would reevaluate their options. This meant another week before they would even vote on an invasion strategy, which still had not been formulated. Any plan they had would hinge on the organization and mobilization of the Joint Politia Forces. They argued about what facilities were adequate in both size and location to amass a coalition large enough to invade. And if they did arm and mobilize sufficient forces, everyone knew the invasion was contingent upon their ability to break the dome's lockdown codes.

Dante Labov listened diligently as the heads of various politia divisions discussed statistics, forces, numbers, weapons, ships, and transports. He heard the facts. What he didn't hear was a plan.

He felt his chest tighten, and as large as the room was, the walls seemed to close in. He needed air. Dante rose and walked to the rear door. He stepped into the large antechambers that were used to receive and transmit various data updates and prepare dignitaries who were being brought in for briefings, presentations, or meetings. As he walked out of the tension of the main chamber, he felt a different kind of energy. Though not as adept as his wife or Riana at reading auras, he sensed a strange feeling of anxiousness that emanated from the far corner.

Dante moved closer passing by the various desks and holoscreens, buzzing conversations, and clicking fingers on touch keyboards. There in the far corner sat several newly commissioned officers: pilot captains, ensigns, and lieutenants barely out of the Academy who had been brought into the headquarters. Dante couldn't help but think they hardly looked old enough to fly. He crossed to the first officer and read his nametag.

"Captain Tennis Kalop?" Dante asked.

The young officer rose to his feet and stood at attention. From the luminescent Triumvirate medallion Dante wore, Kalop knew who had spoken to him. The officer gave the V salute, which Dante returned.

"Ensign, Triumvirate Labov. I'm not a captain yet," Kalop said with a wry smile.

"You know who I am?" Dante asked.

"Ever since Triumvirate Avery was lost and you were commissioned, Triumvirate. You're kind of all over the Vybernet."

Dante smiled. He looked at the young officer. He had a strong, honest face and an air of confidence that radiated through his wide eyes. He exuded charm and arrogance. There was no doubt he was a jet jockey with a new set of metal wings.

"May I speak with you, Ensign Tennis Kalop?"

The young officer shot a look to his flight mate, a female splicer with feathers and large orange eyes. She gave a quick glance, and then set her gaze forward.

"Obsidian, Triumvirate. That's my call sign. Born on Eron in the Corporate Islands," Obsidian said, squaring his shoulders proudly.

Dante smiled. "Well, Obsidian . . ."

Dante stepped away and Obsidian followed.

". . . how long have you been with the politia?" Dante asked as they walked.

"I graduated Tosadae this winter and received my orders a month ago."

"Whose squadron?" Dante asked.

"Tarsiers under Commander Yu. We fly FX-80 Lightning Bolts."

"You've just been transferred to Station Nine on Anastasi Island."

"I guess being Triumvirate means classified information doesn't . . ."

"I just saw the report," Dante said.

"They're amassing a lot of troops on the island. Haven't stopped since we arrived a few days ago."

"Are they all as young as you are?" Dante asked.

"Don't let our youth worry you. We have a thousand hours of simulator time under our belts, and I don't think the Black Guard are ready for us or our technology."

"I hope you're right, Obsidian."

"Triumvirate, will we be going in to take back Atlantia?"

Dante stopped. He turned to look at the fresh-faced young man before him. The harsh reality that he was about to send him in harm's way to fight a foe they barely understood sent a cold chill up his spine. Dante took a deep breath.

"Yes, Obsidian, we will," Dante responded.

"Good. 'Cause they're about to find out we humans are still in charge of this planet."

Dante looked from Obsidian to the other ten officers and sent a silent prayer to the Universal God he was right.

35

THE GATHERING

LAZER AND A SEVERELY wounded Striker stumbled down the jagged mountain trails and switchbacks. The wall that separated the infamous south end of the island wove its way from shore to shore, cutting through the jungles, ending and beginning at the foothills on either side of Mount Quilliani. Whatever they wanted to keep inside the southern region of Passage Island wasn't going anywhere, Lazer hoped.

Tired and hungry, they stayed their course, following a path that was lit by the glow of the Southern Cross and a smattering of distant stars. Lazer knew if they stayed true to their course, it would lead them to Striker's rendezvous coordinates. The issue was time; any other route was not an option.

They left the ambling foothills and reached the ring of jungle that anchored the mountains to the flatlands. There they encountered a number of other students. Lazer listened as they shared their stories. They'd come from various colleges, universities, and academies around the globe and even the domes cities of Panazia under the sea to experience their own Rites of Passage. Like Lazer and Striker, they had also encountered ravenous creatures unresponsive to the PAR protection devices they all wore. Most had survived the insane terrors that had befallen them on Passage Island. Lazer and Striker listened as they shared their stories of how they were assailed by wild, rabid beasts. A pretty girl with almond-shaped black eyes named Jem told how she witnessed another girl killed and devoured before her eyes. A boy named Rhys, whose caramel skin and soft features reminded Lazer of Cashton, shared his ordeal with a bilyon. They lit fires, shared food, and listened to one another's nightmarish stories then started walking again.

Over those hours, they collected fifteen students who had all managed to stay alive. Their tales of horror each ended with the reality that their PAR devices did not anesthetize the creatures. Even more devastating was the report that splicers and mega creatures that were not even allowed beyond the southern sector's goliath wall were roaming free. Lazer couldn't shake the feeling that the creatures hunted them as if guided by an abnormal force. He saw the fear in their faces and decided he'd keep his theories and his feelings to himself.

The little band of refugees stumbled across a pile of half-eaten, human limbs. A girl threw up. They helped her and kept going as a pack of hynocots—a vicious cross of hyena and coyote—ignored them and went for the rotting feast that filled their nostrils.

With constant but gentle nudges from Lazer, the students pressed on. Those that had Visionistic powers used them. When they were exhausted, those that didn't have powers, hacked through the ring of trees that formed the dense jungle. The caravan dropped down into a small gully that rain and time had carved into a shallow river and drank. Lazer noticed it created a natural path that looked like it would lead them directly into the immense, rotting ruins of the Temples of Narez. As they got to the first gates of the temple, one of the older young men, with black and dark eyes named Santiago, stumbled upon a half-buried case of ancient swords and machetes. It was obvious it had been left eons ago by the pirates that ravaged the original people who existed here long before it became Passage Island. His scanner had detected the metal box at the root of a banyan tree under layers of rock and mud.

Lazer touched the carvings in the wall looking at the pictographs that told stories of those who built and lived and died here. One girl told them she'd read the original inhabitants had been monks who came here after a great volcanic eruption akin to the eruption that sank Atlantis and blackened the entire sky for years devastating the earth. She said the monks carved the temples from the rocks but vanished because the island began to sink. A millennium passed before the second planetary shifts that caused the Great Quakes and once again the seas shifted. They rose and lifted many of the islands they had swallowed up from the waters including Mu, Atlantia, and land that became Passage Island. Those humans, who had survived the Great Quakes and the long list of tsunamis, earthquakes, and volcanic eruptions that had redefined the earth, came and made Passage Island their home.

Lazer and the others listened intently as she told them how, after months of darkness, other survivors came and joined them. Together they discovered peace and many settled amongst the ancient ruins of the island. They were rebuilding their shattered lives and starting over. For the first time, they had hope.

She talked as they walked, happy to have her story make the time go faster. Lazer studied their faces watching as they each let the story captivate them.

The girl went on to say the people lived in peace, coexisting in perfect harmony with one another and nature. For more than a century, they farmed the land and raised their families until they were discovered, ravaged, and massacred by the marauding sea pirates. These monstrous men came, saw, and conquered the wondrous little island, obliterating the people within a matter of months. The island served as a secret sanctuary for them until the politia tracked them down and arrested them for crimes against humanity.

Striker added, "Yeah, yeah, yeah, I read that too. I heard the island stood abandoned until it was claimed by the Corporates and donated to the Passage Committee."

"The same Passage Committee who took an oath to clear this place of all unnatural dangers," another student said.

A tall, thin young man said, "Right, and pledged any animals left on every Rite of Passage territory had to be tagged to control their aggressive instincts so they could protect the students."

There was silence. Lazer saw in their faces the harsh truth they'd all learned since they arrived—the committee had either lied or lost control. The question was: so who had failed or what changed?

The rock the boy was using to smash the old lock failed. The girl used her Visionistic powers to melt the rusted metal and the lock fell away. Lazer leaned forward and watched as they pulled the old swords and machetes from the tar-covered sacks. The weapons had been pre-served in oils and dry sand to keep them from rusting.

"No blasters?" Striker asked.

Lazer felt grateful for the weapons but like Striker, wished more than ever they would have found a couple of modern-day blasters.

"Something is better than nothing," Lazer told them with an exhausted smile.

The students took the sabers and machetes and armed themselves. Lazer found flint rocks and, shattering them into pieces, told them to take the stones and sharpen the blades of their weapons, just in case they encountered any more creatures.

Hour after hour, they walked in droopy-eyed silence, too tired and afraid to speak. The tap and scrape of metal weapons sliding against rock became the strange, haunting music that played in rhythmic counterpoint against the eerie intermittent calls of night creatures that roamed the hills and jungles of Passage Island.

Just as they reached the center of the ancient ruins, Striker sat down to rest on a pile of rocks that looked to be the crumbled remains of the main entrance to the temple's courtyard. A huge section was sparsely covered with odd black reeds that grew over the uneven terrain. Lazer sat next to him. He watched Striker lay back. It was easy to see he felt relief from the rocks that had been cooled by the night air, and the chilled wet stones must have numbed the pain in his back. Lazer has been worried about him. The pained expression on Striker's face had affected his every motion since the archeop attack. For the first time in hours, Striker took a full breath.

Lazer looked back and sighed. They had to keep moving. There wasn't time to stop. But he could see in their faces they were exhausted. He signaled to the group to take a rest and crossed back to Striker.

"We can't stop," Lazer told him.

"I know," Striker replied. "Leave me. I'll catch up. I . . . have to rest."

"I'm not leaving anybody. Come on. I'll help you," Lazer bent down to gather him, stumbled, and fell onto the soft, uneven ground.

Striker began to chuckle at the absurd image of an exhausted Lazer helping him and offered a hand to help Lazer up from the ground.

"You can barely help yourself," Striker said with a chuckle.

The absurd notion that Lazer could carry Striker anywhere made Lazer burst into laughter too. He laughed so hard he sprawled on the soft ground, clutching his stomach. Striker joined in and fell next to him grateful to be prone. The laughter grew into such hilarity their eyes filled with tears. They laughed so hard they could no longer speak.

One by one, the other students joined in, some not even knowing what was funny. They succumbed to the infectious guffaws, enjoying the release the laughter gave them. The whole situation became one of uncontrollable merriment, and the levity took with it the fear, pain, and anxiety they had carried inside them since the journey began.

Just the act of stopping seemed to make him and everyone else feel better. The laughter that rose from the group was so rousing it made all of them miss the rumble that shook the ground below their feet.

It was Rhys who realized the earth beneath them was moving.

"Lazer!" Rhys shouted.

Lazer reached down, doing his best to make sense of the situation. The soft earth trembled and rose, lifting and knocking them off balance.

"Run!" Lazer shouted, grabbing Striker.

Before anyone could decide which way to retreat, the mound of earth they clung to dropped down into the dirt with unbelievable speed and carried them into a giant tunnel that seemed to run beneath the courtyard.

"It's alive!" Striker shouted.

"What the spit is it?" Rhys shouted.

"We have to get out," Jem cried out.

"Hang on until it stops," Lazer yelled back, looking at the black reed-like hairs that grew from the creature's back.

It moved with the speed of a bullet train. Blackness closed in around them as they caught glimpses of the huge tunnel they were being carried through. Everyone held onto the strange black hairs and prayed for the creature to stop.

"It's moving too fast," Rhys shouted.

"Just hold on and stay low," Lazer commanded. "We have to stay together."

As they thrashed around in the dark, Lazer could see several of the students' light rings come on to assist them. In the blur of motion, they could see markings etched into the tunnel walls and across the ceilings. *Maybe the ancient monks had carved them,* Lazer thought.

There was a bump, and the creature started to move down, carrying them farther into the labyrinth of larger, darker tunnels.

"It's taking us deeper," another student shouted with a yelp.

"Lazer, we've got to get off this thing," Striker insisted.

"No! Just hold on!" Lazer shouted at them.

They sped along for a few moments more until, with a jolt, the creature stopped.

Lazer could see they were deep inside a large cavern.

"Now," Lazer shouted. "Jump off!"

One by one they slid off, holding onto what Lazer had assessed to be the bristly hair shafts crawling over bulbous warts of what could only be described as a giant grub or caterpillar. It waddled forward, slithering into the water. They all watched as it swam into the center of the black, seemingly bottomless lake and dove beneath the surface. The water swallowed the caterpillar and stilled itself back to a flat, glassy pool. Everyone stood in shocked horror. Only the heavy breathing and the steady drip of water from some tributary far off in the rocks above could be heard. It echoed softly around them. Lazer listened harder. The distance of the echo instantly made him realize the vastness of the caverns. He could see in their faces they all understood they were most certainly, hopelessly lost.

"Is everyone okay?" Lazer asked. "Did we lose anyone?"

One by one, they assessed themselves and reported in.

Lazer attempted to get his bearings using his GPS, but the grub had gone too fast and they were now too deep under the ground to pick up a feed.

"Now what?" Striker asked, flinching at the pain in his back.

"I'm sure it was taking us west the whole time," Rhys said. "And that's west."

"You know that for a fact?" one of the boys asked with a hint of a condescending tone.

"I have perfect sense of direction, and that's west," Rhys snapped back. "If you don't believe me . . ."

"We believe you," Lazer stepped in, calming everyone's nerves with just the right blend of control and authority. "And I say we keep heading west until we find a tunnel that goes up."

"No, we're lost. We're probably farther away from the pickup point than before. Why should we listen to you?" a young girl named Asia asked. She was shorter and younger than everyone else and had only qualified for her Rite of Passage one day before departure.

"Because he saved your life and mine, that's why," Striker confronted her pointing at Lazer.

"Look, we're all in this together, but I think Rhys is right," Lazer said and pointed to what looked like a man-made cave that opened in the direction Rhys had pointed. "Underground or above, we need to keep heading west if we are going to make this retrieval point. I say we go that way until we figure out how to get out of here."

"How do we know the cave goes through?" a frightened voice shouted from the shadows.

"Our only other option is to go back the way we came," Striker chimed in, defending Lazer's plan.

"That will take days," the students grumbled.

"Then let's stay together and keep moving west."

There was a silent agreement and everyone got to his and her feet, preparing to move forward.

"Drink some water and fill your aqua tubes and canteens," Lazer said.

They drank from the lake and washed the grime of the trek from their faces. Jem brought Striker some water in a cup, and he thanked her with a pained smile and a nod. Lazer could see he was pale and weak from the strain and tension of the journey, and the grub's encounter had only made things worse.

Striker arched his back in pain. His wounds were bleeding again. Striker told Lazer he would be okay if he could just rest for a little. They both knew he would have to bear the pain and keep moving or stay and die. That latter was not an option.

Lazer felt Jem's thoughts. Jem told him she'd learned the art of empathetic readings from her mother. Lazer suspected she was able to feel Striker's pain. He could see Jem cringe as she let the pain wash over her. Lazer watched Jem stand, her eyes were focused and her face looked determined as she crossed next to them. Lazer knew what she wanted to ask. She wanted to offer to care for Striker. Jem knew Lazer was reading her thoughts. She gave a sad nod as she told Lazer, "Why don't you use the time alone to figure how to get us safely to the pickup point. I got this. Okay?" With that, she crossed back to Striker.

"Hi. Why don't you let me take a look?" she said to Striker. Striker nodded and peeled back what remained of his suit exposing his wounds.

Jem flinched at the sight of Striker's exposed back. The wounds were vicious and raw, and worst of all, they were infected. A bouquet of white pustule on red scratches covered his back. She pulled a small tube of salve from her utility strap and gingerly squeezed the gel into the most infected areas.

"Do you trust me?" she asked him.

Striker looked at her. In the past, he had trusted no one, especially a splicer. But in this present trial that had now become his life, he knew he needed to trust everyone that was on this incredible journey. He had let go of the past with Lazer—and Lazer had saved his life. Now he had to release the fears and prejudices he had been taught by his father and trust someone who was not of his kind.

"Yeah," he whispered, never taking his eyes from hers until he turned away and exposed his back to her.

"I need to cover these wounds. The silt from this lake will act as a barrier. It's got some kind of clay in it, so as it dries, it will pull the infection out," she explained with a caring smile.

Striker nodded. Jem scooped up a small handful of the clay and gently covered the wounds. It felt cold, and even her most gentle touch sent shocks of pain that charged his body, but Striker held still. He chose to believe that whatever she did would protect him from further infection. He let her finish.

"Thank you," Striker said.

Jem smiled at him, making whatever she was spliced with a little more obvious. He couldn't tell her added genetics and suddenly realized that he didn't care. She was truly kind and her kindness made her beautiful.

Lazer focused on the brave band of students. They needed food and rest, but every one of them knew time was running out to make the rendezvous. They had no choice but to move on, find a way out of the tunnels, and get back on track to reach the rendezvous point on time. They had a plan, and for now, everyone was in agreement. Lazer made sure the whole group's energy refocused on the tasks at hand. They worked together and, with his leadership, moved past any fear and doubt that could shift them out of their state of unity. Almost simultaneous with the shift in thought, a symbiotic connection to the environment occurred. With their calm came a spontaneous blossom of phosphorescent blue green algae that covered the ceiling and walls of the tunnel like a constellation; a beautiful, turquoise haze of light.

The students gave a gasp of complete awe.

"Look," Rhys said.

"It's showing us the way out," Lazer said. The algae's growth path flowed along the ceiling and walls of the cave as if giving them a sign; "This way out" it seemed to beckon them as it lit the passageway and told them, without question, that Lazer and Rhys had chosen well.

36

TRANSMUTATION

"YOU HAVE TO wake up," Cashton commanded Musette. "Wake up! Now!"

The panting, open-mouthed faces of the two leopard seals moved closer.

"Please, Musette, wake up," Jude pleaded along with the others.

He could see her eyelids flutter as she fought her way back into the conscious world. As she regained consciousness, Cashton could actually feel the pain of the battle wounds that stung her body. It was if he could read her thoughts, and they said she needed a host to transfer her powers. Cashton blinked; he was the closest. Without explanation or permission, she jutted her hands through his skin and inside of his chest.

Cashton gasped, sucking in the chilled air. He had no sensation of pain, only the stunned reality of what had happened. He looked at Jude.

"You have to commit," Jude told him.

"Say yes, hurry," Musette said.

Jude's eyes were filled with a strange sadness that sent a different kind of shiver through Cashton.

It took years for Cashton to let anyone through his emotional barriers—and Musette was physically reaching inside his chest. The roar of the leopard seal and the helplessness of the situation filled him with everything he needed to release himself to her. Unsure of what was happening, Cashton knew he had no choice but to surrender. He shouted, "Yes."

The sound of a great wind filled his ears. A hard pressure crushed against every inch of his skin. Cashton thought he was going to explode. He screamed. The sound vibrated in his chest and reverberated through his entire being.

Cashton opened his eyes. He looked down. Musette was gone.

"She's given you her powers. Use them! Hurry! If you die, she can't get back out," Jude yelled up to him.

Cashton looked at his hands. He wanted to create a blaster of some kind but the shape would not form. "These are her powers, not mine," he said.

"Do as Musette had done," Jude said.

Cashton created a sword of solid ice, five feet long. He held the sword in one hand and summoned the ice particles to re-form into a second ice broadsword. He turned to face the leopard seals and felt the rush of a primitive, ferocious anger. Cashton turned to face the sea leopard, gave out a chilling war cry, and attacked.

The sea leopards stood their ground as Cashton advanced brandishing his swords with the precision of a well-trained knight. He imagined all the medieval video games and ancient world 3-D history lessons to which he'd dedicated untold hours.

The first leopard seal, the larger of the two, took the initial blows. The sword sliced into its right shoulder. It wailed, and then snapped at him. It bit into his leg. Cashton hacked into its face until it released. The second seal reared up onto its back flippers, and with one enormous swipe, Cashton's sword sliced into its belly flesh. Entails poured out but it did not stop. Cashton turned from one beast to the next. He swung, backhanding one seal's face. It snapped around and bit into his hand. Cashton shouted in pain. Blood gushed but the rush of ice stilled the pain and gave him strength entering his body feeding through Musette and rushing back into his arms and legs. He felt Musette guide him with her thoughts. "Turn," he heard her voice shout. Cashton turned, watching the larger leopard seal advance while he battled the other.

The second leopard seal came at him again and again. Cashton has to keep his focus forward.

"Behind you," he heard Musette shout into his thoughts.

Jude ran forward to help him. He had saved her life and she wanted to return the favor, but she was too small to take on either creature. She had no weapons, and the best she could offer were a few basic healing arts—if he survived. Without turning or looking behind him, Cashton imagined the creature behind him and in a giant arc, brought one sword down backward over his head with the force of a pile driver and released it. The ice blade pierced into the animal's left flipper and the weight and force of the ice blade drove it into the ice. It was pinned. The force of the blow cracked the ice.

The first leopard seal snapped and bit into Cashton's side catching his vest. It jerked him forward and dragged him across the ice. As Cashton fought, he summoned a ten-inch ice knife to manifest into his hand and plunged it into the leopard seal's left eye. The creature wailed releasing him.

A few feet away, the second leopard seal ripped his flipper from the ice sword and shot over. With a vicious snap, it bit into Cashton's leg. He was outnumbered and outmaneuvered. He couldn't wield his weapons with enough coordination to defend himself. He flailed and kicked as together the leopard seals dragged him toward the sea. If they could get him into the water, they would drown him. Cashton battled them with every ounce of strength he had, kicking one creature loose and then the other. Inch by inch, they dragged him closer to the edge when suddenly, the ice beneath them cracked.

Ciliana, the youngest girl, stared at the scene. Terror filled her eyes. Saying nothing, she ran forward to Jude.

"What do we do?" she shouted.

"Viz Arts," the last girl, Megan, said as she trailed behind them. She was frail and looked like she could be of minimal help at best.

"Whatever it is, use it!" Jude demanded.

"Gimme your survival cords," Megan told them.

The cords were belts that held all their survival supplies. Megan lashed them together into a single rope and then went negative—vanishing before their eyes. Like a thermal heat wave rippling above blacktop, she was barely perceptible to the naked eye. She raced into the brawl and got as close as she could to the thrashing limbs, gnashing teeth, and snapping jaws. Megan threw the rope around the leopard seal's neck and pulled. She was no match for its strength, but she managed to jerk it off balance.

It hung on to Cashton with the force of a rabid pit bull. Jaws locked on his leg as blood spewed in every direction; it dragged Cashton farther away from the girls.

Help us, they all heard Megan's thoughts cry out.

Jude and a reluctant Ciliana ran forward and grabbed Megan. Together they pulled the leopard seal closer to the edge of the ice.

It released Cashton and turned. It snapped at them, then turned back and lunged at Cashton, ripping the survival cords from the girls. The sea leopard was at Cashton's neck, only his crossed ice sword and knife barring the inevitable. Cashton smelled the acrid, metallic scent of blood. The foul stink of filth, fish, and damaged flesh filled his nostrils. His arms were weakening.

Give yourself to the power of ice, Musette's thoughts told him.

Cashton felt a surge of power from the ice. He dropped both weapons and pushed his arms up. In one swift motion, he grabbed the seal by the neck, flipped it, and slammed it to the ground.

Behind him the second leopard seal struggled to get back up. Suddenly, the ice gave a series of loud, definitive cracks as a huge section broke off, taking Cashton, the girls, and one sea leopard adrift.

Cashton swung and connected with the second leopard seal, knocking it into the water.

The unstable slab of floating ice dipped and wobbled. The leopard seal slid off, dragging Megan with it. Jude and Ciliana let go of the rope. They grabbed for Megan. They missed. The freezing cold water sent a shock through her and broke her concentration. Megan sank, and then reappeared.

Ciliana and Jude looked back at the ever-widening chasm as the ice drift pulled away from the frozen land mass in one direction and Megan in the other. Megan swam toward them, reaching for the edge of the ice drift.

The second leopard seal, wounded and bleeding, was swimming toward them when Megan got both hands on the ice float. She slipped and grabbed on again to pull herself up.

"Hold on to my feet and sit," Jude told Ciliana.

Jude lay flat. She crawled to the edge of the ice while Ciliana sat digging in her heels and holding Jude's feet. They struggled for balance. Megan grabbed Jude's hand just has the leopard seal propelled forward, leaping up from the icy water. It grabbed Megan snatching her from Jude's grasp and dragged her down into the water. She never had the chance to scream. Ciliana dragged Jude away from the edge as the second leopard seal reappeared.

Cashton was on his feet. He grabbed the enormous ice sword and again summoned the power of the ice. Cashton swung with all his strength. In one graceful motion the blade severed the head of the leopard seal and sent it into the water. The headless sea leopard's body fell limp and crashed onto the ice at his feet.

Cashton kicked the headless body into the sea and watched as it slipped under the water. The first leopard seal had already dragged

Megan into the icy black abyss. There was nothing any of them could do.

Ciliana and Jude held each other on the ice and wept for their friend. They turned with grateful eyes to Cashton, who sank to his knees, weak and bleeding. Instantly, Musette folded out of him. She fell unconscious on the ice.

Cashton could see from the moment she separated that Musette was in trouble.

"Do something," Cashton said.

"Universal God, she's dying," Ciliana said as she crawled closer.

"No, she can't," Jude said.

Jude moved next to Musette and Cashton, tears streaming from her eyes.

"You have to save her," Jude told Cashton. "You have to."

Bloody and breathless, he looked at the two surviving girls and then at Musette. They were adrift on an ice float headed out to sea, and he knew he didn't have the first clue about what to do.

37

TREASURE

LAZER AND THE GROUP moved down one glowing tunnel after another, trying to forget that they were still hungry, possibly lost, and stuck who knew how many hundreds of feet beneath the surface. He listened as they chatted amongst themselves about school, home, friends, and the various odd experiences that had happened to each of them since they began their treks on Passage Island. Lazer thought about telling them it would conserve energy if they didn't speak, but the dialogue made the time go by faster and helped them ignore the hunger pangs that gnawed at their stomachs.

They walked for what felt like hours through the tunnels, some tall enough to walk in, others only a few feet high. For a long stretch, the ceiling of the cave was so low they had to traverse on their hands and knees.

Lazer began to notice every now and then a strange symbol was etched into the walls of the tunnels, guiding their choices and reminding them the tunnels wove their way beneath the sprawling temples.

They walked and crawled until finally no one could take another step.

He checked his locator. They were too deep to even tell if they were still heading in the right direction. He looked at the calendar. They had been underground for two days, and he could feel the tension building; people had started to get anxious. Hungry and exhausted, they once again stopped to rest.

Rhys and Lazer went with two other students to scavenge for food. They caught and killed two large albino newts the size of fat chickens. Jem and Striker, along with everyone's eager assistance, made a resin fire, cooked the newts, and shared the feast between them.

During their meager meal, Lazer, Striker, Jem, and Rhys hypothesized that the monks must have built the tunnels. Everyone had commented on the amazing symbols that had been etched into the walls of the tunnels, how they looked foreign to anything any of them had ever seen or read about. Lazer could not help but feel he had seen the signs somewhere before. There was something more to these tunnels—something at once ancient and yet timeless.

Momentarily satiated, they agreed to rest for a few hours. Rhys offered to stay awake and watch for any predators lurking in the tunnels. Lazer and four other students agreed to share hourly shifts. He offered to take the second-hour watch, so right now he needed to sleep.

Beyond any exhaustion they had ever known, most of the others instantly fell into a deep sleep, allowing themselves to escape the reality of their situation.

Lazer stretched out on the cold, hard rock and guided his mind into a meditative state. He wasn't particularly good at meditating, but the last thing he wanted was to spend any time on the useless task of worrying. He did his best to ignore the reality that they were trapped somewhere inside an enormous labyrinth of hidden tunnels and secret passageways that ran beneath the lost temples of Narez.

Again and again Lazer shifted, searching for some small spot of comfort as he lay against the cool, hard rocks. Finally, his mind drifted into a distant, semiconscious state. Even in sleep, he tossed and turned in the throes of a fitful slumber. He dreamed of spring on Atlantia's western shore, the warm sand and sea. He imagined the vivid colors that painted the rocky cliffs south of Vacary and recalled in his mind the fields of lavender blue flowers that covered the sandy countryside just east of Vacary. Lazer imagined himself standing on the dunes and remembered the chilly, ever-present winds that blew the tall brown grasses so consistently that they grew leaning to the east. The wind blew so hard it bent the tall, slender poplar trees forcing them to grow at a forty-degree angle. The constant wind and tall cliffs reminded him of his aviation books and their tales of the Wright Brothers and how the constant winds at Kitty Hawk must have inspired them to build wings and fly. He thought of how Kyla liked to fly off the cliffs and the thought made him sad when he remembered her wings were gone. He missed her. Her face. Her laugh. Her strength. *She was safe and healing,* he thought. That was the only solace inside his memory.

Lazer let his thoughts shift to home and a calm washed over him. Lazer smiled as he imagined himself looking up into a blue, cloud-filled sky behind his habitat in the Vacary Settlement. He imagined he was a great, soaring eagle looking down on his homeland. He had chosen an eagle, like his father, as his animal spirit when he was seven. It was part of their Anastasi heritage, a heritage of an animal spirit that bound them to their ancestors and connected the fifteen-thousand-year-old genealogy to their bloodline. Not only could he see the land of his physical birth, but he could see the silver thread, human timeline that led back to the common genetics held by all humans piercing into the cradle of civilization at the heart of mother Africa. It was so real. If only he could astral project himself home. Fly like Kyla through the billowing clouds that cluttered Atlantia's skies until he found himself drawn back to Earth where his feet would settle solidly upon the soft, rolling foothills that stretched out north of Vacary. Something moving caught his eyes. In the distance, he saw someone walking toward him. There was no question, it was a woman. The wind pulled at her long dark hair and ruffled her clothes. The figure seemed distorted and frightening, but Lazer felt himself drawn to move closer. It was not his eyes but his heart that first realized this woman was his mother. His heart raced to her, and in a moment, she was standing directly in front of him.

Her face was filled first with sadness, then with joy at seeing him. Tears fell from her eyes, which were hardened, grave, and filled with fear and anger. Her clothing and her right cheek were smudged with blood. She carried a weapon in her hand. Lazer wanted to look down to see what kind of weapon his mother, who had believed so completely in peace, carried in her hand. But he could not take his eyes from her face.

Detra looked at her son. His mother, who had loved him all of his life, had wiped his tears away, and had nurtured his wounds both physical and emotional, stood before him now as a warrior. He wanted to comfort her, to let her know he would find his way to her, to fight for her and lift the burden of any battle that confronted her. But before he spoke, he heard her voice.

Detra spoke to him, but her lips didn't move. It was just as in the visions with Masta Poe. He didn't need words; he knew her thoughts. He knew then, as he knew now, he was looking into a prophecy of some probable future. This gift of prophetic sight was one of his true powers. It had come to him when he stood before the Orbis Gnorb at the age of seven. When he was young, he feared and blocked the images that created themselves in his mind. It wasn't until Masta Poe's teachings that he began to find the courage to face these futuristic visions without fear or judgment. Lazer took a deep breath and opened his mind. He was more willing to look at what was shown to him with an open heart and a clear mind, for he understood that knowing the future meant there was time to change it. As Masta Poe had taught him, reality hasn't happened until it occurs. He clearly understood this vision was from his mother. He wondered if he could help her and affect change. The wind stopped. The blue skies turned gray, and Lazer felt a heavy, cold rain falling down on them.

Detra stood before him, beautiful, sad, now drenched in the sudden downpour. She carried a weapon. He looked into her eyes. She looked exhausted. It was then he noticed she was bleeding from a small cut above her left eye. Lazer lifted his hand, but it passed through the illusion before him. He ached to make her sadness go away. In an instant, Lazer was filled with a knowing more clearly than ever before: his mother was alive, and now, more than ever, she needed him. Fear, the one emotion that blocked all good, engulfed him.

Detra spoke, but only the sound of falling rain filled his ears with a deafening roar. Lazer called out to her, and in a blinding flash of light, Ducane Covax stood protectively behind her holding the white Gnorb. Lazer panicked. He grabbed for the Gnorb, but it stayed just out of his reach. He looked in Covax's face. The anger swelled inside him. Lazer grabbed for Detra's gun. He had to shoot this man who was responsible for his father's death, this evil monster that he was positive stood at the core of Atlantia's peril. He had to save the Gnorb. Detra held fast to her weapon, refusing to let go. Lazer ripped the weapon from his mother's hand, raised it, and fired. Just as he pulled the trigger, his mother stepped between them and she turned into Elana Blue. The blast slammed into Elana. The bullet tore into her flesh and into his and her wounded body fell against her father's. Together, they tumbled to the ground as the white Gnorb floated away, dividing into all four Gnorbs. Then, they all vanished.

"No!" Lazer screamed.

He released the weapon and dropped to his knees. Lazer pulled Elana off of Covax, but as he turned her lifeless body over, he saw not his beautiful Elana but his mother, wounds gone, face washed clean by the rain. Detra smiled and reached up to touch his cheek as if he had awakened her from a pleasant dream.

There is something you must know, her thoughts said to him.

He felt strength and bravery in her touch, but with it came a profound foreboding that filled his every fiber. I don't want to know, he told her. Then, like a watercolor washed away by a summer rain, her image faded from his arms. Again Covax appeared standing over him with the four Gnorbs floating out before him. Masta Poe and a beautiful young girl he did not know stood on either side of Covax. The Gnorbs, blue, white, red, and yellow hovered in the center. Lazer looked at their faces, and a strange feeling of calm touched him. This man was not his hated enemy. He was afraid and desperate, fearful of something unseen. Masta Poe was his mentor, and somehow he knew the young girl would someday be important in his life. They all faded, leaving only a large puddle of water that reflected his image back at him. The face that looked at him was older, the eyes harder, the clothes different, but it was him. Lazer jumped to his feet, and the rain fell harder and broke the image into a million pieces. He stepped back. He wanted to understand what he had seen, but the message of the vision eluded him.

Just as suddenly as it had started, the rain stopped, and once again the wind slapped at his face. Lazer fought to awaken from this bizarre nightmare. Moment by agonizing moment, he felt himself being dragged back to the hard reality of the cold stone floor on which he was laying. He tossed and turned and, with a bump, knocked loose some stones from the wall. They fell away and exposed a narrow crack in the structure.

Still half asleep, Lazer felt the wind from the dream as it pulled at his hair. It blew the unbraided Rite of Passage lock across his cheek. But this wind was no dream—it was cold and fast and real. His hair was caught in some slipstream of cool air blowing past him with incredible force. Finally, Lazer woke from the sticky mire of his dream world. Eyes wide open, his mind cleared. He shook the last remnants of his nightmare away as the pieces of the real world slowly came back together. He lifted his hands against the flow of air. It was real—a vent or shaft. *A way out,* he thought. Lazer pulled at the rocks and stone. More air came at him.

"I think I found a way!" he whispered, waking Jem and Striker.

Together they ripped the rocks away and exposed a three-foot-wide hole. The air flowed stronger. Lazer pulled out one large stone, causing a mini-avalanche of rocks, which opened the hole into a five-foot-wide shaft. He stuck his head inside and looked around. As his glow ring ignited, he saw above him a long narrow vent that led straight up. There was no light in sight, but the constant flow of air told him without a doubt that this hole went out of these wretched caves. Lazer had uncovered a passage big enough for them to fit through. He crawled inside.

"There's a shaft . . .; it's a passage," Jem shouted to everyone.

The students struggled from their sleep and, learning what had been discovered, buzzed with excitement. All of them came to the opening, eager to help.

Lazer was inside the shaft. Striker, his wounds too painful and his strength depleted, stayed back until they were sure the shaft would lead them out. Jem waited with Striker while Rhys crawled in to assist Lazer. The rush of air as it passed between the rocks made him smile with excitement and hope.

"Let's get out of this pit," Rhys shouted.

One by one, the other students followed him in single file. Finally, only Striker and Jem were left.

She saw the concern and pain in Striker's face.

"You'll be okay," she assured him. "I'll be right behind you."

The warmth of her smile calmed his heart and gave him courage. He had already realized how truly beautiful she was, and now her kindness and inner beauty radiated more brilliantly than ever. He smiled back at her.

With Jem's help, Striker headed in. He struggled with each step and arched in pain every time the passage narrowed and caused him to scrape against the sharp rocks. She stayed close behind him, offering her hand under his boot or setting his foot so it wouldn't slip until he found the strength to pull himself up.

At one point, they reached a wide opening, and she had enough room to sit and rest with him. She noticed fresh blood oozing through his shirt. The microfiber was designed to act as a bandage if it detected wounds. But it, like everything else on this Rite of Passage, wasn't working properly. At least with the clay, the shirt didn't stick to Striker's wounds.

Jem carefully peeled back the fabric of his shirt. In the dim light, she could see his back was raw and swollen and the wounds, pulled open by the stress of climbing, had become more infected. The stripes of scabs over ripped skin branched out and flowered into hundreds of tiny pink pustules. His back reminded her of the twisted old cherry trees as they blossomed in the early spring near her home outside of Station City.

Above them, they could hear Lazer and Rhys tearing more rocks away to make the chimney wide enough to get through. There was still no sign of light, but the shaft twisted and turned relentlessly upward through the dark rocks. It had to be the way out.

"Can you see where it goes?" Jem shouted from below.

"Not yet," Lazer shouted back.

The wind inside the shaft was persistent. It pulled at their hair and clothes. It was cool and wet and carried the hope of freedom. All that mattered was they were getting out. Lazer could feel it as sure as any knowing he'd experienced.

Rhys was right behind him and gave as much light from his glow ring as possible. Several of the other students' glow rings had lost power completely, and the few that still worked were dim at best. If they didn't get out soon, they would be feeling their way up in total darkness.

Relentlessly, they all followed Lazer and Rhys through the vertical crack as it wound its way through a continuing maze of jagged rocks until suddenly it became too narrow to continue. Lazer's heart pounded in his chest. This had to be the way out. They had climbed for over four hours, and Lazer knew they couldn't go back. The rocks above him were solid, yet the air still moved past him at an incredible rate.

Rhys and the others were at his heels. Everyone held their positions.

Lazer placed his shoulder under the rocks that blocked their path and pushed with every ounce of strength he had. Nothing moved.

Someone bumped Rhys to keep going.

"Stop," he whispered, halting the students.

"What's wrong?" Asia shouted up.

Lazer and Rhys exchanged a look in the dim, shadowy light of the fading glow ring. Lazer placed his shoulder against the rock again and pushed with all his strength.

"Use the Visionistic Arts," Rhys whispered. "I'll help you."

"What can you do?" Lazer asked.

"Let's find out," Rhys smiled.

"Maybe this is what people mean when they talk about moving mountains," Lazer said with a nervous smile.

"It is today," Rhys smiled back. "Let's separate the matter and create a path. Hold that image."

They readied their minds, and when they could see into one another's eyes they were in sync. Lazer placed his hand under the rock just above his head and focused his energy.

Their minds linked together and gave a push of collective energy directed at the rocks. Nothing happened. Lazer tried again. Still nothing.

"This has to work," he said.

Lazer braced himself, adjusting to get a better position. He moved his legs into a perpendicular angle and wedged himself between the rocks, hips against one side, his feet pressing on the other. Just as he was about to raise his hands against the rock above his head, his feet moved forward, pushing the rock in front of him. With a giant whoosh, the boulders shifted, falling away and exposing a large opening.

Without hesitation, Lazer crawled into the blackness. Immediately his glow ring illuminated with a surge of light so brilliant it seemed it had been charged by a thousand volts of electricity. The blinding light hurt his eyes. Rhys stuck his head in. He, too, averted his eyes from the harsh glare. As soon as he entered, his glow ring flared into a luminous halo as well.

They looked at each other in complete awe. They had entered a huge hidden chamber with the same unusual hieroglyphs they had seen on the tunnel walls. Painted and carved pictographs filled every inch of the smooth granite that formed the chamber's towering walls.

The students climbed inside, stumbling to their feet behind Lazer and Rhys. Every jaw dropped at the majestic beauty that lay in the artwork.

"What is this place?" a boy named Skyler asked. His voice was hushed in a reverent whisper. It mirrored the wonder reflected on all of their faces.

It was Lazer who put the puzzle of the images together first as he pointed to the strange letters.

"That's Celian," Lazer told them. "Look. There and there," he said as he pointed. "I've seen the Orbis Gnorb of Atlantia and the blue Gnorb of Mu. Those are Celian symbols."

"Look on the walls. These symbols are Mesopotamian and these are Egyptian. We studied them in early Earth history," Asia chimed in, her voice filled with fascination and excitement.

"Lazer, these are ancient Harappan symbols of the Inus Valley. They predate Sanskrit and go back to something like 2700 BCE," Rhys told them as he ran his fingers across the collections of symbols.

"These might be Tamil from Old Dwarka," Jem said.

"That's Mayan," a dark-skinned girl with green eyes and jet-black hair muttered back, staring at the far wall. "I'm sure of it."

Striker and Jem were the last into the chamber. The rush of power charged their glow rings as it had done for everyone else and made the room even brighter.

Striker was beyond exhausted. His legs and arms trembled from climbing. Even with the help of three other people he sank to the floor.

Lazer crossed to him and knelt down. "You all right?" he whispered.

"Ask me again when we're out of here," Striker whispered back as he tried to hide the waves of excruciating pain that obviously ripped through his body.

"Lazer, look," Rhys said.

Terracotta artifacts lined the smooth, polished walls. In the center sat some images that were reminiscent of the kind that graced the thirteen-moon calendars of the Incas, Mayas, ancient Egyptians, Polynesians, and the Lakotas. The geometric forms and symbols of the thirteen-moon, twenty-eight-day lunar cycle were set inside what looked like circles, squares, quadrangles, and multisided stars that formed Metatron's geometric flower of life. Others images were shaped like animals. They resembled ancient pottery from all around the world. The pots, bowls, pitchers, and urns cluttered the floor and were stacked along each of the thirteen immense walls that formed a perfect geometric shape. At the center of the room, thirteen huge cylindrical pillars with detailed hieroglyphics anchored the chamber and stood like silent stone centurions bearing the etchings and lost secrets from untold millennia.

The students, humbled by what lay around them, sat or walked in silence for a long time, marveling at their discovery.

Striker studied the corner of a wall next to him. "Almost looks like the old Druid markings at Stonehenge," he said. "How come the Passage Island excavators never found this place?"

The polished walls stood thirty feet high. Pictographs told stories of events that had been recorded by someone. What they couldn't decipher was by whom? One section of the wall showed thousands of people who stood together holding hands in a huge circle in what appeared to be a vast barren desert. From the tops of their heads, beams of light or streams of energy that had been drawn as wavy lines. Each line shot up into the sky and then bent back to form a colossal arch. In the next picture, clouds formed inside the arch. In the next, rain fell and filled the space inside the massive ring of people, forming a lake. In the last pictograph, people toiled by the banks of the lake they had commanded into existence. Plants grew in the vast fields they had created, and the people gathered and shared the bounty.

"They were hydrating the deserts," Striker said.

"They knew how to join their minds to control the elements," Jem added.

"Look over here," one girl called out and pointed.

Another series of pictures showed multiple volcanic eruptions, earthquakes, and huge sections of land ripping apart and sinking. People were weeping and dying.

"They prophesied the Great Quakes," Rhys said as he touched the etchings.

"Maybe these quakes happened before," Jem replied as she studied a detailed map of the world on another wall.

"Why didn't they use their collective thoughts to stop this?" Asia said and began to cry.

"Maybe they couldn't," Lazer said.

"But why?" Asia asked.

"Maybe they forgot how to work together," Jem answered.

She followed a series of pictographs that showed the population spreading across the landscape into separate directions and battling with one another. "They divided and started wars."

"Look here. Their anger at each other caused the lands to split apart, and when they knew they were doomed, they sent out emissaries," Lazer said.

He spoke as he explored the last wall of pictures.

In front of him, etched into the stone, ships filled with different groups of people, plants, and animals were launching. Each ship carried a huge stone plaque with glyphs, letters, and numbers.

"Call me crazy, but do those look like some kind of Noah's ark and this a Rosetta stone?" Rhys said, tracing his finger over the arch-shaped rocks each ship carried.

Each of the stones looked to be the same dark, pinkish gray granite of the famed Rosetta Stone of Memphis, Egypt.

"Earthquakes, floods, eruptions: something happened and destroyed their continent . . . and . . . it sank," Jem said. She touched the wall and felt the pain they had suffered.

"Noah's legend wasn't about one ark . . . it was about six arks!" Lazer added.

His voice filled with wonder.

"These plaques were the foundation for every culture that has evolved since. Mayan, Egyptian, Harrapan, Chinese, Lakota—who knows what else," Rhys said.

"They sent out knowledge, not gold or jewels, but knowledge. That was the greatest gift they had," Lazer said.

As he traced his fingers on the markings, he could feel them vibrating into his fingers.

"Masta Poe remembered these knowings and built them into the Visionistic Arts. She said they were in our genetic memory. She said they were always ours."

"Look at this. The answer to paradise on Earth is right here in this room," Jem said.

Lazer crossed over to look at a dense block of letters and detailed symbols. "Can anyone read this?" Lazer asked as he struggled to remember the Celian symbols from his experiences.

Now he thought. Please now. He stood, opened his arms, and made himself ready to accept the message the universe had tried to impart to him at least three times before; first as a child when he was in the Orbis Temple with his mother, then fighting to free the white Gnorb in Temple Mountain, and finally when he touched the blue Gnorb at Tosadae with Masta Poe.

Lazer heard the wall breathing. He too took several deep breaths and brought himself completely into the present moment. Intuition told him to put both hands on the wall. A warm vibration ran up his arms and became an audible tone that grew into a chord and the chord blossomed into a kind of song. It was the same kind of song he had heard the first time he touched the white Gnorb as a child. It was celestial and even more beautiful than he remembered.

"Everybody, put your hands on this wall and listen," Lazer told them. His voice was filled with a strange symbiotic rush.

With help from some of the others, Striker managed to stand and join them. Everyone placed his and her hands on the wall. Lazer could see the awe on all of their faces when they heard the single tone and watched as their eyes widened when they heard it grow into the glorious song. Arising from the vibrating tones carried in the rocks, voices rose and began to sing to them. Lazer furrowed his brow. At first, the words were completely alien, but the wondrous tones were filled with such grace and power no one could do anything but listen:

"*Oloragi tati ma. Obana ne she vo reaom*," a solo siren's voice called.

Suddenly Lazer understood the words.

"We are doomed. It is through no fault but our own," a second voice sang beneath the first in the strange, hypnotic language.

"I understand them," Jem whispered in amazement.

"Me too," a girl named Vedi added.

Every one of them understood the meaning of the beautiful song that echoed from the walls.

"*Oloragi vioswe paschne presg morvaba s Celian ommol . . .*"

"*Ti obrdu titik liageakiowa univa, tatam bledsash u ominima oloragi va.*"

"We held the secret to it all and it filled us with all the love and power of the universal source energy we needed. We were equal. We were one."

"First there were beings of kindness and knowledge that had come light years before us. They were the first to enjoy the miracle of life on this paradise. They lived here in harmony, felt sadness and joy, wept and laughed, and lived. When they were full of life, they left but promised to return when they were needed."

"When humankind was born into existence and lost their way, the Celians returned and gave us the Gnorbs to light our way. They saw our fearful and primitive souls and yet they showed us the secrets of the universe. They would help us remember and save us from extinction as a parent would protect their young."

"They taught that each of us is pure energy, part of and connected to the great, all-knowing, all-present universal source. They lifted us up and gave us strength to stand, by our free will, between all energy that is good and evil."

"They shared the power of all things imagined. They told us we were worthy to be at one with the source."

"They left us a precious imprint of how to use our minds to connect with this mighty empowering source and, in turn, with each and every living thing that exists—past, present, and future. In case we should lose our way, they placed the key to understanding the great knowings inside the four Gnorbs of understanding. Most important of all, they instructed us to love one another. Through the power of our collective souls, they told us we must live in harmony with this planet, for only then can we keep our connection with our universal oneness and understand why we were brought into being."

"We used this great universal knowledge to build our temples, moving immense stones with the power of collective thought. We built our homes and raised our children and kept the great traditions of sacred music. Re-empowered each time, we honored our oneness with humility and bliss and joined into the awe-inspiring power of the universal source. Then darkness fell in shades of greed, selfishness, and jealousy and they brought us to hatred. Many stood in grace but those who lived in fear hated them and divided us into those dark fractions of ourselves that pulled us into the chaos that led us into our destruction."

"In our selfishness and greed for power, we separated the Gnorbs and hid them from one another. We changed the thirteen-moon, twenty-eight-day calendar and broke our rhythmic connection with nature. To move back into universal harmony, we must reinstate this calendar, let go of greed, and join together. But the truth comes too late and for us it is too late."

"We polluted our bodies, our minds, and Earth after we were given paradise by our source energy. We destroyed our bliss, separated and lost the wisdom of the Gnorbs, and now we stand at the brink of destruction as the architects of our own annihilation. We were rays of sunlight that forgot who we were and that we would always be part of the same sun."

The chorus of sirens' voices swelled in a wail of sorrow.

"The great change comes, and those who have the eyes to see the future weep with joy, for if you have found these words and understand—prepare."

"Our day is done, and with our tears, we can only send out into your world our greatest minds. Take our deepest knowings, and our most wondrous understandings of unity, power, life, and love. These are the knowings that come from and live in the very essence of our being; this is the core of our true humanity. It was lost, and now, by you, it is found."

"We send this message to you in the hope that this great gift will survive the twisting rivers of time. Remember what we foolishly forgot: love of the universal self, love of one another, and love of all things that are one with your heart. Let all align."

"To you who find this knowledge, understand that the human mind is capable of anything if it is in harmony with the great universal source. Through the path of love, we can be one with all that is, and the gathering of the Gnorbs will reunite all.

"Carry on human life in perfect unity and balanced harmony, for only through the all-knowing universal source can we find peace and live in the bliss of love forever."

"*Fodu strat fage pasch. Ank naniba lochlaan.*"

"This is our gift. Go in light and be one."

Lazer felt the warm tears that fell down his face as the musical vibrations swelled into a perfect harmony, building into one climactic crescendo as if a mighty universal orchestra and a wondrous choir of celestial beings had reached the pinnacle of their performance. The sound rose like an offering, folding finally into one single sustained note that hung in each of their hearts. Then, like a receding tide, it faded back into a peaceful silence.

In the wake of the vast quiet that followed, tears of joy fell from all who had listened not only with their ears but with their hearts, minds, and souls. Lazer looked around and saw in each of them that they knew, at the core of their being, they had been touched by a great and profound universal wisdom. Quietly they sat down in a circle, took one another's hands, and their spirits became as one.

38

SCARABITES

IT SEEMED AS IF hours passed and time had lost its relevance until one small voice spoke out.

"I'm starving," Asia said. "I would love some vegetables with wild rice . . ."

". . . and a two-inch wild bilyon steak with gravy!" Santiago added.

Laughter broke the silence. The students went around and all added their favorite entree, dessert, fruit, and pastry to the incredible menu they were creating.

"Mmmm. Does anybody smell what I smell?" Asia asked, her mouth watering.

"It's delicious," Jem added and licked her lips.

"It smells like . . . honey," Lazer said.

"Look!" Rhys pointed.

Rhys walked to the far side of the room and studied the shinny liquid that coated the rock wall. It was a brilliant amber color that oozed from what once had been a doorway.

Lazer and some of the others stood and moved across the room.

When they reached the corner, they found a gigantic, honey-laden, six-sided honeycomb wall industriously built into the arched doorway.

"That's the exit," Lazer said.

Lazer could feel warmer air coming through the small breaks in the wax structure that oozed gallons of fresh amber honey.

"I agree. It's an exit, but that massive wall of honey and wax is blocking our path," Rhys said

Rhys reached out and touched the rich, thick, and gooey substance. It clung to his fingers and hung like strands of golden threads. He raised it first to his nose then stuck out his tongue.

He put the honey to his mouth and tasted. It was manna from heaven and a sound of delight was all he could share as he licked the delicacy from his fingers.

"Mmmm. Oh Mmmmm!"

The other students dug in. They broke off large, waxy chunks and devoured the amber nectar.

"Hey, you think we can eat our way out of here?" a girl with an infectious laugh said.

At first, Lazer did not partake in the sweet treat. Something inside him made him feel the need to warn them. But warn them about what he could not articulate. Still, the feeling of foreboding tugged at him.

"Well, you can stand there and starve or eat something and have the strength to get out of here. If that's the exit, we can make the transport pickup," Rhys told Lazer.

"I agree. Our ticket out of here is on the other side of this honeycomb," Striker said, and everyone agreed.

Torn between his gut instincts and the hunger pangs in his stomach, Lazer grabbed a handful of honey-laden wax and ate the sweet nectar. The taste was unbelievably delicious.

"Honey this pure and unprocessed is filled with a multitude of nutrients and vitamins and will give us huge amounts of energy," Skyler said.

"And keep us hydrated," another student said.

"And most of all it will stave off hunger!" Rhys said with his mouth so full that his voice was almost too garbled.

Lazer looked through the small hole they were creating and saw behind it a glow of light. He tore away at the wax, breaking off large chunks. The wax was strong but incredibly pliable, and the bites of honey had given him an energy rush. Lazer raised his hands and used the Visionistic Arts to draw heat into a ball. He gently pushed the ball forward. He was using it to melt a narrow path that cut through the wax and at the same time melted the golden nectar into globs of oozing liquid honey.

"Be careful," Jem shouted to Lazer as he disappeared into the crevasse he'd created.

"Wait up. I'm coming right behind you," Rhys called to Lazer and followed him, squeezing into the narrow opening.

In a few minutes, Lazer poked his head back in, covered in honey and smiling.

"Come on. Just be careful," he told them. "Wait until you see this."

On the other side was an enormous hive constructed inside a huge cavern. It was one hundred feet high and meticulously followed the natural rock arch.

Again, he felt the strange rush of trepidation as it coursed through Lazer's veins. He just couldn't shake the question that had haunted him since he entered the hive: what kind of bee could make a hive this large and this deep in the ground?

"Does anybody remember the bee epidemic that swept the planet?" he asked.

Rhys nodded. "The entire species died off for no apparent reason."

Jem took a finger full of the delectable treat. "Real honey. I don't think I've ever had real honey. I mean the synthetic stuff is pretty good, but this is unreal!"

"Back before the Great Quakes, there was very little honey left and no one could afford to buy it. I've only had the fake honey my whole life," Santiago said.

"Yeah. Me too," a chorus of agreement echoed back.

"I remember reading about the epidemic in genetics," Rhys said, licking his fingers.

"Some kind of parasite," Jem added.

"Varroa mites got blamed, but no one was sure. Stress from pollution was the other school of thought and electromagnetic waves from early cell phones," Striker added. "I remember because I got it wrong on the final."

"Wait. If bees are extinct, what made this honey?" Lazer asked.

"Maybe some splicer scientists cross-engineered a new species and created a new honeybee."

"The only splicer strains capable of generating this much honey are . . . scarabites," Lazer explained.

"You've got to be kidding!" another student said, her mouth dropping open at the realization of what Lazer was driving them to understand.

"I saw some the first day here," Lilani said.

"Me too. They're huge," Asia added. "I saw a swarm pick the bones of a carcass clean in a matter of minutes."

"Meat eaters?" Lilani said. "Great."

Lazer knew of scarabites: fist-sized part bee, part hornet splicers. One strain that had been intentionally bred on Atlantia were part hawk. All the scarabites, at least the known varieties, were meat eaters.

"Uh. We need to get out of here before the drones get back," Rhys said.

"What if we run into the queen or her nest?" Jem asked.

"We don't," Rhys said.

"Okay, that's out. How do we get up there?" Lazer said as he pointed at the opening.

Everyone looked up at the impossible ascent. The narrow hole in the very top was punctuated by a stream of morning sunlight that poured in and painted the enormous honeycomb in warm white light that turned to gold as it reached through the liquid amber. *If it weren't so dangerous, it would have been breathtakingly beautiful,* Lazer thought.

"I can levitate . . . sort of," Asia said, ". . . with maybe one person. Maybe."

"I say you and I go up and get some hemp or, even better, a bunch of thick vines to lower back down inside. Then we use that old crate in the other room to hoist everyone out," Lazer explained.

"That will take forever," Santiago complained.

"You got a better idea?" Striker asked.

Lazer watched Striker wince. He was trying to find a comfortable position to stop the pain in his back.

"If so, share it. If not, stop complaining and help out," Striker said.

"Yeah? Help out," Santiago said back. "You're the one holding us back."

"Enough," Lazer said cutting in and diffusing the tension. "We can do this if we do it together."

Lazer had kind of a plan, and, if it worked, it was pretty much their only hope of escaping.

"You think you can handle that crate?" Lazer asked Striker.

"I'll be fine. Just get us outta here," Striker said.

Lazer nodded with a smile. He instructed everyone to gather as much honey as they could carry for later. They stuffed their cuff cups and pouches and stepped back to give Lazer and Asia space and time to prepare for their ascent using the Visionistic Arts. Lazer knew getting into the frame of mind to levitate had its challenges, especially under such dire circumstances.

Lazer looked over as Jem cleaned Striker's wounds and replaced the mud with honey. He knew it would act as a natural coagulant and keep out any infection. That would help in the long run. Jem laid hands on Striker and meditated. It was obvious she was a natural healer. He watched as she talked and cared for his wounds telling him she too was a freshman at Sangelino University, studying for her healer's degree. It was obvious to everyone there was an attraction between them.

Seeing them together made Lazer think of Elana. He missed her and hoped she was safe in Sangelino. Maybe she had heard through the Vybernet about what had been happening to them on Passage Island. The thought of Elana Blue lightened his spirits but the light turned cold. His thoughts were yanked to Kyla and a wash of fear hit him. Something was wrong. The moment he opened his thoughts to both of them, a cry for help flooded in. Kyla's was clearest. His heart raced. *No!* he thought. He knew he couldn't give his energy to what she was sending. He needed to focus on getting everyone out. Lazer pulled his thoughts away from the barrage of feelings that would have to wait outside of what he had to do.

He saw Asia as she focused her energy inward, imagining good things; her family, the horseback riding on a sunny day she's told them about while walking. He could see her body slowly shift as it began to lift. She floated upward, drifting toward the small opening at the top of the hive.

A moment behind Asia, Lazer shifted his thought to home, days with his father and mother, riding his Zakki across the Atlantia outback. He started his ascent.

Below, Lazer could see that Rhys had gotten the crate from the other room and had taken command.

"Everybody, find as much hemp, loose wax, and sticks as you can and help us bind them together around this crate. Hurry," he told them.

"I feel like Hansel and Gretel at the witch's house right before they were . . .," Lilani was saying, until the buzzing sound of a thousand wings stopped her cold.

Everyone looked up from the floor of the hive as an army of scarabite drones poured in through the opening, blocking out the sun. They swarmed into attack formation, circling into a living black twister.

Lazer and Asia were ten feet in the air when Rhys's call broke their concentration.

"Scarabites!"

Lazer sank, and then countered, controlling his descent as best he could. Asia panicked and fell. Lazer reached out and grabbed her as she passed. Her weight and velocity increased his speed, and they slammed down into a mound of thick honey and wax seven feet above the floor. Lazer knew the honeycombs broke their fall and saved their lives—for the moment. Lazer scrambled to his feet and grabbed Asia's hand.

"Run!" Lazer and Rhys yelled in unison.

The swarm of fist-sized scarabites poured into the hive. There were thousands of them: yellow and black bodies with a streak of cobalt blue shining between their sheer wings.

Lazer and Asia grabbed Striker and, with the help of Jem and Rhys, raced across the chamber floor as fast as the thick sticky goo would allow. They reached the rest of the students who were in a panic, pushing and shoving to get back through the doorway. The weight as they struggled through the opening at once was too much for the wax to hold. It collapsed. Everyone was coated in gallons of honey that held them like a vat of glue.

The scarabites came in stinger first. Lazer could see they were ready to stab the sea of flailing arms and kicking legs below. Somebody had to do something before they were stung to death and, worse, devoured.

"Hold your breath and dive under the honey. Make sure you grab hold of one another," Lazer ordered through the chaos and then vanished under the honey.

All of them submerged, holding a collective breath. Lazer threw a bubble shield, which expanded around them. It was covered by globs of dripping liquid-gold honey with enough room for everyone to stand together in a clump.

"Everybody in?" Lazer shouted, breathless from the ordeal.

"Where's Rhys?" Jem yelled as she looked around.

Lazer searched inside and out. Other than Rhys, everyone stood linked together, covered in honey. Each face held a look of terror as the swarm of angry scarabites buzzed around them. Again and again, the scarabites slammed their stingers into the energy shield.

"Over there," Striker pointed.

They all turned to see Rhys in his own energy shield ten feet away.

In his head Lazer heard Rhys's voice say, *I'm going to drop my shield and throw a fireball.*

How will you hold them off? Lazer thought back.

You have to distract them long enough for me to manifest and grow the fireball. I can start it inside but I'll need room to expand, and that'll mean releasing my shield, Rhys thought to himself.

Distract them how? Lazer thought back.

I don't know how. Just do it!

"Can we move?" Jem asked suddenly able to hear Lazer and Rhys.

"I don't know. Where?" Lazer responded, looking for the new voice that filled his head until he knew it to be Jem.

"Look over there," she pointed.

A large tunnel lay open across the hive floor.

"What if that's the main egg chamber? The queen will be there," Striker said.

"Even better. They'll come protect it," Lazer responded and expanded the shield to give them a tiny bit of room to move. Somehow, they would have to get the bubble across the floor.

"We'll draw their attention as soon as we start moving," Lazer told them.

"Make sure he's ready," Striker added.

Lazer sent a telepathic message to Rhys, and he sent one back. It was time. With one hand, Rhys created a ball of energy that ignited into fire and grew. It would eat up the oxygen, so he had to release the shield or suffocate. What would happen after that, Lazer could only guess.

"Everybody put your hands on the shield and roll us that way," he ordered.

Like matchsticks in a row, they all lay flat. Lazer held the shield and levitated inside the bubble. He pulled his legs up and crossed them, which gave the signal to roll the ball of energy.

The motion of the energy bubble drew the scarabites' attention away from Rhys. They would, at all cost, protect the queen.

The angry swarm turned full force, like a single black entity rather than a thousand individuals. They attacked, covering Lazer's bubble and stabbing it with their stingers. Ten, then twenty, then hundreds enveloped them, blacking out the light. It made the task of moving through the honey arduous, but not impossible. The motion kept the scarabites off balance. Through the tiniest of spaces left by the frenzy of scarabite bodies, Lazer could see Rhys.

Fireball in hand, he sweated from the intense heat. Suddenly, he began to gasp for air. He needed oxygen.

Throw it, Rhys, Lazer thought. But Rhys's eyes rolled back into his head and he blacked out. His energy bubble popped, leaving him exposed.

Face down in the honey, he would suffocate before he was discovered by the scarabites—if he were lucky.

"Lazer, Rhys fainted," Jem yelled.

"Turn left! Roll us to him," Lazer ordered.

The direction of the energy bubble shifted on Lazer's command. He searched his mind for some way to gather Rhys under his shield and get them all out. It was impossible to get him inside without opening the bubble and risking everyone.

Nothing's impossible, a voice in Lazer's head prompted him. Imagine.

"We've got to pick him up," Striker said. "Drop the shield long enough for me to grab him and get him in here."

"No!" several students screamed.

The bubble was covered in scarabites. Lazer knew that if he dropped the shield they would all be at risk.

They reached Rhys, who lay in a puddle of honey, his face turned sideways. He was breathing but unconscious.

The scarabites ignored him, concentrating on breaking the bubble shield. Lazer could feel the tiniest sensation of pinpricks in his hands. The shield was a direct extension of his energy field, and he could feel a distant version of what it felt. Lazer's mind spun, searching for a solution. He needed a weapon, and only fire made sense.

"Jem, can you create a shield?" Lazer asked.

"Yes. No. Maybe. I don't know. I've never tried it for real."

"Everybody who thinks they can, get up and try. Everybody that can't, grab on to someone who can and give them your complete focus," Lazer insisted.

Three of the students, plus Striker and Jem, cupped their hands.

"This is impossible," one student whined.

"You're already defeated if you believe that," Lazer told them.

"Jem got an energy spark!" Striker shouted, still trying.

Lazer talked her through it as Masta Poe had done with him. He told her step by step what she needed to do as she and the other students listened.

The flicker of energy she held in her hands began to grow. When it was the size of a zoccair ball, Lazer told her to push one hand inside it but not before everyone grabbed hold of her. In an instant, all the students were inside Jem's bubble shield—all but Striker, who held onto Lazer's shoulder.

"I'm staying with you. Whatever you're gonna do, I'm guessing you might need a little help," Striker said.

Lazer destroyed his shield with a loud pop that momentarily scattered the scarabites. Exposed, Striker grabbed Rhys, still keeping a firm grasp on Lazer as he re-shielded. Lazer gathered them all inside before the scarabites regrouped.

A few scarabites got in, and Striker battled them with one hand. He slammed one with his fist, then grabbed the body of another and used its stinger to kill the other three.

"Wake up," Striker shouted to Rhys.

No response. Striker picked up the still-unconscious Rhys and threw him over his shoulder. The dead weight fell against Striker's back. Lazer could see him flinch when Rhys's weight sent an excruciating shock of pain through him that buckled his knees. Lazer watched Striker will the pain to subside. Striker forced himself up and nodded to Lazer that he was ready.

Lazer smiled. It was nice to have a friend on his team. He also knew whatever adrenalin-driven strength Striker had summoned would be short-lived at best. They would have to act now.

"Push," he told Striker.

Together they walked, using their hands and feet to roll the bubble shield.

Roll into that entrance, Lazer ordered Jem telepathically. We'll meet you there.

Jem nodded.

The scarabites were in a frenzy of rage. They divided their forces and attacked both energy shields. Most of their stingers were broken, but they still had double pincers. They were meat eaters and would rip the flesh off their prey.

Lazer shifted control of the shield to one hand and created an energy ball with the other. Striker had watched him destroy the archeop. He had even helped. His palms still showed the burn marks, and he knew he would have to do it again. Striker held out one hand, completing Lazer's cup, and their energies collided into one. Guided by Lazer's power of matter manipulation, the core of antimatter manifested into matter and then ignited into a sphere of fire. It grew larger as they expanded the space between their hands. Striker could feel the heat singe his face. The air, thinned by the hungry blaze, made his lungs struggle to work. Lazer stayed focused.

"Drop down and hold on," he said to Striker.

Get ready, Lazer sent a thought to Jem, and then shouted at the same time. "NOW!"

He dropped the shield, then extended, opened, and fanned his arms. The fire exploded upward in an arch of flames, igniting the scarabites.

Lazer re-shielded. They watched the burning bodies of the creatures consumed by the flames as they flew up to escape their doom. One by one, their charred wings vanished in smoke, and their tortured burning bodies rained down to the floor in hundreds of smoldering mounds of flesh.

The blaze suddenly began to spread as the wax of the honeycomb ignited into flames. A flash fire sent a blaze through the entire hive, and everything went up in a flaming inferno. The intense heat of the waxy fire melted the honey and turned it into a scalding river. Gallons of boiling liquid lifted up the students' shield bubbles and carried them through the opening of the tunnel.

The two bubbles crashed into each other. Flames from the wax shot up all around them, yet they remained unscathed.

They coursed through the tunnel, watching the enormous scarabite queen as she tried in vain to save herself.

The bubble shields were carried into a series of randomly turning and twisting tunnels. The passageways were no longer man-made but were carved by time and Mother Nature.

"We're going down again," Striker said.

Rhys was beginning to revive. He shook himself back to consciousness.

He and Striker held onto the sides of the shield, each keeping a hand on Lazer, who struggled to keep the bubble shield upright and balanced. They stared into the dim light, imagining what dangers might be waiting at every turn. Jem and the others were ahead of them.

"What do we do?" Striker shouted.

"Just hang on," Lazer said. His precognitive abilities gnawed at his gut, telling him some kind of imminent danger lay ahead. A clairvoyant image of smoke and water filled his head, but it was too late. Both bubble shields went over a cliff.

They dropped like an elevator on a horrifying death descent.

Hold on, Lazer thought to Jem.

I am, she thought back with complete resolve.

They crashed hard into fast-moving water. It carried them on a swift current and dragged them deeper underground. Steam rose from the surface and the shoreline bubbled. They were on a boiling, thermal, subterranean river.

The bubble shields protected them, but they could feel the heat. As they moved, they crashed into one another, but no one dared let go. Everything was getting hotter, and the water was moving faster.

Striker, whose eyes had been riveted on Jem's bubble shield, lost sight of her.

"I lost them!" he shouted.

Lazer and Rhys felt a rumbling that called to them from ahead. Striker felt it a moment later.

"What the hell is that?" Striker asked.

"Lock arms," Lazer said.

They locked arms and were sucked backward, then just as furiously pulled forward and slammed into a rock wall. The bubble shield jerked down with such velocity and force that the three of them were slammed against it. The g-forces crushed them, pinning them to the floor.

"Hold . . . on to the . . . shield," Rhys said through a grimace.

"Losing it!" Lazer yelled. "Help me."

It was getting hard to breathe, and the pressure was making Lazer's limbs shake. He was sure he would black out.

Rhys and Striker could do no more than hold on when they were abruptly bounced off the ground and into the air.

The bubble shield slowed and danced on a spout of water one hundred feet above the jungle floor. The geyser stopped, and the spout of water dropped away, splattering across the muddy ground below. They hung suspended for a moment then plummeted to the ground. The bubble shield hit with a thud and bounced across the steamy, hot, gray mud.

Lazer's concentration broke, and they all tumbled out into the shallow waters of a hot spring.

The rumble started again, and the geyser exploded. Lazer and Rhys grabbed Striker and scrambled across the scalding mud and onto a mound of land away from the steaming hot-water spout. Their shields and environmental suits had once again saved their lives.

The other bubble shield had preceded them. Everyone inside was stunned but alive, scattering and tumbling in every direction. A few fell into a nearby freshwater stream that ran parallel to the thermal geyser.

The water in the tributary was cool and about knee deep. It was moving fast.

"Grab something and pull yourselves out!" Santiago shouted. "Hurry."

Thirty feet ahead, a single horrendous scream echoed, then faded away. Everyone stopped. Someone had fallen over Universal God knows where. No one spoke. The little band of students clung to the rocks and helped one another out.

Lazer, Striker, Rhys, Jem, and the rest gathered together and managed to pull everyone out of the rushing water.

They collapsed, exhausted, on the shore. One boy threw up. A girl wept. With a gentle touch, Asia comforted her. They were out of the caves and, save for one, still alive.

39

CLOSER

EVERYONE SLEPT THROUGH the morning and into the early afternoon. They were near the edge of the eastern jungle, farther south than they had hoped, but their rendezvous location was within reach. The smell of burnt honey permeated the air, and plumes of smoke billowed up from the temple ruins miles behind them.

They found food, ate, drank, and assessed the damages. They realized it had been Lilani who had died in the fall. Lazer and a few others followed the river to a moss-covered cliff where the river ended and turned into a deathly waterfall that emptied into a giant sinkhole. Those brave enough to look peered over into the abyss. The bottom was not visible, lost in the blackness below. Lazer kicked a few large rocks over the cliff and listened to the rush of the falls until the rocks crashed onto the bottom hundreds of feet below. Still they called and listened, but the sound of crashing water told them any attempt to rescue her was futile.

Lilani was pretty, quiet, and helpful. She had been a team player every step of the way. Someone who had spoken to her said she was part splicer and that she had been a student at Panazia College of Aquatic Technologies and Genetic Arts. They didn't know her last name. Her death made the journey even more somber than it had been.

They drank from the mountain tributary and diverted enough hot water from the thermal spring so they could wash the sticky globs of honey from their skin, clothes, and hair and feel human again.

The lumps left by the scarabite stings still hurt. The honey they ate acted like an anti-venom serum against the bites. They even found that when applied topically, the honey slightly dulled the painful lumps.

Bit by bit, they gathered their strength. Late in the afternoon they started walking again. Lazer let Rhys lead them as they traveled through the hues of sunset and into the inky darkness of night. Lazer calculated they had been traveling for nine days. The rendezvous was set for tomorrow at 11:00 a.m. That was hours away and Lazer looked up at the stars and moon, glad they were there to guide them. He pushed hard and they walked for hours until the last star sank below the horizon. Pre-dawn, the blackest hour before the sunrise, covered them, but even in the shadows he could see all of them hiding their sorrowful and exhausted faces. They walked in silence watching the pearly gray of the day's first light break the darkness. Finally, they reached the sandy edge of the desert.

Lazer lifted a hand.

"Rest," he said.

One by one they sat. They would take one hour. Lazer knew they would need their strength for the remainder of the journey. He laid his head on a pile of cool sand. Again, Lazer fell into sleep. It was the same deep, dreamless sleep and for that he was grateful. He woke itching. The swollen bites, welts, and bruises covered his cheek, neck, arms, and left leg. His body ached but when he looked at Striker he knew he had it a thousand times better. Striker had fared far worse by turning his back on the scarabites to protect Rhys when Lazer dropped his shield. The pain from their stingers aggravated the infected lacerations left by the archeop. His bravery against the scarabites had saved both himself and Rhys. Thanks to him they were alive . . . for the moment.

Jem and Santiago, who had been on watch, gently woke everyone and got them to their feet. Rhys and Lazer plotted the last stretch of the trek and confirmed it with Lazer's locator, recalculating their time and distance. A few attempted to send messages to the rescue ship, but no one got a response.

"What if they don't come?" Jem asked.

"What if they can't come?" Santiago added.

"They'll come," Lazer said. "They have to."

They stopped to eat only once, gathering edible berries and fruits and drinking the milk from coconuts they hacked off the slender palm trees in a tiny oasis at the edge of the next sand dunes. The pale sand stretched for miles in front of them. Lazer nudged them onward. From now on, there would be no more rest. He drove the exhausted students with a gentle but firm voice, reminding them their only chance of salvation was Striker's rendezvous. For all the obvious reasons, no one tarried for fear of being left behind.

After three straight hours of walking, Striker stopped and collapsed.

Lazer gathered him up and draped him over his shoulder like a lifeless yoke and continued to walk. Striker's weight crushed him. The sun was climbing and the temperature was too. Lazer struggled to keep his balance on the uneven sands of the desert terrain. Rhys and several of the other students offered to help, but Lazer declined. He could see they were as exhausted as he.

"In a little while," Lazer said.

Lazer was relieved that Striker was unconscious and could no longer feel the pain that racked his body. He was pale from blood loss and obviously tortured by the gaping wounds that splayed open the exposed flesh along his back. Even through the honey patches, he could see the wounds were deeply infected. Rhys and Jem watched the ribbons of raw, open flesh turning pink and gush with pus as they glistened and cooked in the cruel morning sun. Jem grabbed a palm leaf she'd been carrying food in and opened it, holding it over the flesh.

Lazer's body ached. He ignored the pain that bit into his back and arms with each agonizing step. His tired legs moved relentlessly forward. *Home,* he thought over and over again. All that mattered was getting to the pickup point and going home. Somehow, the image of getting home and finding his mother filled him with a new strength and drive to get there. He knew he had become a very different Lazer from the young man who left Atlantia. He was no longer the boy who had played and laughed in his homeland. That boy had fallen away like an old familiar cloak, and from its youthful wonder, a man had been born. The aches came over him and he almost stumbled. The image of the Black Guard filled his brain and with it a surge of anger energized him. He knew he was still fueled by the same searing hatred that burned in the pit of his stomach. He recalled the feeling of hated at the murder of his father and all the other innocent people who were burned alive at the mines. He hated that his Rite of Passage had been marred by whatever was happening that made Passage Island unsafe. Lazer hated that all the guardians who had promised to protect him had failed and students died on their watch. His felt no remorse as the hatred consumed him because he believed that same hatred gave him strength.

Beware, Lazer heard Masta Poe's voice as it echoed in his mind.

She had warned him his anger would be a detriment to him even more than the fear of failure that haunted him. He knew the negative emotions would block his powers and keep out all that the universe promised to give him including the love of those who believed in him.

"Let it go," Lazer said softly to himself.

As he spoke he fought the darkness that gnawed at him. He knew the feeling of love but not the sweetness of passion, but he understood the call of desire. His thoughts went to Elana, and like an angel of mercy, her image filled him with the hope of finding her, loving her, and spending the rest of his life with her. Striker's weight lightened, lifting with each step. Was it this sliver of hope that reached out from his heart and filled his head with images of Elana, his mother, his friends, Kyla and Cashton, Masta Poe, and home? The love empowered him and had it not, he knew he would have been consumed by the anger that cloaked itself in vengeful hatred.

"Kyla," Lazer whispered. "Give me strength."

He saw her face and her love kept open the door to his heart, for without them the icy wind of revenge would have turned him into a wall of stone.

The night before, Lazer had followed the bottom star that formed the Southern Cross. Kyla once told him it was their star; their twin star. Divided by fate and destine to reunite. He'd laughed at her, but right now it was Kyla's strength, not Elana's, that filled him, guided him, and empowered him. That star had guided them out of the jungle to the outskirts of the harsh dunes that formed the undulating sands of the desert terrain. Lazer looked up at the merciless sun as it climbed in the sky and beat on their faces and backs with its relentless, fiery heat. With Rhys's perfect sense of direction, they kept moving.

A few daunting miles more and they would reach the pickup site with half an hour to spare. Just knowing how close they were gave them all strength. Lazer could feel it as they all picked up their pace. They walked, pushing forward, ignoring all that had passed and focusing only on the rescue that lay ahead.

After all those unbearable hours, Lazer looked up and saw in the distance the small oasis that was the center of the rendezvous coordinates. Banatek Oasis was just that—a tiny watering hole, anchored by a few palm trees and a variety of tan- and jade-colored grasses that stood as erect as the quills of a giant sleeping porcupine. The tiny sanctuary represented survival not only to the students but also to the various animals that lived on this part of Passage Island.

Lazer imagined how each day, the creatures came to drink: lizards, vultures, and packs of riders. At the far end of the water, a flock of baby archeops played.

"They're breeding here, and the Passage Committee doesn't even know," Lazer said to Rhys as he pointed to the archeops.

Lazer wondered if these were the young offspring of the two creatures he had fought and killed only ten days earlier. *Had it only been that long,* he wondered. It seemed as though months had come and gone in those last relentless hours. Lazer was grateful that his powers had brought him through the harrowing ordeal. He was grateful to Masta Poe and all that she had taught him. For the first time, he wanted to return to her tutelage—to learn everything he could—to be the best he could be. But it would have to wait until after the war. If she would have him, he would return to her.

Some of the other students came and helped carry Striker the last few yards, laying him at the tiny shore of the oasis. They all rushed into the shallow spring to drink the cool water, wash the sweat and dust from their faces, and breathe a sigh of relief. Beaten and bruised and too tired to celebrate, some wept. Each gave silent gratitude for the good fortune, grace, and survival skills that had kept them alive. In the quiet moments before the retrieval, they turned their eyes to the horizon in search of the transport that would rescue them.

Lazer gazed beyond the life-giving waters of the little oasis and saw the miles of sand dunes that stretched behind them. It was almost over. He knew in a few hours that the ocean of sand would become a blistering furnace. But by then, they would be gone, rescued, saved. They'd made it to the rendezvous. Now they had to wait.

Lazer brought Striker a cuff full of water and gently poured it across his parched lips; Striker drank, choked, and coughed. His eyes fluttered open and he stared at his one-time rival turned friend and tried to speak. Only a dry whisper of gratitude was possible.

"You saved our lives," Striker whispered.

"Couldn't have done it alone," Lazer added.

"Yeah, you could have," Striker spoke with a newfound humility and deep respect. There was a long pause held by the tears that filled his eyes. "Lazer, about your dad. I . . . I would have never taken the key card if I'd known my father wasn't there. I'm sorry." Striker extended his trembling hand in friendship.

Lazer looked at the open hand and felt a twinge of the old blame he had so often aimed at Striker for his father's death. He took the key card. *He made me stay,* the old voices in Lazer's head insisted. But Striker had not made him stay; that was his own choice, and neither he nor Striker knew Mr. McMann had left for Sangelino with the primary key card that day. *A handshake won't bring back my father!* the old voice screamed in his head. But this time it was followed by another, softer voice. *And neither will hating Striker for a past that can't be changed.*

Lazer took Striker's hand, shook it, and smiled at him. Striker gave him a weak smile back. They had completed their Rites of Passage and emerged as citizens of the world and best of all, friends. Lazer stretched his aching body on the ground beside Striker, closed his eyes, and relaxed for the first time since he had landed on Passage Island. A moment later, the crickets went silent.

On the far side of the oasis, all the creatures that had been at the water's edge scattered in a hundred directions. They abandoned their midday ritual to one much more important: survival.

Santiago pointed at the horizon. A wall of moving black shadows was closing in on them from perhaps a hundred yards away. In the blinding light of the midday sun, the formless wall began to take shape. They were creatures, splicers, at least thirty of them. They were different species, seemingly hunting together like a well-coordinated pack. And they were moving in fast for the kill.

"That's impossible," Lazer said as he pulled himself to his feet.

They all knew one thing: they had to stay alive until the transport arrived. Lazer checked his chronograph: twelve minutes until rendezvous. They would be dead in ten.

He knelt down by Striker, leaning close to his ear. "I'm putting you in the water," he whispered. He pushed him into the shallow banks of the water, hiding Striker in the tall reeds that lined the banks.

"We'll be back," Jem said and kissed his lips. She broke off a long hollow reed, stuck it into his mouth, and gently pushed him beneath the surface. Striker understood what to do.

The creatures advanced: lions, bears, bulls, and tigers crossed with wolves, snakes, bats, hyenas, zebras, horses, and crocodiles—freaks of man's genius both hideous and wondrous at once.

"Stay together," Lazer whispered to the terrified faces that looked to him for guidance. "Move out to solid ground and keep together."

Those who still had machetes and swords drew them.

"Why don't we get in the water?" a brown-skinned girl begged, wiping the tears from her eyes as she raised her sword.

"Some of them are part crocodile. We wouldn't stand a chance in the water," Lazer said. "Stay together. Keep your backs to one another, and don't let them get inside our group."

"Where's the transport?" Santiago's frightened voice called out.

"They'll be here. We just have to stay alive until it arrives. Link arms," Lazer spoke with the calm authority of a seasoned warrior. He slowly laid down his sword and brought his wrists together.

The splicers slowed their run a few feet away from the tangle of students. One by one, the creatures stalked forward. Their motions were as graceful and defined as a well-choreographed ballet. The larger ones lowered their bodies into a crouching stance and held their positions, eyes fixed on their prey. Then, as if on command, they sprang at the students from every direction.

In the instant before contact, Lazer and Rhys threw an energy shield that encapsulated the students. The animals were repelled, falling and tumbling away, startled by the force field that zapped them with a jolt of electricity. The students, for as long as Lazer and Rhys could hold the shield, were safe. A cheer rose up from the group. Everyone was yelling with delight until Lazer noticed that two of the girls had not been in close enough to be covered.

"Jem!" Rhys said, seeing her and Asia outside the field.

Asia tried to throw a shield around herself and Jem. Before she knew what hit her, she had been snatched by the tongue of a crocull, a seven-foot-long bull spliced with crocodile. It coiled her into its slithering tongue, then opened its huge jaws and swallowed her whole.

Jem was alone. She raised her sword hoping she could somehow save Asia from the belly of the crocull. She swung and hacked with all her might into the pointed face of the crocull, which lunged at her. The blade ripped into its sand-colored flesh. The creature retreated a few steps then roared furiously at her. It prepared to attack as the rest of the animals that had been circling the bubble shield turned to heed its call. Three more creatures turned their attention on Jem. Out of nowhere, Striker appeared. He grabbed Asia's fallen machete and stepped in beside Jem. Together, they battled all three creatures. Two more splicers gathered around them and headed in to attack. Jem and Striker were outnumbered. Arms and weapons flailing, they held the creatures back. How Striker was standing was a miracle Jem would give thanks for as soon as she had a moment to do so.

Lazer and Rhys had no choice. They had to release the shield.

"We can't leave them out there," Lazer said.

The other students saw him lower his hands.

"Please!" two of them screamed.

"I won't leave them out there," he shouted back. "Stay together! Rhys, throw a new shield, and I'll shield again as soon as I get Jem and Striker!"

The creatures came in for the attack. Rhys threw a shield, but nothing happened.

"Rhys," a redhead named Arcturia shouted.

"Do something!" a dozen more voices pleaded.

"I'm trying!" Rhys replied. "Weapons up. Now."

Everyone dropped their linked arms and lifted their weapons to defend themselves.

A few yards away, Striker and Jem were fighting a pair of creatures as they stood back to back.

Lazer raced to them.

In a last desperate attempt to shield, Rhys tried again. Nothing happened.

"Concentrate!" Santiago shouted, swinging his sword.

It was useless. Rhys grabbed his machete. All he could do now was fight for his life.

Lazer leapt in front of Jem and Striker. He pounded his wrists together and a blast of energy arced out and stunned the creatures. It knocked two of the creatures to the ground and stopped the others in their tracks, buying the three students a few precious seconds.

"We need to get back to the group," Lazer commanded.

They turned to find that several of the larger and stronger creatures had stepped between them and the other students.

Again Lazer pounded his wrists together and sent out an arc of energy. He could feel he was getting weaker. The force field was not as powerful as before, nor did it extend as far.

The creatures shook off the concussion, scrambled to their feet, and rushed back in for the kill.

Two of the more muscular boys worked together and battled back the bear creature with huge bat-like wings. It rose onto its hind legs, looming more than ten feet above them.

Together, they plunged their swords into the creature, piercing its heart and stomach. It fell forward, flailing. The boys scattered moments before the creature landed, almost crushing them. They retrieved their weapons and fought on.

Four other girls stood in a tight circle; they too were back to back, fending off three smaller creatures that circled them with dizzying speed looking for an opening to get in and kill. The girls sliced and hacked through two of the creatures and turned to face the third together. The last creature hissed, looking for a way to divide them. The girls held their ranks, keeping the creature at bay until one of them slipped around from behind and decapitated it.

Lazer, Striker, and Jem stood together and fought with a relentless strength they did not question. They swiftly killed two creatures and turned to face the same crocull that had devoured Asia. Behind it, a zebra mixed with lion roared in. The crocull instinctively turned to defend its back.

Lazer ran up the back of the crocull's tail and along its spine. He jumped off its snapping snout and flipped like a swimmer in a high-dive competition. He landed feet first, face to face between the two eight-hundred-pound monsters. A huge paw swung at him. Lazer jumped back. Its razor-sharp claws swiped out and tore through the leg of his protective suit, slicing into his skin and knocking him to one knee. He scrambled to his feet and locked his wrists together to send a blast of energy. Nothing happened. His energy depleted, he had lost his focus. He was fighting on primitive survival instincts.

The crocull snapped at Lazer from one side, advancing at lightning speed. Lazer dropped and rolled back, narrowly missing the lash of its whip-like tongue. The creature roared an ear-shattering, unearthly bellow. It lunged in its relentless advance, snapping and swiping its huge paws wildly, inches from Lazer's face. Lazer jumped, twisted, and ducked, avoiding the creature's every move with the grace of a matador. Again the tongue lashed out, this time snatching Lazer's sword.

"Spit," Lazer said.

He tried to shield. Thrusting out his hand, he willed his mind to send a pulse of energy to knock the creature back. Again, nothing happened. It was all going too fast. He couldn't focus. In the mass of confusion and carnage, his powers had abandoned him. Another snap from the splicer's tongue and Lazer would be caught. The crocull's jaws hinged open. Spittle splattered across his face. A frustrated roar, rank with the scent of rotting flesh that hung in its razor-sharp teeth, wafted past as Lazer was about to be devoured.

"Lazer!" Striker shouted and tossed him his machete.

Lazer grabbed it in midair, swung the weapon, and sliced off the tongue that held him. The crocull screamed in pain, and Lazer fell, pulling the disembodied tongue from around him. He looked up to see the crocull still alive and enraged.

Striker grabbed Lazer's fallen sword and turned back to help Jem finish the creature they were battling. Then they raced over to help Lazer finish the crocull. Jem raised her weapon and Striker his; together they stabbed into the crocull's left and right flanks. Another ear-splitting roar, and the crocull spun with lightning speed, snapping first at Striker and then at Jem. The momentary distraction was all Lazer needed. When the crocull swung back its head, he was ready. With a powerful lunge, Lazer drove the sword sideways through the crocull's eye and into its brain. It roared, backed away, and dropped dead.

A tiger-faced horse with enormous fangs and paws that sprang from its hoof-like feet galloped in and reared up as it kicked and swatted at Jem. The razor claws ripped into her arm and knocked her to the ground. The beast reared up on its hind legs in a death dance, ready to trample her.

Lazer hurled his sword with all his might directly into the heart of the rearing creature. It screamed out in pain as it thrashed and screeched and stumbled forward, caught in the throes of its demise. Jem saw the shadow of its body expand across her. She scrambled back, her feet slipping and sliding beneath her in the sand. It was too late; she was about to be crushed. At the last second before the enormous weight of the tiger-horse would have slammed down on her, Striker shoved her out of the way. The creature fell across Striker's legs, pinning him.

Lazer and Jem struggled to pull him free. Striker heard his shinbone snap. He grimaced and threw one arm around Lazer and the other around Jem. They ran toward the group. Three of the students lay dead, but they were winning. There were only seven splicers left.

Lazer, Striker, and Jem reached the others as the remaining creatures circled, preparing to attack.

"Back to back!" Lazer shouted.

The students obeyed and huddled into a protective circle.

The creatures held, watching them as they paced.

Lazer looked at them. They acted like a well-coordinated pack of wolves waiting for their leader to signal the attack with a single command. He knew that what he was thinking was impossibly absurd. These were a wild mismatch of genetic splicers. There would be no way to coordinate their actions.

For some reason, the splicers had stopped, and Lazer saw a chance to re-shield. He dropped his sword and joined his wrists together. Again, nothing happened. It was as if he'd forgotten everything or the universe had abandoned him. Maybe he was filled with too much terror to manifest. Hadn't he been terrified on the mountain and in the caves? Why now? Lazer tried again, as did Rhys and Jem. None of them could make a shield manifest.

Their animal adversaries stared at them . . . waiting. Waiting for what? Each paced, breathless from the fight and seemingly waiting for the other to make the first move. When they did it would be a battle to the death. Lazer had no intention of ending his life as splicer food.

In the short respite of silence, Lazer heard the deuterium engines of the transport whining in the distance, growing louder with each second. Their salvation was minutes away. But like all cavalries, they were about to be too late.

Lazer had to do something now. He glanced at the distant transport and then at the bared teeth of a panting, hyena-faced hynocot splicer that glared at him. Its brindled coat and enormous teeth caught the sun. Then Lazer saw it. The creature's eyes were blank.

It's waiting for an electrical signal, he thought. He was suddenly certain of what was happening. Someone was controlling the creatures through their tags, and there had been a communications glitch. The moment was now or never.

"Attack!" Lazer screamed and lunged forward, rallying the others into their final battle.

With two wild swipes, he decapitated the creature that faced him.

The other students followed his lead and attacked the befuddled creatures. Driven wild by panic and fear, they unleashed a fury and decimated the remaining splicers. The creatures hardly defended themselves. Those creatures that fought back did so out of reflex, caught in some kind of confused state. Again and again, the students sliced and hacked into them until they all lay dead. Not even a twitch could be seen from the heap of carcasses that lay at their feet.

Finally, everyone stopped. They were panting, breathless, and trembling. All but one: Santiago. He was in a state of hysteria. He yelled and screamed with tears streaming down his face as he stabbed at the dead crocull again and again. He split it open, reached in, and pulled Asia whole from its spilled entrails. Seeing her face made him stop. She was dead. One of the other girls gently reached out and turned him to her. They embraced as they wept and held on to each other.

Lazer walked to the lifeless Asia and lifted her out of the spilled innards that fell in huge mounds from the splayed creature. He laid her on the sandy shore at the water's edge just as the transport positioned itself and landed.

40

THE RETRIEVAL

THE SANGELINO TRANSPORT arrived. It stopped, hovered gracefully down on its vertical landing pods, and sent a mushroom of dust and wind billowing up into a soft, cloudy haze that caught the midday sun. It landed in front of the surviving students; filthy and desperate to climb inside and get off of Passage Island. Lazer listened as the whine of the massive engines engulfed the silence of the oasis. He turned and looked at the wide-eyed students as they watched their salvation; a set of ten-foot, double-cargo doors as they hissed open. The Sangelino University's elegant black, white, and silver emblem with its classic columns and swirling green earth—the symbol of life and knowledge, proudly emblazoned on the school transport's smooth chrome surface split apart allowing the light inside to spill out.

One by one, the retrieval team emerged from the transport and stepped into the sunlight. They faced the group of dirty, blood-soaked young warriors who all stood around Lazer, each still gripping the weapons that had saved their lives. Beyond the students lay the carnage of

253

their battle. Their look of stunned horror left no question of what the entire retrieval team was feeling.

The students turned to Lazer. All of them waited patiently in reverent silence for their leader's final command.

"Let's get out of here," Lazer said softly as he nodded them forward.

The bedraggled students moved to the transport, carrying the wounded who could not walk and the bodies of their fallen. They too deserved to go home. Santiago held Asia. The retrieval team joined them, giving a helping hand with gurneys and floaters to assist them inside.

Lazer lifted Striker with Jem's help, and together they carried him to the transport. Two more members of the retrieval team rushed over to lend a hand.

Jem followed, then stopped at the top of the ramp. Lazer had turned back for one last look at the island and the carnage that had almost taken their lives. In the harsh glare of sunlight, he noticed something strange about the pile of dead creatures that lay no more than ten feet away. He squinted, shading his eyes to get a final look. They were dead but were still twitching, their muscles responding to some unseen command sent too late.

From the jungle, a large swarm of scarabites rose up and descended on the dead splicers. They began to scavenge their flesh.

"Come on, Lazer," Jem said. "This Rite of Passage is done."

She was right. The creatures of Passage Island were no longer any of his concern. Lazer dropped his sword.

Jem walked into the transport. Lazer followed, and as he stepped through the door he was hit by a single welcome reality: he had fulfilled his promise to his parents, completed his first-level Rite of Passage, and now he could go home.

41

NEWS OF HOME

LAZER STOOD ON THE Sangelino University transport and looked around. It was elaborate compared to the Spartan military look that defined its Tosadae counterpart. This one was slick and ultramodern, with state-of-the-art technology. Lazer didn't have time to appreciate the grand conveniences like vapor showers, suspension sleepers, full kitchens, and complete medical facilities; all he cared about was getting off as close to Atlantia as fate would allow.

Lazer slipped away from the tangle of people asking a thousand questions and ducked into a private bathroom. Alone for the first time since he landed on Passage Island, he closed his eyes and took a long deep breath. He has survived the horrors of everything that had been thrown at him. He didn't understand why, even though every student on the island had been under attack, he felt that everything that had happened there was directed at him. Maybe it was arrogant or maybe there was a bigger picture that no one was able to see. This was a feeling—a knowing as Masta Lia Poe would have said. He needed to speak

255

with her to share the churning inside him that felt like something or someone wanted him dead. It was the feeling he got when he touched and connected to both of the Gnorbs. They were trying to tell him, warn him but of what he couldn't be sure. He felt so tired and yet he knew this battle for his soul wasn't over and neither was his fight for Atlantia.

Lazer opened his eyes. He studied his face in the efficient bathroom mirror that reflected its truth back at him. He couldn't help noticing that he appeared older. The stress of all he had experienced had made him into a man. He hoped he was wiser, but he knew for certain he was forever changed by the ordeals he'd faced over the past few weeks. He touched the dark circles hung beneath his eyes. His fingers dragged down his cheeks. They seemed hollow and gaunter than he ever remembered.

Lazer turned the shower from mist to rain and stepped in letting the crusted dirt, sand, and dried blood wash away from his body. He wanted it to take with it the memory of all who had died today. The liquid soap smelled of pine and the lather felt clean and slippery as he washed his hair, face, and body. He wanted to scrub everything bad away, but he knew that was an impossibility. He thought of his father who once told him, "You can't change the past and you should never dwell inside it but never forget what it has taught you or, like history, it will repeat itself." Lazer sighed. He missed his father. He felt a well of tears beating against the back of his eyes, but he pushed them away and brought his thoughts into the moment. His eyes fell to the floor, and he watched the rivers of blood and filth flow into the water and disappear down the drain. When the water ran clear, Lazer turned off the flow and let the hot air blow over him. It was the first time in a week he'd felt warm. He stepped out and brushed his teeth. He combed and dried his hair, and, out of habit, braided the six-inch lock of hair that hung at the nape of his neck. It was a ritual he had done since he was old enough to make the braid straight. But instead of tossing it back over his shoulder, he held it in his hand. Lazer studied the thick lock of dark hair his mother and he had kept and cared for since the day he was born. It represented his youth and innocence. Those were gone. He thought of how, ceremoniously, after completing the first-level Rite of Passage, schools would invite parents to join their offspring in a grand ceremony in which wise speakers came and stood before the class. They would share words of profound wisdom, bravery, and accomplishments. They would speak of new responsibility, and honor that these young men and woman had achieved adulthood in the eyes of the Collective. There, before family and friends, the braid was cut off to signify the student had severed from all things childish and immature. They were, by the laws and standards of the Collective people of planet Earth, adults, welcome and worthy of all rights the status represented.

Lazer needed no ceremony to tell him what he already knew. He was a man. He had saved and taken lives and he has survived. He grabbed the scissors from his courtesy grooming kit, cut off his passage lock of hair, and threw it in the trash. The moment he did, it released all the anchors and memories it represented. The quiet intake of air surprised him. Then a cool calm came along with a slow release of his breath to set him free.

Lazer looked one more time at his face, opened the bathroom door, and walked out. He moved down the corridors of the transport, following the signs to the infirmary. Once inside he saw several of the students he'd fought with being cared for by the healers. At the far end of the room, Striker lay on a floater in an isolation chamber bathed in a soft orange light. He had been the most severely wounded.

Lazer shot a look to the healer who was walking out.

"May I speak with him," Lazer asked.

"For a little while. He needs rest," the healer said.

The healer nodded to a stack of sterile protective gowns. Lazer took one, slipped it on, and stood by the door.

"Hey," Lazer said, leaning into the room through the archway.

Striker opened his eyes, focused, and brightened when he saw Lazer.

"Hey. You almost look human," Striker said, trying to remain oblivious to the multiple rows of acupuncture needles that stuck out from his arm and neck. They had been meticulously placed to dull the pain, speed his healing, and help him sleep.

"That makes one of us. You look like a porcupine," Lazer laughed. "How're you feeling?"

"Better," Striker said almost cheerfully, but his expression quickly faded into serious concern. "Lazer," he whispered, "I heard the healers talking about the Black Guard. They've taken control of Atlantia and the dome."

"They don't know how recent the data is," Striker lowered his voice. "They said the Triumvirate is nervous about something bigger happening. Global. They just don't know what or when."

"I'm past nervous and they're all fools," Lazer said. "Anything about what the Collective is saying?" he asked.

"I don't think they know what to say," Striker told him.

"That's impossible. The Freedom of Information laws wouldn't allow them to hold the truth back," Lazer said.

The lead educator assigned to the shuttle stepped into the room and held out his hand.

"Cadet Lazerman? I've been looking for you. Doctor Laurant Bouvier," the man said. "I've heard a lot about you. It seems from all the debriefing, you are quite the hero."

Lazer shook his hand.

Lazer knew Doctor Bouvier's name and face well from all the years of press, awarded published papers, inventions, and countless articles and interviews on ANN. He also knew Dr. Laurant Bouvier was the head of Aquatic Studies at Panazia Institute and Resident Dean of Technology at Sangelino University. He was Cashton's idol and Cashton had told Lazer many times how Bouvier had been responsible for implementing some of the world's most ingenious theories and cutting-edge inventions including many of Bouvier's more provocative theories. Lazer's favorite of Bouvier's extensive research was regenerating the mastodon and woolly mammoths. He was cloning them from frozen blood cells retrieved from thirty-thousand-year-old carcasses that had been held inside the ice until the melting permafrost gave them up. The work was started by a Russian scientist whose concept to bring back the massive beasts was conceived in Siberia a century earlier to help restore the polar ice caps. The scientist's plan had almost failed due to poachers killing the cloned species for personal trophies and the sale of their tusks for profit. Bouvier revived the research after the Great Quakes using Ducane Covax's DNA splicing solutions when he was only nineteen years old. Cashton had raved that Bouvier wrote his study when he was just a student, studying for his engineering degrees at Panazia Institute of Aquatic Technologies and Genetic Arts.

Lazer couldn't help noticing that Laurant Bouvier was strikingly handsome with prematurely snow-white hair and a narrow beard that traced his jaw. A few distinguished wrinkles accented his chocolate brown skin.

"It's a pleasure to meet you, Doctor Bouvier. I've read your papers on aquatic molecular solidification," Lazer said as he finally released Bouvier's firm handshake. "Will it work? Can you convert water to a substance stronger and lighter than any metal we have on Earth?"

"In theory. Human beings are thankfully back in vibrational alignment with Earth's 528 Hz frequency, thanks to the thirteen-moon Mayan calendar. That has definitely allowed us to realign with the universal vibrations, and those are the connections we need to shift water into its next physical incarnation," Bouvier said.

"My best friend, Cashton Lock, said your T-7829 process will work," Lazer added.

"That is supposed to be secret. I'm guessing your friend is a hacker," Bouvier said.

Lazer smiled knowing Cashton was guilty as charged.

"I think we're still a decade away from any real proof. Suffice it to say we're making progress. Panazia's aquatics research division is working on the first prototype. An interstellar ship. Tell your friend he should come check it out. If he understood the science, I'd like to meet him," Bouvier said.

Lazer could tell the good doctor was impressed that Lazer knew of his research, and he couldn't wait to tell Cashton that not only had he met his idol, but he had accidently arranged a possible meeting between them.

"We are starting our decent. Please secure all objects and take your seats," a voice said over the speaker system.

Lazer knew he needed to change the subject. The transport was heading the wrong way for him to get to Atlantia. And he needed Bouvier's help if he wanted any chance of getting home.

Bouvier lifted a small data shard to eye level. "This was an amazing series of deadly encounters you students reported. You're sure those animals were tagged?"

"Every one of them. And they were standard issue tags. I checked," Jem interrupted as she entered the room.

"We think someone hacked into the tags and took control of the animals," Lazer said.

"The creatures are out of control down there, sir," Striker added.

"We believe you. The most concerning part was that it wasn't only on Passage Island that this occurred. The past three retrievals have had similar tales. We believe every passage has been compromised," Bouvier said. "We're still missing several Panazia and Sangelino students, and Tosadae is missing two."

"Anyone from the ice field trials?" Lazer said, fearful that it might be Cashton.

Bouvier shook his head. "I haven't heard back on the ice field passage."

"How is any of this possible?" Striker asked.

"We don't know . . . yet. Our best intelligence is linked to a satellite override no one can triangulate. Everything looked normal at Passage Control so for a week we missed anything being wrong. But now that we know some kind of hack happened. We've only been able to do a partial trace and unfortunately it leads to a dead end. We know someone hacked in to Passage Control, shut down the monitoring and PAR systems, and took control of those creatures," Bouvier said.

"They took control of every tagged creature and splicer on every Rite of Passage location," Striker said shifting uncomfortably.

"But the hackers have been identified," Jem asked.

"No. We can't trace the feed to the final source. Add to that, we believe, starting as far back as three weeks ago, at roughly six-hour intervals, we discovered numerous transports vanished unreported, snatched off the ocean surface and out of the sky," Bouvier said.

"Vanish?" Jem asked. "How is that even possible?"

"Who have you found out has been taken?" Lazer asked. Concerned filled his voice.

"So far we know of a high level, political convoy. Intel won't release who was on it when it disappeared. There was a Sangelino-bound Tosadae Academy transport. It was reported to have been snatched somewhere just outside of Atlantian airspace," Bouvier said. "That one was more blatant than any of the rest."

"Is there a passenger list? What was the date?" Lazer asked.

His heart raced. *Please don't let them have snatched the transport Elana and Kyla were on*, Lazer thought

Lazer, Jem, nor Striker could respond. Lazer could see by all their expressions they knew things were much worse than they had suspected.

"I wish I could tell you more. You've been through a lot and I, for one, feel you deserve to know everything that's happening," Bouvier said.

"Thank you, sir," Striker replied.

"Have our parents been told we are all right?" Jem asked.

"As delicately as we can. Yes. We're setting it up now for you to speak to your families. Get some rest, cadet," Bouvier said to Striker.

"You two do the same," he added, pointing to Lazer and Jem. "Cadet Lazerman, we'll be landing in Station City in about two hours. I was able to divert our return to take you to the Alliance. Commander Hague at Tosadae said he's sent a private transport from Mu for you. It will be waiting to bring you back to the Academy."

"Station City and Mu are the opposite direction, sir. I need to go to Atlantia!" Lazer said.

"Atlantia's been domed and not by the Collective or the politia. Sorry, son," Bouvier said to Lazer.

Bouvier turned to leave. Lazer blocked his way. "Dr. Bouvier, sir, I need to borrow a sponder. My mom lives on Atlantia and . . . I just—"

Bouvier pulled Lazer into the hallway. "There hasn't been any direct communication with Atlantia since the dome was launched," Bouvier said. His tone was as compassionate as he could make it.

"But there has, sir. I think when they open the dome to grab those transports, some messages leaked out. I got one from my Mom," Lazer said.

"Show me," Bouvier said, very interested.

"I can't. My sponder was taken from me before I made the jump to Passage Island. My instructor has it. Please, sir. I have to get home. My mother's in danger."

Laurant Bouvier took a long hard look at Lazer.

"I understand your concern. My seven-year-old son and wife escaped Atlantia a few months ago. They were on the last transport out before . . .," Bouvier stopped. "I have known this situation has been wrong since . . . I lost my sister in the Orbis Temple attacks. As far as I'm concerned, something should have been done a long time ago," Bouvier said.

Bouvier released the magnetic latch, flushed the information, and handed Lazer his wristsponder. "Take it. Maybe you'll have some luck getting through."

Lazer took the sponder. He said nothing as he watched Bouvier leave. Lazer stepped back into the doorway of Striker's room. From Lazer's look of absolute desperation, Striker knew there were no words he could say that would help. Lazer knew Striker's parents had moved out of Atlantia right away after the Vacary Mine attacks. They were safe in Sangelino, waiting for his return.

"I gotta go," Lazer told Striker and Jem. "Let the Collective know what's happening."

"You have my word," Striker told him.

Jem nodded in a silent pledge, and the three shared a V salute.

"Take care of each other," he said as he left.

Lazer slipped down an empty side corridor. In the dim silence he spoke into the sponder. He used a sequence of verbal access codes to boot the system into the data configuration he had set in place for himself. He kept walking as he waited for the satellite hookup and the requested data to drop. The wristsponder flashed, download complete. Lazer pulled up a 3-D holo-projection of his V-mail and searched for anything from Atlantia. He could see numerous old communications from Masta Poe, various teachers, Cashton, Kyla, and Elana Blue; all had been sent long before the incident at the battle forum and well before his departure for his Rite of Passage. Worst of all, there was nothing new from his mom. When he clicked on her access, all that came back was a hiss of white noise. He tried again. Static. Lazer input the code for another digital address, then a second, and then a third. Still nothing. Finally he input the pass code for a secret mailbox that held the most recent communication from Detra. It opened and with it the sponder flashed a frantic, red signal.

"Communications alert. Status Red. Cole Lazerman."

Detra's face appeared in the holoscreen. It was the same communication he had seen on the Tosadae transport to Passage Island. She looked frightened, and behind he could see and hear a battle raged outside.

She spoke the same words he'd heard before as she glanced over her shoulder. The look of terror in her eyes ripped at Lazer's heart. He could tell she knew she was running out of time. When she turned back, her eyes filled with tears. "Stay away from Atlantia! I love you, Lazer. I love you."

The transmission went into a blur of static. Lazer's heart pounded so hard he felt it would explode out of his chest. He turned around and started running. He raced back through the transport to find Dr. Bouvier.

Lazer stopped and asked a dozen people until someone finally pointed and said, "He's on the top Deck, upper level briefing room."

Lazer raced through the transport, up the stairs, and onto the top deck. It was a huge transport. He reached the briefing room and burst into the cabin, breaking all protocol. He was desperate. Dr. Bouvier stood with his staff, going over several reports they had compiled from the survivors. Lazer could see floating in front of them a new set of navigation charts where they had changed course to drop off Lazer in Station City. Lazer knew that the change could also help them stay well away from the electromagnetic gravity beam that had pulled Kyla and Elana and the others into captivity on Atlantia.

"Dr. Bouvier, I have to get to Atlantia. My mom's been taken prisoner."

"You got through?"

"Yes. I mean . . . no. It was an old message that got out. I don't know from how long ago. But I know she's alive and I've got to get home. Please help me," Lazer said, his voice was breathless and taut with desperation.

"They were dropping the dome to hijack transports. It would make sense that Vybernet communication could leak out. Report that to the Triumvirate," Dr. Bouvier said.

"Yes, sir, but we can't go to there. There are no transports allowed within a hundred miles of Atlantia, son," the assistant shuttle commander said. "I'm afraid your request is impossible."

"It's not impossible! Nothing's impossible!" Lazer argued back.

"May I have the room?" Bouvier said.

The knot of people stepped outside so Bouvier could speak to Lazer privately.

"Lazer, we suspect the Black Guard took the dome's control towers," Bouvier explained. "Son, the Black Guard hacked into the access codes that seal the dome. You understand, we've all been locked out."

"I can get in," Lazer asked. "You said yourself, anyone who ventures within a few hundred miles of Atlantia has been sucked out of the sky or off the sea by a huge electromagnetic gravity beam. I'll take a chance they will grab me.

"I can't risk this transport and you know it. By order of the Triumvirate, no one is allowed inside Atlantian air or sea space. No, Lazer, I can't take you there," Bouvier said.

"My mother's in there! That's my home!" Lazer said. "I have to get in, sir"

"I understand, son, but the politia can't open a shield they don't control and neither can I."

"The Collective can't leave the people of Atlantia trapped in there. Covax and his Black Guard are murderers. We both know they won't stop at conquering Atlantia either. Or is the Triumvirate planning to seal in any Black Guard sympathizers as well? That would mean whole sections of every continent on the planet," Lazer said. "It has to be stopped."

Bouvier could see Lazer had no intention of going to Mu or staying locked out of Atlantia.

"Listen to me, Cadet Lazerman. I am not at liberty to discuss what the politia are doing. You're just going to have to trust that there are plans underway to take Atlantia back," Bouvier said.

"How? When? Those are third- and fourth-generation Black Guard. I've seen them firsthand. Why can't we just shut them down with a massive EMP? One electromagnetic pulse big enough to shut them and every system on Atlantia down including the dome," Lazer insisted.

"Even if an EMP would work through the dome, which it won't, intelligence says the rebel Black Guard may be equipped with surge protectors and possibly engineered without embedded regulator chips to re-imprint them. That would shut everything down *but* the Black Guard. You'd be leaving the Wave without weapons or communications," the commander said.

"You're Detra Bryant's son? I see her all over you," Bouvier said.

"You know my mother?"

"And your father. She worked at the Covax splicer labs right after Aleece Avery left him," Bouvier said. "Your mother was his only friend."

"My mother was Covax's friend? My mother never worked for Ducane Covax and neither did my father?"

Bouvier fell silent and the look that washed across his face unnerved Lazer. Lazer could tell there was something Bouvier knew about his mother's past and now obviously Lazer's that Lazer had never been told.

"My father's dead, Doctor Bouvier" Lazer said. "He was killed by the Black Guard at the Vacary Mines attack."

Laurent's eyes searched Lazer's for something Lazer couldn't imagine. Lazer knew what Bouvier was saying wasn't making any sense to him.

"Look, son, Triumverate Aleece Avery, Dante Labov, and a lot of other people in Sangelino believe the biodroids have gone sentient. If they've started to self-generate and create more sentient A.I., we're all in danger."

"They have, sir. I've seen it," Lazer told him.

"Can you give me proof?"

Lazer said nothing. Proof meant admitting he, Cashton, and Kyla blew up Temple Mountain.

"Without proof your accusations are conjecture," Bouvier said

"I've seen the Black Guard production facility. I tried to destroy it once and I won't stop until I destroy all of the Black Guard before they destroy us. I have to get home!" Lazer blurted. "I won't let them entomb my mother or my home inside that dome and not fight to get them out! Please! Help me, Dr. Bouvier!"

Bouvier had not stopped searching Lazer's eyes. Lazer looked back at Bouvier matching his stare. Lazer made sure his wild, angry stare was filled with a relentless determination that would not be deterred by Bouvier or anyone else. Lazer was on his mission to get home and save Atlantia.

The magnetic seat warning sign illuminated, announcing their preparation for landing at the capital of the republic. Station City sat on the easternmost edge of the continent.

Bouvier pulled Lazer closer to him. "There is a splicer named Pushkin Tao," he whispered, "in Station City. He is a big-time professional game banger who owns one of the high-end interactive clubs, or at least he used to. Supposedly, he ran guns into the Lost Territories. He'll know the underwater routes and maybe even the deep-water trenches. They're dangerous, but the satellite radar tracking devices can't penetrate those depths. Maybe he can get you deep enough to get under the dome if that fancy transport of his can withstand the depths. Listen to me carefully, Lazer, Pushkin's a water pirate. He's mean and dangerous, but if anyone knows how to get you onto Atlantia alive, it's him. I saved his life once, and he owes me a life debt and a thousand platinum chits. Tell him I'll erase both debts if he helps you."

Bouvier took his old wristsponder from Lazer and punched in Pushkin Tao's contact information. He added enough chits for Lazer to buy food, water, and lodging in Station City until arrangements could be made. Lazer looked at him, grateful, relieved, and frightened.

"There are enough chits to get you to Mu if Pushkin can't or won't help you," Bouvier said.

"I can beam these chits back to you as soon as I can," Lazer said.

"Keep them, son. You'll need all the help you can get out there. Pay it forward or find me when this is all over," Bouvier said. "Bring your hacker friend."

Bouvier added a post-Rite of Passage ID card number and with it an all legal chip. Lazer was grateful it would allow him access to Game Bangers Alley without requiring an implanted micro ID cylinder chip, still mandatory in Station City. Implants had been outlawed by almost every other city in the Republic and the Alliance. The United Co-Federation and the Euro Common Market had abolished the chip and the I.I.I. tattoo it left. It was a pre-A.Q. hated dictator's mark used during the reign of the last American president. Without it you couldn't buy food, get a job, own a home, or a have a family. Bouvier handed the sponder back to Lazer.

"If you make it onto Atlantia, I understand there are underground fighting forces called the Wave. They were just getting organized when we lost contact. Be sure and ask for Eddie Ping. Remember, Eddie Ping," Bouvier repeated. "Tell him, *ank am naniba* and that I sent you. Good luck, Cole Lazerman," Bouvier said.

"What's *ank am naniba* mean," Lazer said.

"Go in light," Bouvier replied.

Bouvier placed a fatherly hand on Lazer's shoulder but firmly shook his hand like the warrior he knew Lazer had become. Lazer nodded an unspoken thank you. The restraint bell dinged again demanding they both return to their seats and prepare to land.

"Sir, the story you started about my father?" Lazer asked at the last moment.

"Is not mine to tell," Bouvier said and hurried away.

Lazer walked to the lower deck. He reached an empty seat, strapped in, and waited for the transport to descend. He felt the shift in gravity and began to visualize what might be on this next chapter in his odyssey to get home. Lazer knew he needed a plan. He would have to locate and somehow convince the pirate Pushkin Tao to take him across the seas, somehow get through the Black Guard controlled dome and onto Atlantia. Lazer looked out the transport window as the sprawling, futuristic Station City rose up beneath him. It was massive and like nothing he'd ever seen on Atlantia. He felt strangely excited and fearlessly ready to face whatever awaited him. Lazer took a deep breath in and released it as a long, courageous exhale. He let the words of Masta Lia Poe and the teachings of the Visionistic Arts fill his mind as he asked the Universe to connect. *Ank am naniba*, Lazer thought. It took a second to realize the words came into his mind not in English, but in perfect Celian. The translation for *ank am naniba* was ***go in light***, and he was sure this peaceful knowing was a confirmation that all the powers of the universe were igniting inside his body, mind, and spirit. He knew he was, in that instant, at one with the Universe. It would ebb and flow until he was strong enough to hold it. He also understood, without question, this connection was the first doorway to his destiny, his Vision Quest, and this was only the beginning.

CELIAN LANGUAGE

By Deborah M. Pratt
Lexicon Guide by: Dr. Katie Petruzzelli

THE CELIAN LANGUAGE is one of flowing words—one rolling effortlessly into the next. To those fortunate enough to hear and understand—every calming word is a peaceful song.

Let this guide to the Celian language help connect you to the oneness of the Universe. Go in light.

PRONUNCIATIONS AND TENSES

c—*c* is always pronounced as a *k* sound. Therefore, the word Celian is always pronounced with a hard C as in *Kelian,* and not as *Selian.*

x—*x* is always pronounced as an *s* sound, making the word Xhin pronounce as *S-hin,* and not *Zhin.* The one exception to this rule is the word *Xelian* which is still pronounced as *Kelian* as shown in the English spelling of the word.

a—*a* is always pronounced as an *au* sound, as in "trauma." Making the word *Alan* pronounced as *Au-laun* and not with the pronunciation of as the name "Alan."

e—*e* is always pronounced with the short vowel sound of *e* such as in "tender."

i—*i* is always pronounced as a hard *e*. Making the word *Garin* pronounced as *Gar-een* and not as *Gar-in.*

o—*o* is always pronounced as a hard *o,* as in "home." Making the word *lio* pronounced as *lee-O.*

u—*u* is always pronounced as an *oo* sound, as in "broom." Making the word *fodu* pronounced as *fo-doo.*

y—*y* is is not often used, and has the same rules as the letter *i.*

271

PLURALS

Removing the last consonant and vowel from the end of a word and replacing it with *-um* will make the word plural. Example: *Orah* (Gnorb) becomes *Orum* (Gnorbs). If the word ends in a vowel, only that last vowel is removed and the *-um* is added. Example: *Aliomi* (History) becomes *Aliomum* (Histories). If the word is two letters or less, *-um* is simply added to the end of the word. Example: *Ma* (Doom) becomes *Maum* (Dooms).

There is a singular use and a plural use of the word *the*. *Lai* (the) is used when the word following it is singular. Example: *Lai tatam* (The power). *Fi* (the) is used when the word following it is plural. Example: *Fi tatum* (The powers).

ADDING -ING

Adding *-wa* to the end of a Celian word is equivalent to adding "-ing" to the end of a word in English. Example: *Morran* (Know) becomes *Morranwa* (Knowing).

PAST TENSE

Adding *-ne* to the end of a Celian word will make the word past tense. Example: *Alan* (Unify) becomes *Alanne* (Unified).

CELIAN GLOSSARY

Celian to English:

A
Alan: Unify
Alanne: Unified
Aliomi: History
Aliomum: Histories
Am: Inside
Ank: Go
As: Incarnation

B
Bledash: Source

C
Cassim: Become
Cha: That
Che: Give
Chene: Given
Clay: Day
Clayum: Days

F
Fage: Our
Fan: If
Fatsi: It
Feriate: Perfection
Fi: The (*plural*—example: *fi tatum*/the powers)

Figgii: Part
Fodu: This
Fume: Longer

G
Garin: Fearful
Ghi: Human
Gighe: Call
Gighum: Called
Gleotopa: Let
Ganna: Pathway
Gredia: Command

H
Hane: Cause

I
I: Into
Ima: Have
In: I
Inu: Soul

K
Kachiti: Understand
Kilonye: Embodiment

L
La: Chose
Laan: One

Lanna: Single

Lai: The (*singular*—example: *lai S*/the Universe)

Leom: Look

Leitt: Real

Liageakiowa: Everything

Lio: Oneness

Lipa: Truth

Lith: Will

Loch: Be

Lochlaan: Be One

Lome: Way

Lon: All

M

Ma: Doom

Maage: You

Maagan: Your

Magien: Belong

Magium: Belongs

Mai: Physical

Manro: Find

Masi: Of

Maum: Doomed

Maya: Pure

Me: Vision

Morran: Know

Morranne: Known

Morranwa: Knowing

Morvaba: Mind

Morvabum: Minds

N

Nane: Allow

Naniba: Light

Ne: A

Nu: No

Nun: Not

O

O: And

Obana: Through

Obrdur: Held

Oloragi: We

Ommol: Elevate

Ommolne: Elevated

Onamm: Lonely

Ongam: Darken

Ongamna: Darkness

Orah: Gnorb

Orum: Gnorbs

Ori: Make

Orine: Made

Orinima: Energy

P

Pae: Keeper

Pug: Greed

Pasch: Gift

Paschne: Gifted

Paum: Keepers

Presg: Us

Q

Qua: Spirit

R

Rah: Every
Re: Back
Reage: Revenge
Reaom: Own

S

S: Universe
Sapharono: Great
Savi: Anger
She: Fault
Shovate: Each
Shum: Lost
Sho: Lose
So: Sensation
Stali: Life
Stamus: Breaths
Strat: Is

T

Ta: With
Taan: Future
Tash: Must
Tati: Are
Tatam: Power
Tatum: Powers
Te: Who
Ti: Secret
Titik: For
Tu: To

U

U: Universal
Umlin: Heart
Univa: Love
Uti: Wonderment

V

Va: Needed
Vi: Explore
Vici: Hatred
Vie: Eternal
Vioswe: Paradise
Vo: Solely

X

Xelian: Celian
Xihn: Do

English to Celian:

A

A: Ne
All: Lon
Allow: Nane
And: O
Anger: Savi
Are: Tati

B

Back: Re
Be: Loch
Be One: Lochlaan

Become: Cassim
Belong: Magien
Belongs: Magium
Breaths: Stamus

C

Call: Gighe
Called: Gighum
Cause: Hane
Celian: Xelian
Chose: La
Command: Gredia

D

Darken: Ongam
Darkness: Ongammna
Day: Clay
Days: Clayum
Do: Xihn
Doomed: Maum

E

Each: Shovate
Elevate: Ommol
Elevated: Ommolne
Embodiment: Kilonye
Energy: Ominima
Eternal: Vie
Every: Rah
Everything: Liageakiowa
Explore: Vi

F

Fault: She
Fearful: Garin
Find: Manro
For: Titik
Future: Taan

G

Gift: Pasch
Gifted: Paschne
Give: Che
Given: Chene
Gnorb: Orah
Gnorbs: Orum
Go: Ank
Great: Sapharono
Greed: Pug

H

Hatred: Vici
Have: Ima
Heart: Umlin
Held: Obrdur
Histories: Aliomum
History: Aliomi
Human: Ghi

I

I: In
If: Fan
Incarnation: As
Inside: Am

Into: I
Is: Strat
It: Fatsi

K

Keeper: Pae
Keepers: Paum
Know: Morran
Known: Morranne
Knowing: Morranwa

L

Let: Gleotopa
Life: Stali
Light: Naniba
Longer: Fume
Look: Leom
Lose: Sho
Lost: Shum
Love: Univa

M

Made: Orne
Make: Ori
Mind: Morvaba
Minds: Morvabum
Must: Tash
Needed: Va
No: Nu
Not: Nun

O

Of: Masi
One: Laan
Oneness: Lio
Our: Fage
Own: Reaom

P

Paradise: Vioswe
Part: Figgii
Passed: Cleh
Pathway: Ganna
Perfection: Feriate
Physical: Mai
Power: Tatam
Powers: Tatum
Pure: Maya

R

Real: Leitt
Revenge: Reage

S

Secret: Ti
Sensation: So
Single: laana
Solely: Vo
Soul: Inu
Source: Bledsash
Spirit: Qua

T

That: Cha
The (*plural*): Fi (example: *fi tatum*/the powers)
The (*singular*): Lai (example: *lai S*/the Universe)
This: Fodu
Through: Obana
To: Tu
Truth: Lipa

U

Understand: Kachiti
Unify: Alan
Unified: Alannne
Universal: U
Universe: S

V

Vision: Me

W

Way: Lome
We: Oloragi
Who: Te
With: Ta
Wonderment: Uti

Y

You: Maage
Your: Maagan

CELIAN ALPHABET

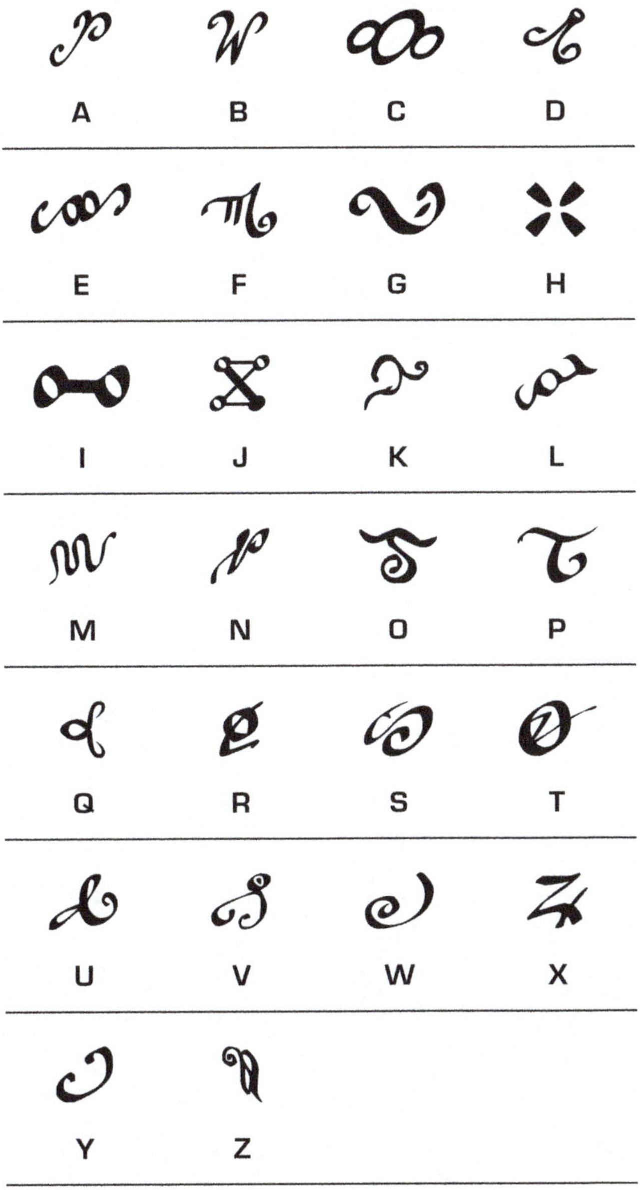

A	B	C	D

E	F	G	H

I	J	K	L

M	N	O	P

Q	R	S	T

U	V	W	X

Y	Z		

ABOUT THE AUTHOR

 **DEBORAH M. PRATT** is a significant force in Hollywood. She's an American director, writer, producer, and actress. Ms. Pratt is a graduate from Webster University with a degree in psychology and theatre. She was co-creator, executive producer, and head writer on the iconic series ***Quantum Leap*** for NBC and ***Tequila and Bonetti*** for CBS. She also created for TV and became executive producer of ***The Net*** for the USA network. Ms. Pratt wrote for multiple television series including ***Magnum, P.I., The Pretender,*** and ***Airwolf.*** She is an award-winning graduate of the American Film Institute's Directing Workshop for Women and made her directorial debut with ***Cora Unashamed*** for the BBC, PBS, and *Masterpiece Theatre's The American Collection.*

Ms. Pratt is a five-time Emmy nominee, a Golden Globe nominee, and the recipient of The Lillian Gish Award from Women in Film, The Angel Award, The Golden Block Award, and six Black Emmy Nominees awards.

A published novelist, she breaks the mold of science fiction and creates a genre of science fantasy with the vision of a new, unified Earth and the keys to human empowerment. The books are intricately layered with scientific fact and imaginative fantasy. ***The Atlantian, The Academy, The Odyssey, Panazia,*** and ***Salvation*** are due to be released this year. ***The Vision Quest*** series is a critically acclaimed, exhilarating journey into the future of our world. Ms. Pratt is a pioneer in trans-media entertainment and is developing the world she's created in her books and films across multiple platforms. Her latest book, ***The Tempting: Seducing the Nephilim,*** is book two in ***The Age of Eve*** novel series.

Deborah currently lives in Los Angeles, has two children, and considers herself a citizen of planet Earth.

Visit these sites to learn more:

TheVisionQuest.com • TheAtlantianVQ.com • DeborahMPratt.com

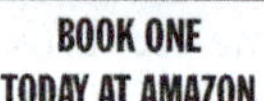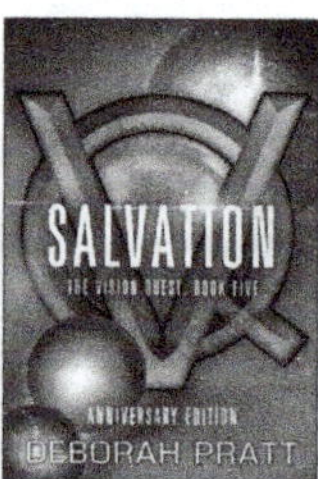

BOOK ONE
TODAY AT AMAZON

BOOK TWO
TODAY AT AMAZON

BOOK THREE
TODAY AT AMAZON

BOOK FOUR
COMING 2017

BOOK FIVE
COMING 2017

THE VISION QUEST SERIES: In the not-too-distant future, Earth has unified into a brave new world. Humans have crossed their genetics with an array of creatures and these amazing new species have helped us to remember the powers humans forgot. But they also crossed their genes with machines, and our mechanical creations have become sentient and determined to change the world as we know it. On the risen continent of Atlantia, three friends—Cole Lazerman, Kyla Wingright, and Cashton Lock—are thrust into Earth's next evolution and forced to be part of the battle for humankind. Friendship, family, love, and a call to destiny, command them to find the courage to stand and fight or die. **This the journey of the Vision Quest and these are the heroes we've been waiting for.**

Visit these sites to learn more:
TheVisionQuest.com • TheAtlantianVQ.com • DeborahMPratt.com

Made in the USA
Monee, IL
09 April 2024